HATE ME

ASHLEY JADE

First published in USA, January 2021
Copyright © Ashley Jade

This is a work of fiction. Names, characters, businesses, places, events and incidents are either the products of the author's imagination or used in a fictional manner. Any resemblance to actual persons, living or deceased, or events is purely coincidence.

Hate Me

Photographer: Scott Hoover

Cover Design: Lori Jackson at Lori Jackson Design

Editor: Kristy Stalter

Proofreader: Lilypad Lit

Hate Me

"The Devil hath power
To assume a pleasing shape."

— William Shakespeare, Hamlet

Prologue

9th grade

Aspen

*F*uck *this.*

I rub my sweaty palms on my skirt and inhale a shaky breath that fails to calm my nerves.

Not only did I get my period for the first time ever this morning, it's my first day at Black Mountain Academy.

Looking back, it should have been a sign.

Stepping out of my dad's car, I hike my backpack onto my shoulder. I hate that he's forcing me to go to this elite private school with a bunch of rich kids, instead of the public school across town that I was attending.

Then again, it wasn't like I'd be here for long, since my family's financial situation was *unstable* at best.

One month we're eating filet mignon and lobster for dinner, and the next we're lucky if we can afford a jar of peanut butter and a loaf of bread for sandwiches.

Every time I asked my dad what was going on and why things were so *weird,* he'd quickly assure me everything was fine before changing the subject.

And now here I am.

About to enter what I'm positive will be the tenth circle of hell.

My legs feel like jelly as I glance around the empty parking lot.

School started fifteen minutes ago.

"Come on, Aspen," my dad says. "You're late."

Stomach knotting, I spin around to face him. "I can't do this."

His brown eyes soften. "You'll be fine, kiddo."

I shake my head, the bad feeling in the pit of my stomach growing. "I don't think so."

Sighing, he chuckles. "It's just nerves." Reaching into his pocket, he pulls out what appears to be a jewelry box. "I was going to give this to you after you came home, but I think now might be a better time."

Raising an eyebrow, I reach through the passenger side window and take the box from him. "What is it?"

"Open it and find out."

I stare down at the necklace in confusion. "Pearls?"

It's not that I'm not grateful for the gift, but I'm fourteen…not eighty.

"Not just any pearls. *Real* ones," he declares proudly.

That only makes me feel worse. Unlike my mother, who only cares about her wine and that my dad buys her nice things all the time to keep up appearances, I don't want or need any of that from him.

"Dad, this is too much—"

"It's fine."

"But how can you afford—"

"Don't worry about it."

I level him with a look. "Dad—"

"Your Uncle Leo and I got a few more investors for that retirement home I was telling you about." He waves a hand. "Now quit drilling me and put them on."

Uncle Leo was my dad's best friend, and the lawyer for my dad's company. However, he was also the one person I could turn to if I had any problems.

Unlike my dad, Leo never kept me in the dark or treated me like a little kid.

He treats me like I'm special.

Stifling the urge to drill him, I fasten the string of pearls around my neck. Given we're required to wear uniforms consisting of a white button-up shirt and a plaid skirt, I'm positive I look like even more of a preppy nerd now, but I don't care.

It was sweet of him to get me this necklace, and I don't want him to think I'm not appreciative.

I wave goodbye and turn around, but his next words halt me.

"Aspen, I didn't make you change schools to be mean. I just want the best for you." He darts his gaze to the giant building behind me. "This is the top high school in the state and with your grades…" his voice trails off, but I know what he's getting at.

While I was used to the public school I attended, it wasn't the best one for a student like me.

At this point I knew more than most of the teachers did and I was so far ahead of the curve, classes were becoming boring.

Not only did Black Mountain Academy have the potential to advance my education, it looked great on college applications.

Not that I could afford to go to a decent college.

Well, not without a scholarship.

Dipping my head through the open window, I kiss his cheek. "Love you, Dad."

"Love you too, kiddo." He holds my stare. "Now go in there and show them what you're made of."

"I will."

I start to turn around again, but he snaps his fingers. "Oh, by the way, Leo said his nephew goes here."

My stomach flips inside out before falling to the ground.

I met Trenton Knox once when I was eight.

Given he pushed me so hard into a swing set he knocked my front tooth out and then tackled me to the ground while I was crying and took a pair of scissors to my ponytail…it didn't go well.

I warned my parents if they *ever* forced me to play with that psychopath again, I'd call the police.

I can feel every ounce of blood drain from my face as I stand there frozen.

"Relax, Aspen," dad says. "I know you two didn't hit it off, but you guys were just kids back then."

My dad has a point…but still.

Something about him rubbed me the wrong way from the moment I first laid eyes on him. And seeing as he called me *carrot top* before shoving me and hacking into my hair…it was clear the feeling was mutual.

Then again, that was six years ago. People change.

After waving goodbye to my dad, I make my way inside the building.

Everyone's eyes are glued to me the moment I enter the classroom, and I can hear them all whispering amongst themselves.

"Fresh meat."

"New girl's kind of cute," someone says.

"Damn. She's a ginger," another guy declares. "You know what they say about those."

A girl sitting to the left of him laughs. "That they have no souls?"

More laughter. More teasing.

"Nice pearls," a girl seated on the other side of her taunts. "Did your grandma give you those?"

Feeling like a fish out of water, I quickly shuffle past them to the only open seat I can find in the back of the room.

A moment later, the teacher resumes her lesson, and everyone quiets down.

I force myself to take several cleansing breaths as I pull a notebook and pen out of my bookbag.

Only…I don't have a pen.

Or a pencil.

Because I left them on the kitchen counter.

I mentally curse myself for being an idiot.

I turn to the guy sitting next to me. "Can I borrow a pe—"

Words die in my throat when he tilts his head and those intense eyes—one cobalt blue and the other emerald green—slice through me like a hot knife through butter.

I've seen those haunting eyes before.

Dread has my stomach coiling because I know exactly who I'm staring at.

Trenton Knox.

Knox

When an animal is shot by a hunter but doesn't die, the humane thing to do is put it out of its misery and kill it.

However, it's way more fun watching them suffer.

I'd almost laugh at this turn of events if it didn't piss me off so much.

Aspen Falcone—the irritating little girl my parents once forced me to play with when I was a kid—has found her way inside Black Mountain Academy.

Only she isn't so little anymore.

The last time I saw her was at the beginning of the summer. She was at a bookstore in the mall with a friend...leafing through a copy of *Hamlet*.

She'd been every bit as skinny, hideous, and annoying as the first time I'd laid eyes on her—and despite my inability to tear my gaze away—the sharp sting of hatred had burned just as strong.

But it's obvious the ugly duckling syndrome is long gone now that her nose finally grew into the rest of her face and she filled out in all the right places.

Briefly, I let my gaze fall to her tits. Her perky D cups strain against the white fabric of her shirt, threatening to pop out at any moment.

However, it's the utter fear swimming in those bright green eyes that makes my dick hard.

The room grows silent—so silent I can hear the sound of her heart beating like a freight train.

Fuck. Aspen looks terrified. Her ivory skin is coated in a sheen of sweat and her two crooked front teeth dig into her plump bottom lip as she steals a nervous glance at the door, no doubt debating whether she should make a run for it.

Too late.

The energy in the classroom buzzes with anticipation as everyone looks on with bated breath...awaiting my next move.

Each and every one of these losers fears me, and if I make it clear that she isn't to be messed with…they wouldn't dare cross me.

I could do the noble thing and draw the line in the sand.

I could take the scared little bird under my wing and protect her.

I could show my new wounded animal some mercy.

But mercy wasn't something I was capable of.

I hold her gaze. "You need a pen?"

She visibly swallows. "Yes."

My lips curl as I pick up my pen and throw it across the room. "Go fetch, fire crotch."

The room erupts in snickers and howls as she slinks down in her seat.

My mother once told me that the first time she saw my father, it was love at first sight.

It was the exact opposite for me when I saw Aspen Falcone.

I hated her face and the stupid freckles lining the bridge of her nose.

I hated her smile and her crooked teeth.

I hated the carefree way she giggled and how the wind blew her long red hair as she swung on the swing.

I hated the way she looked at me when our gazes collided—like she could see all the demons taking up residence in my black soul.

I hated her for prying and asking shit she had no business asking.

I hated her for breathing the same air as me.

I hated her for existing.

10th grade

Knox

Anger boils my blood as I watch them in the empty classroom.

Aspen's pointing to something in a textbook, attempting to teach Ken Ruckman—an offensive lineman on the football team—how to do math during her lunch period.

But the dumbass is too busy focusing on her.

My hands clench into fists when he leans in way too fucking close for my liking. "Sorry, it's still not making any sense."

Aspen looks up. "Oh." She digs her teeth—teeth that now have braces on them—into her bottom lip. "Let's try a different approach."

Grinning, he sets his pencil down. "Or…how about you come to my house later and tutor me there?"

Irritation crawls up the back of my neck.

Every guy at school knew to stay the fuck away from Aspen.

Not because I was jealous.

But because ruining her life was the only thing that brought me any kind of satisfaction.

And right now, she was a budding flower that needed to be plucked from the dirt before it could blossom.

"Um." A pink blush stains her cheeks as she tucks a strand of hair behind her ear. "I mean, I guess I could."

The douchebag grins. "Great." His gaze drops to her chest. "Maybe after we can watch a movie and hang out?"

Over my dead fucking body.

Aspen

Oh. My. God.

Was Ken Ruckman *flirting* with me?

Holy crap. I've had the biggest crush on him ever since last year when he recovered a fumble and saved the game against the Vikings.

And now he's asking me to tutor him at his house and watch movies.

I want to pinch myself to make sure this is actually happening because I'm not the kind of girl football players ask out on dates.

I'm the kind of girl they avoid.

"Sure." My cheeks heat, and I'm positive I must be blushing. "That would be—"

Words get trapped in my throat the moment I see him…looming over us like a dark storm cloud.

Instantly, my heart pounds with dread.

Trenton Knox—or just *Knox,* as everyone calls him—is the bane of my existence.

Not only did he go out of his way to make my life a living hell every day…he made sure I was a social pariah who had no friends.

I should have known he'd be lurking nearby, no doubt searching for more ways to make me suffer.

God, I hate him.

So much so, I find myself constantly wishing for him to either get hit by a bus, or get caught doing something stupid and be thrown in jail. Unfortunately, the latter would never happen because his father is an FBI agent.

I glare at him. "What are you doing here?"

Ignoring me, he shifts his attention to Ken.

Suddenly, Ken stands up and snatches his backpack off the desk. "On second thought, tonight won't work. I have this…thing."

My mouth drops as he heads for the door, and it takes everything in me not to scream.

Knox didn't even have to utter a single word to put the fear of God into him.

I know he's intimidating and scares everyone at school—hell, make that the entire freaking town— shitless of him, but this is ridiculous.

Furious, I slam my textbook shut. "I hate you."

As usual, the asshole stays silent.

Because he never says a single word to me.

Not unless it's an insult.

I'll never know what I did to make him hate *me* so much, but I will not waste precious moments of my life trying to figure it out.

As much as I'd like to make friends and go out on dates—especially with hot football players—there are more important things I want out of life.

Like to get a scholarship and be able to attend a good college.

Have a stable career.

Because it would be nice to not see an eviction notice taped to the front door every few months.

Not sparing him another glance, I grab my things and march out of the room.

I'm changing out books in my locker when someone seizes my arm.

"What—"

I don't have the chance to finish that sentence because Knox tugs me down the empty hallway.

"Are you out of your damn mind? Leave me alone."

I might as well be speaking another language though, because he only tightens his grip and walks faster.

A minute later, he opens the door to what looks like a storage closet and shoves me inside.

Trepidation twists my stomach. Knox has terrorized me since the moment I stepped foot inside Black Mountain, but he's never *trapped* me before.

As if sensing my fear, his lips curve in a malicious grin.

I hate the way my breath catches.

Because while he's the biggest asshole on the planet...he's also dangerously attractive.

Full lips, tan skin, dark hair shaved close to the scalp, a sharp jawline that looks like the gods carved it from granite, prominent cheekbones...a stubborn chin that's currently clenching in contempt.

However, it's those unusual, *piercing,* harsh eyes that never fail to hold me captive.

I'd give just about anything to know why—despite how intimidating and scary he is—he looks like the most broken person I've ever seen.

Shaking that thought from my head, I make for the door.

However, he stands in front of it, blocking me from exiting.

"What is your prob—"

I don't get to finish that sentence because his hand slides to the back of my neck and his mouth crashes against mine.

What the hell?

Everything freezes…except my heart, which feels like it's exploding.

It's my first kiss..

The fact *Knox* is the one doing it is just…weird.

I should probably stop him. I hate his guts and he doesn't deserve to kiss me.

But I can't…because he's kissing me like he just swallowed poison and I'm the antidote.

At first there's no tongue. Just greedy lips.

But then he growls, low and deep, and *everything* changes.

I rest my hands on his shoulders, my knees going weak as the fingers on my neck tighten and he coaxes my mouth open to feed me his tongue.

He tastes like cinnamon and uninvited desire…wrapped in pure evil.

Head spinning, I fall into the kiss, sinking fast into the black hole he's imprisoned me in.

I should end this madness and make him apologize. Not only for stealing my first kiss—because that's *exactly* what he did—but for all the torture he's inflicted.

I'm about to break away, but his free hand slithers up my leg, disappearing under my skirt.

Despite the need coiling inside me, my chest constricts and my nerves reach new heights.

Especially when he presses me against a shelf and tugs my panties down my legs.

At sixteen, plenty of my peers are having sex, so it's not like this is unusual. However, I'm still trying to wrap my mind around how in the span of a few minutes I'm going from experiencing my very first kiss to…whatever he's about to do.

"I've never done this," I whisper against his mouth, feeling so vulnerable I could cry.

His entire body tenses before he edges away.

A condescending smirk twists his lips. "I can tell."

His words are the equivalent of a slap, but I won't give him the satisfaction of knowing how much they hurt.

Head held high, I go to shove past him, but he opens the door, beating me to it.

I was prepared for Knox to be an asshole, because he always is.

What I'm not prepared for is to see a group of guys from the football team—Ken included—huddled right outside the closet.

Knox holds up my white-cotton panties like a trophy. "She's a purebred fire crotch. The carpet matches the drapes."

A few guys snicker.

Until Knox sniffs his fingers and makes a face like he smells something rancid. "Bitch smells like tuna though."

With that, he stalks off.

And I wonder if it's actually possible to die from embarrassment.

Or from hating someone so much.

11th grade.

Aspen

The priest is talking, but I can't hear a word he's saying.

The only thing I can focus on is the coffin beside him.

The one containing my father's body.

Leo puts his arm around my shoulders and kisses my temple.

As usual, he's the only one here for me.

Sure, my mother is in attendance, but she's buzzing around the room socializing, like my father's wake is a party she's hosting.

The first tear rolls down my cheek, but I quickly wipe it away. I don't want to fall apart in a room full of people. Especially when I hardly know most of them.

My chest squeezes and I swallow the needles in my throat.

I don't understand how this happened.

I mean—I'm not an idiot so I can comprehend that apparently, my father was a swindler.

Evidently, he convinced a bunch of people to invest in a retirement home.

And then stole their money.

He fucked with the wrong person though, because two years later he was found in a parking lot with a bullet in his head.

The man who shot him didn't even try to deny it when the police tracked him down at his house.

He simply said my father deserved it for stealing his hard-earned savings.

And now here I am…at his wake, grappling with the fact that the man I loved more than life itself is gone.

Because he was a conman.

Leo turns to me when the priest finally stops talking. "Is there anything you need? Anything I can do?"

I shake my head, trying my hardest to keep the tears at bay.

Leo lifts my chin, forcing my gaze to meet his. "It's okay to be angry." His eyes soften. "It's also okay to miss him. Your dad went down a bad road, but he loved you, Aspen."

I know he did.

But knowing that only makes the pain worse.

He stole from people to not only support his family, but to make sure my superficial mother had everything she wanted.

And not just her.

He stole to make sure *I* had a better education, clothes, books, a roof over my head, food in my belly…the braces I begged for to fix my crooked teeth.

Absentmindedly, I finger the necklace around my neck. The one I can't bring myself to take off. *Pearls*.

The last time I saw my dad we were eating breakfast—bacon, eggs, and French toast.

I was excited because it meant things were on the upswing again and we had enough money to pay our bills and fill the fridge.

But now I know the truth.

Whenever my family had money…it was never really ours.

"It hurts," I whisper. "Knowing what he did. Who he really was."

"I get it." He sighs heavily. "I wish I'd known so I could have stopped him." Closing his eyes, he shrugs. "He asked me to draw up contracts and make sure everything was legal. After that…"

It was out of his hands.

"He was my best friend," Leo states with a shake of his head. "But now I feel like I never really knew him." He looks down at his shoes. "I also can't help but feel like I failed him…failed *you*."

"It wasn't your fault."

He touches my cheek. "It wasn't yours either, honey."

We stare at each other for the better part of a minute…until something out of the corner of my eye catches my attention.

"What the hell is she doing?"

I watch as my mother—who's obviously had way too much wine tonight—shamelessly flirts with some man.

Upon closer inspection, I realize it's not just any man…it's Leo's brother.

And Knox's father.

Leo mentioned that he asked his brother for help when my dad was found murdered, since he's an FBI agent…but I had no idea he and my mother had grown so *close* in the week since my father had been found murdered.

The anger brewing in my gut burns hotter the longer I stare at them.

For fuck's sake, it's my father's wake. Yet, here she is trying to sink her hooks into the next walking ATM she can find.

Not only was it in poor taste, it was embarrassing as hell.

"Aspen," Leo calls out behind me when I walk over to them.

I ignore him.

"Aspen, hi," my mom says when she finally notices me. However, it's short lived because almost immediately her focus is back on the man she's flirting with. "Trent, this is my daughter. I believe you have a son around the same age."

I grind my molars so hard I'm surprised they don't turn to dust.

Trent smiles before taking a sip of his coffee. "I do. He attends Black Mountain Academy."

My mom leans into him, placing her palm on his chest. "What a coincidence. So does Aspen." Her eyes flick to me. "Aspen, dear, isn't that wonderful—"

"It's your husband's wake," I remind her. "Have a little decency."

She blinks, clearly caught off guard by my outburst. "Excuse me?"

It's all I can do not to laugh.

I'm done with this little act she puts on.

Done with her need to pretend like life is perfect so she can fit in with those she deems significant.

Done with her need to demand shit from others without getting off her ass and working for what she wants.

Done with her being so drunk she ignores the important things.

Like taking care of her daughter.

My mother is beautiful—so beautiful she easily uses her looks to her advantage. I have no doubt it's why my dad stayed with her so long, despite how horrible she is—but her insides are so ugly it makes me physically sick.

"Maybe if you weren't a superficial lush Dad wouldn't be dead," I hiss with every ounce of venom I feel for the woman standing before me.

Her eyes widen. "How dare you."

The sharp sting of her palm slapping my cheek, followed by the audible gasps from people standing nearby, sends me reeling.

She's never hit me before.

"That's *enough*, Eileen," Leo barks, wedging himself between us. "This isn't the time or place."

Trent shoots me a sympathetic look before taking my mother by the elbow and leading her out of the room.

Leo turns to me. "Are you okay?"

I rub my cheek. "I'm fine."

But really…I'm not.

I don't know how to make sense of this loss.

I don't know what I'm going to do without my dad.

I don't know how I'm going to survive on my own.

Because that's exactly what I am now. *All alone.*

"I'm sorry about that," Leo says. "It was completely uncalled for."

"Don't apologize on her behalf."

Frowning, he reaches into his suit pocket and pulls out his wallet. "You know I'm always here for you, right?"

I stare down at the small wad of money in his hand and finally realize why people say it's the root of all evil.

Money equals greed.

Greed made my mother the shallow, vapid woman she is today.

Greed killed my father.

I wonder what it would do to me.

Shaking my head, I say, "I can't accept that."

Leo has a wife who's struggling with ALS. Over the past year, her health has declined so much she can no longer speak or move without the help of a twenty-four-hour nurse.

Even though Leo is a lawyer and makes a decent living, the kind of help she requires is expensive.

"Take it, Aspen," he insists, placing the cash in my hand. "It's the least I can do."

I start to protest again, but he curls my fingers around it. "Let me take care of you."

Those words unleash a surge of agony that's so visceral, I have to clutch my chest.

I can feel my heart physically breaking into a thousand pieces.

My father is dead.

He's never coming back.

I'm on my own.

Heart lodged in my throat, I run out of the room, desperate for air.

The moment I stumble out the back, I lean against the building and drop my head, forcing myself to breathe so I don't pass out.

God, I'm so angry with him for being a thief.

So angry with him for leaving me.

The tears finally fall, and for the first time since I found out he was gone, I give myself over to the heartache and cry.

It hurts so bad. Like someone plunged a dagger straight into my sternum and twisted it until I finally bled out.

A wave of sorrow washes over me and my knees buckle, hitting the ground. I'm so lost in my grief; I don't realize I'm not alone.

Not until a pair of black boots comes into view.

I don't even have to look up to know who they belong to. I always feel his presence…kind of like how some people's bones ache right before it rains.

"What do you want?"

I peer up at him when he doesn't answer.

He's wearing a black hoodie and dark jeans. The full moon illuminates the sharp lines of his face as he takes a cigarette out of a pack and brings it to his mouth.

Silently, he studies me…like I'm some strange new specimen under a microscope.

A puzzle he can't quite figure out.

Narrowing my eyes, I stand.

"What do you want?" I repeat, harsher this time.

Frustration claws its way up my throat when he doesn't respond, and I shove him.

"Why the hell are you here, Knox?"

I go to shove him again, but he backs me against the building, his arms caging me in.

I freeze, my insides seizing up when long fingers curl around my neck and he dips his head.

His rough voice is a menacing rumble in my ear. "Because I knew you'd be in pain." A cold sweat breaks over me and a weird twist goes through my chest when his tongue darts out and he licks my tear-stained cheek. "And I wanted to see it."

His cruel words punch into my heart. "I hate you."

I mean the proclamation with every fiber of my being.

His dark laugh is every bit as callous as he is when he pushes off me and stalks away.

Chapter 1

Aspen

One year later…

*G*rimacing, I adjust the spaghetti strap of my peach chiffon bridesmaid dress, wishing I was anywhere else but here.

My lips twist into a scowl as I watch my mother and her new husband careen around the dance floor.

People smile and clap when he dips her and plants a lingering kiss on her lips.

They look so happy it's nauseating.

Peeling my gaze away from the train wreck, I walk over to the bar stationed in the corner.

"What can I get you, pretty lady?" the bartender asks.

Hoping he takes mercy on me and doesn't ask for my I.D, I say, "Vodka and Sprite."

He looks me up and down, assessing me. "Do you have I—"

"My mother's the bride," I whisper. "I could really use a drink."

Make that twenty.

He fills up a glass and winks. "Okay, but if anyone asks, you didn't get this from me."

Giving him an appreciative smile, I pick up the glass he sets in front of me. "Thanks."

I wander over to the back of the large room, trying my hardest to blend in with the wall. My mother doesn't have a big family and neither does her new husband, so *thankfully* it's not a big wedding. Aside from my senile grandmother and an annoying aunt I haven't seen in years, the guests mostly consist of the men he works with and a few friends my mom made at the country club she recently joined.

Annoyed, I run my tongue over my teeth—teeth that no longer have braces because my mother *demanded* they be removed three months early for the wedding.

God, everything about this marriage is sickening.

My father's body wasn't even cold before she moved on.

Closing my eyes, I take a sip of my drink, hoping the alcohol quells the anger in the pit of my stomach and makes being here a little more bearable.

I'm about to go back to the bar and ask for another one when my phone vibrates.

I smile when I see his name flash across the screen.

"Hey, you," I answer. "Shouldn't you be dancing?"

I hear him chuckle over the line. "I'm too busy looking at you." His voice turns serious. "You look beautiful."

I scan the room but don't see him. "*Very* funny. This dress is hideous…and itchy. I can't wait to get it off."

"Interesting," he muses. "I was just thinking the same thing."

I bet he was.

I amble to the other side of the room, hoping to spot him. "Where are you hiding?"

"I just slipped out the back door, and now I'm headed toward my car…waiting for a beautiful redhead to come out here and join me."

"Is that so?" I tease, placing my empty glass on a table.

"I need you, Aspen," he croaks, and I can't help but picture him stroking his cock as he waits for me. "I've been hard as a goddamn rock since I saw you."

Pinning the phone between my ear and shoulder, I head toward the exit. "Guess I should do something about that then, hu—"

I startle, nearly dropping my phone when someone grabs my wrist.

A surge of animosity flows through me like hot lava when I look up and realize it's Knox.

The asshole isn't just my bully and enemy anymore…

He's my new stepbrother.

Tightening his grip, he escorts me to what appears to be a coat room.

"What the hell?"

"Let's get one thing straight," he snarls, cornering me until my spine meets a row of coats. "Your whore mother marrying my father changes nothing between us."

I almost want to laugh, because I don't like this new *arrangement* any more than he does.

However, it's comical just how much it's ruffling his feathers.

"Awe, what's the matter, *Trenton?*" I taunt. "Afraid I'll—"

Words die in my throat when one hand slams across my mouth and the other one hovers over my throat, threatening to squeeze. "I'm not afraid of anything, *Stray.*"

He utters the last word with so much venom I nearly wince. Out of all the cruel nicknames Knox has given me over the years, this one hurts the most.

Because it's the truth.

Ever since my dad died, I've felt lost and abandoned.

Like a kitten who lost its way and will never find home because they don't belong anywhere.

He leans in close, his ruthless stare burning a hole right through me. "But you should be."

A shiver runs down my spine, not only because of his threatening words and the hostility they're laced with…but the lethal way he's looking at me.

As if he's contemplating the best method to kill me and dispose of my body afterward.

I've heard all the rumors going around school.

His mom was murdered when he was twelve…

And his dad sent him to a mental institution for a year while he covered it up.

Because Knox was the one who did it.

People weren't terrified of him just because he was a bully who got off on terrorizing others.

They were terrified because he was a legitimate psychopath who was capable of homicide.

Until now, I wasn't sure I believed any of the gossip.

At six foot three he towers over my five-four frame, but I force myself to peer up and look him right in the eyes. "Go to hell."

Deep down I'm petrified of the lunatic, but I refuse to let him see that.

My breath hitches when he presses his body against mine and the hand looming over my throat constricts. "I live there."

Live? More like ruled because as far as I'm concerned, he's the devil.

My retort falls by the wayside, though, when he leans in and his mouth brushes mine.

I'm about to ask what the fuck he's doing, but a sharp sting shoots through my flesh when his teeth clamp down on my bottom lip and I taste a hint of copper.

I try to pull away, but that only makes the pain worse.

Thinking quick, I knee him in the balls.

With an aggravated grunt, he finally releases his hold.

I expect him to be pissed so I brace myself, preparing for another attack, but to my surprise there's a trace of amusement in his expression.

His tongue darts out and I see the glint of metal from his piercing as he swipes the blood gathered on his lip. "Welcome to the family, *sis*."

With those cryptic parting words, he turns and storms out.

Chapter 2

Knox

*A*nger warms my blood as I zero in on the Mercedes stationed under a large oak tree in the back of the parking lot.

The black SUV rocks ever so slightly with their movements, and all six windows start to fog up.

Gravel crunches beneath my boots as I make my way over to them.

They're so into their forbidden fuckfest, they don't hear me approach.

I stand behind a tree as one window rolls down and I hear their heavy breathing.

Bringing a cigarette to my lips, I light it, observing their little show.

Long red hair cascades down her back in a mess of silky waves, and her dress is pushed up those creamy thighs as she straddles him in the backseat, riding his pathetic cock to the finish line.

The old man sputters a curse, digging his fingers into her hips. "Shit."

He pants and beads of sweat drip down his face as he reaches up and yanks the top of her dress down, exposing one of her tits.

I ignore the way my dick twitches when he sucks a pale, pink nipple into his mouth.

"Oh, fuck," he sputters. "I'm gonna come, honey."

She speeds up her movements, causing the SUV to rock a little more. "Me too."

I grind my molars when she tilts her head back and moans, the action sounding every bit as fake as she is.

My new stepsister might have everyone at school fooled with the straight A, student body president, goody-two-shoes persona she likes to put on...

But I know the truth.

Aspen Falcone isn't nearly as innocent as she pretends to be.

And in my experience, those people are the most dangerous.

The hypocrites who like to hide who they really are.

Pinching the cigarette between my fingers, I take another long drag, watching as Aspen unfastens herself from my uncle's—and her dead dad's best friend's—dick and fixes her dress.

Smoke pours out of my mouth as I laugh under my breath.

The only thing better than killing a wild animal is catching it in a trap.

Because then they have nowhere to run.

Nowhere to hide.

Chapter 3

Aspen

"*B*reakfast is ready," my mother calls out from the other side of my bedroom door.

I roll my eyes so hard I swear I see my brain. Ever since the wedding two weeks ago, she's been acting like some kind of Stepford housewife.

Because that's what her new husband wants.

Reaching for my pearl necklace, I secure it around my neck.

The holiday break is officially over, which means it's time to go back to school.

Picking up my brush, I run it through my hair a few times before twisting it into a bun and securing it.

I don't bother putting makeup on for school, so it doesn't take me long to get ready.

After grabbing my bookbag off my bed, I head for the spiral staircase.

The only good thing about my new house is that it's big.

Unfortunately, not big enough to keep me away from *him*.

Evidently, Knox's room is in the basement—something I was grateful to find out. However, I have no choice but to see him more than I care to because my new stepdad insists we all have breakfast and dinner together…like we're some kind of big happy family.

Once I enter the spacious kitchen, I make a beeline for the coffee maker because caffeine is pretty much how I survive.

Unfortunately, Knox beats me to it.

I don't miss the smirk on his face as he pours what's left in the coffee pot into his mug and takes a sip.

Bastard.

"Here," Trent offers, pushing his cup toward me when I take a seat at the table. "It's my fourth one so far, and your mother thinks I should cut down."

Leaning over, she kisses his cheek. "I just want you to be healthy."

Disgust rolls through me. I feel like I'm trapped in an episode of Black Mirror that I can't escape.

And even though my new stepdad is trying to be nice, me accepting the olive branch he's extending might make him think I accept his marriage to my mother.

And I don't.

"It's fine," I lie, pushing the mug away. "I'm not a big coffee drinker anyway."

Averting my gaze, I shovel some eggs onto my plate. I'm not hungry, but maybe they'll help push down the bile crawling up my throat.

An awkward silence falls over the table for the rest of breakfast.

Until my mother holds up her glass of orange juice—which I'm positive is actually a mimosa—and says, "Aspen, will you be here tonight, or will you be studying at Violet's again?"

"I'll be at Violet's," I mumble, and she frowns.

While Violet is a friend of mine—well, sort of because I don't really have friends and neither does she—I also use her as a cover-up.

Because Lord knows my mother would keel over and die if she ever found out the truth.

That thought has my lips twitching. *On second thought—maybe I should spill the beans.*

I'm grateful when Trent shifts the focus to his son. "I made you an appointment at the recruitment center after school."

Recruitment center? As in the *military?*

Instantly, Knox tenses, his hand clenching around his fork. I expect him to argue, because he's not one to back down from a fight.

However, to my utter shock he grinds out, "Okay."

Then he gets up from the table and walks over to the sink.

Interesting.

I finish the rest of my eggs and wipe my mouth with a napkin. The bus will be here soon and if I don't hustle, I'll miss it.

"So, your mother and I were talking," Trent says as I grab my backpack off the floor. "We think it's time to get you a car."

It takes everything in me not to slam my plate over his head.

I'm not sure which is worse—the audacity of him thinking he has *any* right to consult with my mother about making decisions for me.

Or the fact he's trying to buy me.

"I'm fine with taking the bus."

Truth is, I've been wanting a car ever since I got my license last year. However, I'd rather crawl on broken glass than let him buy me one.

My stepdad makes a face, clearly displeased with my refusal. "We'll talk more about it at dinner." Swiveling his gaze to his son, he says, "In the meantime, Trenton will take you to school."

The dish in Knox's hand falls into the sink with a loud crash, and I swear I see the tiny hairs on the back of his neck stand on end.

It would almost be comical if I didn't harbor so much hatred for him.

"That's not nec—"

"Do you have a problem with taking your sister to school?" Trent interjects, cutting me off.

Being referred to as Knox's sister makes me want to vomit.

Knox's voice is so low I almost don't hear him respond, "No."

"No, *what?*" his father snaps.

The muscles in Knox's back coil. "No, *sir.*"

Jesus. I knew Knox and his dad weren't particularly close, but their relationship makes the one I have with my mother look like rainbows and butterflies.

Then again, Knox is a sadistic psycho, so I can understand why his dad wants to keep him on such a short leash.

Hell, maybe Knox enlisting in the Army is just what he needs. This way he can learn to have some respect for others, and you know…use his homicidal tendencies for the greater good.

With hands folded in front of him, my stepfather flashes me a terse smile. "Then it's settled. Trenton will take you to and from school until we get you a car."

I can't help but feel like this is some kind of intimidation tactic.

It's no secret Knox and I don't like one another, ergo being forced to ride to and from school with him will no doubt coerce me to accept the stupid car he wants to buy me.

I don't like it one bit.

Unfortunately, I'm late for school so I don't have the time to argue with him about it.

Hiking the strap of my purse up my shoulder, I stand. "Whatever."

"Have a good day at school, kids," my mother calls out as I head for the front door.

Seriously? Who the hell is this woman and why is she suddenly acting like June freaking Cleaver?

Shaking my head, I swing open the door and tread down the cobblestone path that leads to the driveway. Knox is hot on my heels.

"You don't have to take me," I tell him when we reach the driveway. "The bus stop is down the road."

I'm walking past his jeep when there's a sharp tug on my arm.

Next thing I know, he's carting me inside his vehicle like I'm a rag doll. "Asshole."

Jaw ticking, he walks around to the driver's side and throws open the door.

"What's the matter?" I taunt when he starts the engine. "Scared to disappoint daddy?"

The hand around the steering wheel clenches, causing the veins and tendons in his arms to flex. "Do us both a favor and shut the fuck up."

I purse my lips. "And if I don't?"

The look he shoots me could kill a dead person. "I'll toss your annoying ass out of my jeep when we reach the highway." His teeth flash white. "Oncoming traffic will take care of the rest."

He flicks a button on the dashboard. A moment later, a Papa Roach song blasts through the speakers and he peels out of the driveway.

We don't say a word to each other for the rest of the drive.

Chapter 4

Aspen

"*How* ow was your holiday break?" I ask Brie who's seated across from me.

As another resident *outcast* of Black Mountain Academy, we've been eating lunch in silent solidarity together since ninth grade.

Emphasis on the *silent* part because the girl is as timid—and as quiet—as a mouse and rarely speaks.

She looks down at her plate. "Fine."

Yup. That's the most I'm going to get out of the girl.

I twirl my spaghetti around my fork. "You should join student council."

Truth is, I'm desperate for more members. Hell, I'm pretty sure the only reason I got voted in as president is because no one else wanted it.

And if I'm being honest with myself, *I* only wanted the position because it looks great on college applications.

Brie shakes her head, and that's the end of that.

Sighing, I bring my water bottle to my mouth. "I swear it's not as bad as you…" My sentence trails off when Brie's blue eyes widen with fear.

Instantly, I know who's behind me.

I spin around in my seat. "What do you want, Knox?"

My stomach rolls when I see *Shadow*—the freak he's rumored to be hooking up with—draped around him.

33

I take in her heavy black liner, black lipstick, combat boots, the blue-green hair she's wearing in pigtails, and the multiple piercings on her face. Why she doesn't get in trouble for violating the dress code is anyone's guess.

The hand Knox has curled around Shadow's hip tightens. "Be at my jeep at three."

"No can do." I give him a sugary sweet smile. "I have a student council meeting after school."

His nostrils flare with annoyance. "Of course, you fucking do."

Slinging an arm around Shadow's shoulders, he stalks off, but not before I hear Shadow mutter, "Nice pearls, prude."

You'd think someone like her would understand what it's like to be ostracized…but apparently not.

Before I can stop myself, I utter, "Isn't it time for you to go back to your coffin, Morticia?"

Snarling, she bares her teeth at me.

I make the sign of the cross with my fingers. "May the power of Christ compel you."

To my surprise—and delight—a few people in the cafeteria laugh.

Until Knox strides back over.

It happens so quick, I barely have time to register him picking up my plate of pasta before dumping it over my head.

Embarrassment floods my cheeks as the red sauce seeps into my hair and clothes and laughter echoes throughout the cafeteria.

Since I don't have a spare uniform, I'm going to be stuck like this all day.

I peel a few strands of spaghetti off my skirt and throw it at him. "Asshole."

He plucks it off his shirt and licks the sauce from his thumb. "I suggest you stop running your mouth, Stray."

I'd rather swallow glass.

I'm about to tell him so, but he seizes my chin. "Or it will get a lot worse. Trust me."

My eyes burn with anger as he releases his hold on me and grabs Shadow's ass before heading for the exit.

Brie gives me a sympathetic smile. "Let's go to the bathroom so you can clean up."

As if my day couldn't get any worse, the student council meeting ended up running late and the treasurer quit.

Groaning, I take my phone out and text Leo. The late bus left a little while ago, so I'm hoping he has a free minute and can give me a lift.

Aspen: Can you give me a ride home? I missed the bus.

He's usually quick to respond, but after five-minutes pass without an answer, I head outside.

Seeing as the weather isn't bad, I'll just walk home.

Granted, it will take me at least an hour on foot.

I freeze when I spot Knox's red jeep in the empty parking lot.

That's…*weird*. I figured he would have left already. Especially since he has an appointment at the recruitment center.

Even though I probably shouldn't, I walk over to his jeep anyway. The way I see it, giving me a ride home is the *least* he can do after dumping my lunch over my head.

I stop mid-step when I hear the sound of someone moaning, followed by, "Jesus, Knox. Your dick is so fucking big. My jaw hurts."

Yeah, file that under things I could have gone my whole life without knowing.

A rough grunt breaks free. "Less talking, more sucking."

Gross.

Heat rises to my cheeks and I'm about to walk away, but piercing eyes hold mine in the side mirror…almost daring me to watch.

I shouldn't. This is disgusting.

And yet…I find myself unable to move.

I see his lips curve into a smirk before he sticks his arm out the open window and adjusts the mirror ever so slightly.

Shadow's head bobs up and down in his lap, and the muscles in his arms flex as he threads his fingers through her blue-green hair.

I can't see her face, but it's obvious what she's doing to him given the movement and all the gagging sounds she's making.

Knox adjusts the mirror again, and all I can see is him.

His dark eyebrows pinch together before he tilts his head back against the seat and closes his eyes. His mouth parts ever so slightly, the thick vein running along the column of his neck bulging as he forces her head up and down his cock.

Suddenly, his eyes open, pinning me to the spot.

I tense, shame flushing my skin as his gaze burns a hole right through me.

He grips the side of the jeep, the vehicle now rocking as he fucks her mouth.

I swallow hard, my heart hammering in my chest.

A desperate whimper cuts through the air.

I stop breathing, humiliation rolling through me like a boulder picking up speed when I realize it wasn't from either of them.

It was from *me*.

I see the corner of his mouth curve…like he knows he's got me right where he wants me.

Fuck that.

I turn away, squeezing my eyes shut.

A moment later, I hear the jeep door open.

"What the hell, Knox?" Shadow shrieks.

"Get out," he barks.

Jesus. Not only is he a ruthless asshole to me, he's that way to everyone.

Shadow slinks out the passenger door, looking mad as hell.

Only her anger isn't directed at Knox like it should be…it's aimed at *me*.

"Pearl clutcher," she hisses before she walks over to her beat-up Toyota.

I flip her the bird. "Cock sucker."

"Get in," Knox grunts, banging his fist on the side of his jeep. "Now."

I should tell him to go fuck himself, but I really need a ride. Not to mention, I'm enjoying the look of contempt *Elvira* is giving me as I climb into the passenger seat her boyfriend just kicked her out of.

"Quite a girl you got there."

He tugs his zipper up and buckles his belt. "That's some judgement coming from a hypocrite like you."

I have no idea what he's talking about.

Unless…

No. I shake the thought out of my head. There's no way he'd know about me and Leo.

No one does.

As if on cue, my phone buzzes with an incoming text.

I wait for Knox to gun the engine before I read it.

Leo: Can't. I'm stuck in a meeting. I'll PayPal you some money for an Uber.

Aspen: No, it's okay. I found a ride.

Almost immediately, another text comes through.

Leo: Will I see you tonight?

Disappointment flickers in my chest as my thumb hovers over the keyboard.

Aspen: Can't. I'm studying for a big test with Violet. I'm free tomorrow night, though.

Leo: Tomorrow night it is then. Miss you, honey.

A small smile touches my lips.

Aspen: Miss you, too.

I never intended to hook up with Leo. It kind of just happened.

And before you judge me for my indiscretions—I'm fully aware of what it makes me and exactly how society would perceive me if they knew my secret.

Yes, he's married. But he and his wife haven't been together in a very long time, given she's suffering from a crippling disease that's slowly killing her.

Yes, he's old enough to be my father. Which would be creepy to some people, seeing as he was *my* father's best friend.

But the thing is...we all want to be special to someone.

We all want to feel cherished and cared for.

To know you have someone in this world who gives a shit about you.

Leo is that person for me.

And while I would never use him for his money—because I'm not my mother—I do use him for his capacity to care about me.

It makes me feel less alone in the world.

Like I belong somewhere.

And even though I'll go off to college soon and I have no delusions that he'll probably end up marrying a woman who's closer to his age after his first wife passes, right now, what we have works.

It makes me feel a little less dead inside.

Knox takes a cigarette out and brings it to his mouth. "My father's gonna give me shit about not showing up to the recruiting appointment, so I'll need you to tell him the truth."

I place my phone back in my purse. "That you were getting a blowjob in the school parking lot?"

He brings a lighter to the end of his cigarette. "That your bullshit little meeting ran late, and you asked me to wait for you so I could give you a ride home."

Who's the hypocrite now?

"But I didn't ask you to wait for me," I point out.

He makes a sound of annoyance in his throat, looking like he wants to reach over and throttle me. "Goddammit, you're a pain in the balls. Are you gonna do it or not?"

I fold my hands in my lap. "Let me get this straight, you're asking me to lie for you."

A stream of smoke leaves his mouth. "Get off your high horse, Stray. It's not like you've never lied before."

He's right.

But I only lie to cover up my shit. *Not his.*

Besides, he has a lot of nerve asking me to do him a solid after what he pulled today.

I can feel his gaze boring into me; however, I'm not prepared for his next statement.

"Did you enjoy watching me get my dick sucked?"

My cheeks heat. "No."

A cocky smirk pulls at his lips. "Liar."

"I didn't," I exclaim, squirming in my seat. "But I'll cover for you as long as you never bring it up again."

Witnessing that was an unfortunate mishap and the last thing I need is to hear him using it to torment me whenever the urge strikes.

The tendons in his hand flex as he tightens his grip around the steering wheel. "I bet you wish it was your lips wrapped around my cock."

At that, I laugh. "Definitely not." I take out my phone again because having a conversation with him is worse than hearing nails on a chalkboard. "And you're officially on your own now when it comes to Daddy."

Chapter 5

Knox

"What part of you have a meeting after school don't you fucking understand?" my father booms the moment I pull in the driveway.

I suck my cigarette down to the filter and toss it out the window.

I knew he'd be pissed when I didn't show up, but I was hoping I'd be able to get home and sneak downstairs before he started with his shit.

I open my mouth to tell him something came up, but Aspen says, "It was my fault. I asked him to wait for me after school to give me a ride home, but my student council meeting ended up running late and I forgot to tell him."

My dad blanches, clearly caught off guard by her declaration.

That makes two of us.

"Oh." I can tell he wants to scream some more, but he won't because he still wants to make a good impression on her. "I see." His dark eyes zero in on me again. "I'll reschedule for next week. This time you better be there."

You can cut the tension between us with a knife.

Apprehension flashes across Aspen's face before she opens the door and hops out of my jeep. "I'm gonna take a nap before I go to Violet's."

"Aspen," I call out when she's halfway up the driveway.

She freezes. "Yes?"

"What time are you going to Violet's house?"

I bite back a smirk when she swallows thickly.

"Eight."

Liar.

She usually leaves at ten, but she pushed it up by two hours because my dad's still standing in front of us and going to a friend's house to study at ten on a school night sounds suspect as fuck.

"I'll drive you."

She looks like a mouse hovering near a trap. She's starving and wants the cheese so badly she can already taste it…

But she also knows one little bite might kill her.

"You don't have to. I can walk—"

"Walking alone at night is dangerous for a young lady," my dad chimes in. "One of us will drive you."

Choose your poison wisely, Stray.

She looks at me. "I'll be ready by seven fifty."

Good girl.

Aspen probably thinks I'm doing her a solid for covering for me, but I'm not.

I just enjoy watching her squirm.

"She's a beautiful girl," my dad states after she walks into the house. "I'm glad you're being a good brother and looking out for your new sister."

Chapter 6

Aspen

Dammit Violet, answer your phone.

I've been trying to get ahold of her ever since Knox offered to drive me to her house, but she still hasn't texted me back.

Normally it wouldn't be a problem, but I have no freaking idea where she lives.

The only thing I know is that she lives with her Aunt who's loaded.

I rub my hands on my jean-clad thighs and force myself to breathe.

"Everything okay?" Knox questions from the driver's seat.

He's been acting smugger than usual ever since we got in the car.

At first, I thought he offered to drive me as a thank you for covering for him in front of his dad, but now I'm not so sure.

Knowing him, he's only doing it because he knows how much I loathe being near him.

"Just peachy."

"You said she lives on Crystal Court, right?"

I nod. "Yup."

My pulse races when he turns down a side street. "What's the house number?"

"Twenty-three."

We drive past a few houses and he rubs his chin. "Weird. The houses on this block are all in the hundreds."

Dammit.

I bring my palm to my forehead. "Whoops. I meant one twenty-three."

His eyes narrow a little. "Right."

A moment later he pulls to a stop in front of a large house. "We're here."

I grab my purse and knapsack. "Thanks." I bristle when he cuts the engine. "What are you doing?"

"I figured I'd wait for you to go inside before I leave."

Well, shit.

"That's really not necessary."

His teeth flash white. "Just trying to be helpful."

It's all I can do not to laugh. He's not trying to be helpful, he's…

What *is* he trying to do?

My stomach somersaults, and I feel the blood drain from my face with my next thought.

No. There's no way he knows.

How could he?

Pushing the door open, I slide out of the seat.

"What time should I pick you up?" he calls out.

I freeze, scanning my brain for a reply that will make him back the fuck off.

"You don't have to. Violet already said she'd drop me off later."

I can tell he wants to argue, but fortunately he drops it.

Unfortunately, I can feel his eyes glued to me the entire time I walk up the driveway.

My palms turn clammy the closer I get to the house because there's no way in hell Violet will be the one answering.

It's fine. I got this.

I turn around and wave when I reach the front door, hoping he'll drive off, but no such luck.

If anything, the fucker looks amused.

Gritting my teeth, I ring the doorbell.

A sweet old woman answers. "Hi, dear. How can I help you?"

I blurt out the first thing that comes to mind, "Hello, ma'am. Do you have a moment to talk about our Lord and Savior, Jesus Christ?"

Ignoring her confused expression, I muscle my way inside the poor woman's house and shut the door behind me.

"Come on, sexy," the guy says as I grind against him. "Take that mask off and let me see your face."

"Sorry," I tell him. "Club rules."

I never in a million years thought I'd be a stripper, but after my dad died and I had no way to support myself—or pay for college—it was the only option at my disposal.

Working at an ice cream shop after school didn't pay the bills or fit around my hectic school schedule. And I'd rather die than rely on my new stepdad or accept the money Leo's always offering.

Stripping at the *Bashful Beaver* doesn't exactly fill me with pride, but at least I'm able to support myself without relying on anyone else.

"What's your name?" the guy asks, and it's all I can do not to stab him in the thigh with my heel.

I thought being on stage in front of everyone sucked, but I'm realizing private dances in the champagne rooms are way worse.

Not only are they too personal for my liking, the customers tend to ask way too many questions when they get you alone.

"Ginger," I deadpan, hoping he takes the hint to shut up and enjoy his dance.

"Your *real* name," he presses.

"That is my real name."

Gripping his glass of scotch, he sighs. "Do you have any other moves, or is this your only party trick?"

Given I've only worked here for two months, I'm still relatively new to the industry, but rumor has it some girls dole out special *favors* to certain customers who are willing to pay.

However, that's not my scene.

The only thing customers should expect from me is a pair of big tits, an okay ass, and mediocre dancing.

I look at the clock on the wall, relieved to see his time is up.

"Sorry, handsome. Party's over."

He slips a five-dollar bill into my G-string. "Learn to play nice next time."

Dick.

Draining the rest of his drink, he walks out.

Muttering a curse, I slip past Bubba the security guard and make my way into the dressing room.

Violet—or should I say *Angel*, because she's donning her usual white angel wings and feather masquerade mask—must see the disappointment on my face because she says, "That bad, huh?"

I hold up the five-dollar bill. "You tell me?"

She winces. "Ouch."

"You'd make more if you weren't such a bitch to everyone," Candi Kane chimes in. "And if you knew how to dance."

She's one to talk. Not only is she mean to every girl who works here, she fell off the stage last week when she attempted to twerk.

"Ignore her," Violet mutters, running her fingers through her long blonde hair. "You're doing fine. Some guys are just douchebags who need to be put in their place."

Amen to that.

Freddie, the owner, pops his head inside the door. "Ginger, you're on stage in five."

Awesome.

Chapter 7

Aspen

a grunt fills the air as Leo grips my hips and pumps into me one last time before he collapses against the headboard. "You're going to kill me one of these days."

We're currently holed up in a hotel room because I refuse to go to his house and screw him while his wife is home.

There are many lines we've crossed by being together but crossing that one just feels…wrong.

Leaning forward, I fold my arms around his neck. "Come on, Leo. You're not *that* old."

Scowling, he gives my hair a gentle tug. "Brat." His expression turns serious. "Did you come, honey?"

"Yeah," I lie, running my fingers through his sweaty salt and pepper hair.

Truth is, the only time I orgasm is in my room at night when I'm touching myself, but Leo doesn't have to know that.

While the idea of fucking him is exciting because it's so taboo and forbidden…the sex between us isn't why I do this.

He runs his hand down my naked back. "Do you have any idea how special you are to me?"

His words make me smile. "No." My nose crinkles. "Why don't you tell me?"

"I'd do anything for you, Aspen." Brown eyes hold my gaze as he tips my chin. "*Anything.*"

I close the distance between us, crashing my mouth against his.

Deep down, I know I shouldn't believe his pretty words laced in lust—because all men lie when they want to hold on to something.

But not Leo.

There are no pretenses between us. We both know exactly what this relationship is and what it isn't.

Grabbing his hand, I place it on my tit and grind my bare pussy against him.

"I'm gonna need some more time if you want to go again," he murmurs against my mouth. "Unlike you, I'm not a teenager."

Edging away, I look down at his flaccid cock. "I bet if I suck it, you'll be ready for me."

Closing his eyes, he groans. "Dammit. You're *killing* me."

I unstraddle his lap and shift so my mouth hovers over his cock. "You can't die on me yet." I lick his crown, tasting myself on him. "I'm not done having my wicked way with you."

His fingers tangle in my messy hair. "Shit."

Pulling his tip into my mouth, I look up at him. "Leo."

I want him to say it.

I *need* him to say it.

My nerves light up when he finally does.

"Good girl."

I slide my mouth down his length, hoping he'll get hard again for me.

"Honey," he whispers after another minute passes. "I'm sorry, but it's not going to happen right now."

I try to hide my disappointment as I flop onto the mattress. "It's okay."

Reaching down, he palms my naked breast and gives it a squeeze. "Tomorrow night."

I'm about to agree, but then I remember tomorrow is Friday and one of the busiest nights at the club.

"I can't tomorrow. I'm studying with Violet."

I can be honest with Leo about most things, but there's no way in hell I can tell him I'm a stripper.

Not only because he'll be upset, but because he'll throw money at me and demand I quit.

Then he'll have me…because I'll need him to survive.

And I refuse to let any man have that kind of power over me.

Because I'm not my mother.

"You've been studying with her a lot lately," he notes as he gets off the bed. "If I didn't know any better, I'd think you were seeing someone else behind my back."

"I'm just trying to maintain my grades and get a scholarship."

It's not a lie. I really am trying to get a scholarship to a good college.

But in case I don't, I have seven thousand saved up in my bank account.

I'm hoping to have at least triple that by the time summer rolls around.

Sighing, he puts his clothes back on. "I already told you I'd pay—"

"I don't want your money." I drop my gaze to the zipper he's tugging up. "Just your dick."

And the assurance of knowing someone in this world gives a fuck about me.

Walking back over to the bed, he dips his head, planting a quick kiss on my lips. "You can have whatever you want from me."

I purse my lips, pretending to think. "How about a cheeseburger and fries then? Because I'm *starving*."

Guilt colors his expression. "Then I suggest you order room service because Lenora's nurse is leaving early tonight, so I have to head back."

"Oh."

A weird twinge of disappointment flickers in my chest, but then I remember that *she's* his wife and he should be there with her.

"Do you want me to give you a ride home?"

I shake my head. "No, it's okay. I'll call an Uber." I make a face. "Or Knox."

Since he's been so *keen* on giving me rides lately.

I don't realize I said that last part aloud until Leo makes a face. "Knox has been giving you rides?"

Nodding, I pick my jeans and sweatshirt up off the floor. "Yeah, Trent basically insisted he take me to and from school."

I don't know what to make of his expression, but it's clear Leo isn't pleased. "I need to have a little chat with my brother then."

"Why?"

God knows I can't stand Knox, but we live in the same house and attend the same school. It makes sense for him to give me a lift.

He pinches the bridge of his nose. "Knox is my nephew, but…"

"But what?" I ask when his sentence trails off.

Something strange passes in his gaze. If I didn't know any better, I'd say it looks a lot like fear.

"He's not right in the head, Aspen."

I bite my cheek to stop from laughing, because *duh*. "Well, yeah, but—"

"But *nothing*. I don't want you around him. He's dangerous."

Dread coils my stomach and my throat locks up.

For some strange reason, I never wanted to believe the gossip.

Probably because despite Knox being an asshole, there's still a tiny part of me that sees a flicker of humanity in him, buried underneath all the evil.

However, it's obvious I'm a moron who's been deluding herself this whole time, given Leo's genuinely concerned for my safety.

"So the rumors are true," I whisper. "Knox killed his mom."

Oh, God.

I know Trent loves his son, and I can't imagine the position he was in after his wife died, but Knox obviously needs serious help. It's clear his year stint in a mental institution didn't do shit if Leo's scared of him.

Leo folds his arms around me. "I'll tell Trent not to let him near you."

Too late.

"You can't," I whisper when it occurs to me.

"Why not?"

"Because then he might think something's going on between us."

Leo huffs. "I'm not just going to stand by and do nothing." Walking to the nightstand, he picks up his wallet and shoves it in his pocket. "Dammit. I told Trent *not* to marry your mother. I told him it —" He shakes his head. "Doesn't fucking matter. What's done is done." He treks over to the door. "I'll figure something out. In the meantime, just stay the hell away from Knox."

With that, he slams the door.

And I'm left wondering how the hell I'm supposed to stay away from someone when we both live under the same roof?

Chapter 8

Aspen

I jolt when there's a knock on my bedroom door.

It's Sunday night, and I've avoided Knox the entire weekend. Not that it was all that difficult considering neither of us go out of our way to speak to one another.

"Come in," I mutter, staring down at my math textbook.

Mrs. Larsen gave us a shit ton of homework this weekend, and I haven't even made a dent in it.

The door opens and my mom pops her head in. "Dinner will be ready in ten minutes."

"I have a lot of homework to finish. Save me a plate."

Or not. Either way, I don't care.

She frowns. "Trent wants us to all eat dinner together as a family. You know this."

Annoyance bursts through me. I have no interest in playing the part of the doting stepdaughter.

"Tell Trent he can go fuck himself."

She closes her eyes. "Aspen."

I'm not sure what makes me cave. Maybe it's the forlorn way she says my name, or the uneasy way she's worrying her bottom lip between her teeth.

"What's going on, mom?"

Her green eyes widen. "Nothing. What makes you ask that?"

"I don't know," I snap, closing my textbook. "Maybe because you're suddenly acting like some kind of Stepford wife."

And like you actually give a shit about being a decent mother.

She looks around the empty hallway, like she's scared someone might overhear the next words out of her mouth.

"Mom—"

She presses a button on the vacuum and the abrupt hum cuts me off.

Before I can question her any further, she walks over to my bed.

"Trent's late wife's parents had a lot of money before they passed. Money Trent and his son inherited after she died." She frames my face with her hands. "That money can set us up for life, baby. We just need to—"

I pull away from her touch. "*I'm* not doing a damn thing."

God, she makes me sick.

Honestly, I should have known better. It's always the same thing with her. *Using men for money.*

"Don't look at me like that," she hisses. "You know how hard things have been since your dad died."

Yeah, hard enough I had no choice but to become a stripper.

Which is still a hell of a lot more noble than what *she's* doing.

"Aspen—"

I shake my head. "No."

I have absolutely no interest in conspiring with her like we're Thelma and Louise. As far as I'm concerned, she's on her own.

"Please," she pleads, her lower lip trembling, "do this for me."

It's on the tip of my tongue to ask her what she's *ever* done for me.

However, guilt prickles my chest. Because whether I like it or not, the woman is still my mother.

I ball my hands, hating the position she's putting me in.

"Fine," I concede. "I'll go downstairs for dinner. But that's *it*. I want no part in whatever it is you're trying to pull."

"Thank you," she says, walking over to the vacuum to shut it off. "I made Trent's favorite—meatloaf and mashed potatoes."

Of course she did.

"How was everyone's weekend?" Trent asks after we're all seated at the dinner table.

Knox and I stay silent.

"I joined a new fundraising committee," my mom chirps after another minute passes. "We were thinking about throwing a party here next month—" her sentence trails off when her husband glowers. "I suppose I can always ask Janine if she'd be willing to host it at her house instead."

"It's fine," Trent says. "Host the party here."

My mom's face lights up. "Really?"

Biting into his meatloaf, he nods. "Yeah. It's about time we did something entertaining around here."

I shift uncomfortably when I feel his attention swing to me. "How was your weekend, Aspen? Do anything fun?"

Took my clothes off for money and spun around a pole.

Gave a few old men lap dances.

Oh, *and* fucked your forty-eight-year-old brother in the back of his car while it was parked behind a grocery store.

That was kind of fun.

"Not really." I push my food around my plate with my fork. "Studied with Violet."

"I see."

I'm not sure what to make of his tone, but I don't have time to dwell on it because Knox pushes his chair back and gets up from the table.

"Dinner isn't over yet, young man," Trent barks.

Knox ambles over to the kitchen sink. "I told Shadow I'd give her a ride to work."

"Don't you think you should have cleared that with me first?"

Geez.

Then again, I can't blame Trent for keeping him on a tight leash.

He killed his own mother.

Knox freezes, the tendons in his arms coiling as he grips the edge of the sink. "I didn't think it would be a big deal."

"Well, you thought wrong." Trent wipes his mouth with a napkin. "You know how important your attendance at family dinner is."

Knox turns around. "It won't happen again." It looks like he's swallowing nails before he utters, "Sir."

"Make sure it doesn't." He waves a dismissive hand. "You may be excused."

Knox starts to leave, but then Trent snarls, "Thank your mother for the lovely dinner she made."

His back is turned so I can't see his face. However, I *do* see his hands clench into fists…like it's taking every ounce of his self-control not to flip the fuck out.

"Thanks for dinner," Knox mutters under his breath before he stalks off.

A moment later, the front door opens before slamming shut.

We finish the rest of dinner in silence.

I'm loading the plates from dinner into the dishwasher when Trent approaches me.

"You don't like me," he notes, leaning against the marble island.

Awkward.

However, I tell him the truth, "I don't know enough about you to form an opinion."

Okay, that's a lie.

I don't like the fact that he married my mother.

Or that he insists we all eat breakfast and dinner together like we're one big happy family when it couldn't be further from the truth.

I also don't like that he referred to *my* mom as Knox's mom earlier. Because she's not.

Or that he thinks he can buy my approval with a car. Because he can't.

"I get that," he says softly, like I'm a bomb he's afraid will detonate at any moment.

Taking a plate from me, he puts it into the dishwasher. "I'm not trying to be your father."

"Good."

Because my dad isn't someone who can be replaced.

Especially by the likes of him.

"But I am hoping we can be friends one day."

I raise a brow. "Friends?"

He chuckles a little. "Okay, *friends* is a bit of a stretch." His expression turns serious. "I'm sorry about your father, Aspen. It was a terrible tragedy I wouldn't wish on anyone. But I'm tired of feeling like I need to tip-toe around you in my own home." He takes a step closer. "I just want to take care of you and your mother."

The words are out of my mouth before I can stop myself, "I don't need you to take care of me."

He drags a hand down his face. "You're not going to make this easy on me, are you?"

I scrub the dish in my hand with more vigor than necessary. "No."

"That's okay," he says, and I feel his breath tickle my ear. "I like a challenge."

Chapter 9

Knox

a sharp uppercut strikes my jaw. The pain is white hot, like a flash of lightning in the dark. It buzzes through me, ringing in my ears.

Smiling, I look the motherfucker who hit me in the eyes. "Is that all you got?"

I want him to get in as many punches as he can.

I want him to think he's winning.

Heckles and shouts surround me in the secluded warehouse, their faces nothing but a blur.

Another punch flies out. This time catching my lip. My tongue comes out and I lick it, tasting my blood.

I point to my chin in invitation. "More."

He strikes me for a third time, and I welcome the rush of pain.

Gimme more.

Rage pushes through me, growing stronger with every breath I inhale.

The pool of blood on the floor.

The colorful bruises marring her skin.

The helpless look on her face.

My fist connects with skin and bone and I revel in the release it gives me.

I plow my fist into his kidney before bashing my elbow into his jaw.

A ragged breath saws in and out of him as his head lolls to the side.

A few people in the crowd gasp. My opponent easily has thirty pounds of solid muscle on me.

The fight should be a cakewalk for him.

But it's not.

A roundhouse kick to his chest has him staggering back, trying his hardest to maintain his balance.

And that's when I unleash the rest of my fury.

Charging at him, I crack my head against his. Were this a legal fight, the move would get me thrown out of the makeshift ring.

But it's not.

My body throbs when his eyes roll back. The lights are on, but no one's home.

Victory is mine for the taking.

I plant a kiss on his sweaty forehead right before he crumbles like a sandcastle on the beach.

People rush to help my opponent off the floor as I make my way over to Jerry.

The dude's a crook, and I can trust him about as far as I can throw him. Which isn't far, considering he's a fat fuck.

However, he's in charge of setting up these fights, so I have no choice but to deal with him.

"Another win," he says, slapping some cash into my hand.

I quickly count it, grinding my molars when I notice he's two-hundred short.

"Where's the rest?"

He shrugs sheepishly. "Money's a little tight this week." Reaching over, he squeezes my shoulder. "You know I'm good for it, Knox."

Bullshit.

If he were good for it, I wouldn't have to fucking ask.

My glare darkens and the nervous way he shuffles his feet tells me it's enough to shake him.

"You have until next week to get me the rest of my money." I lean in. "Otherwise, I'll break your goddamn legs…after I rip your beating heart out of your chest and eat it for breakfast."

My expression must convey how serious I am because the color drains from his face.

"Sure thing, man. You know I always take care of you."

Removing his hand from my shoulder, I spit blood at his feet. "You better."

I wait for him to nod before I swipe my gym bag off the floor.

"You were really something out there," someone purrs.

When I turn around, I see a leggy brunette smiling at me. She's wearing a pair of black booty shorts and her white tank top is knotted just below her tits, showing off her toned abdomen.

But that's not what has me smiling back.

She goes by *Candi Kane* at the Bashful Beaver.

The same place Aspen works.

Her gaze lingers on my bare chest and she worries her bottom lip between her teeth. "You want to get out of here?"

Her breathy tone and the way she's looking at me make it obvious that subtlety isn't her style.

I jerk my chin toward the door. "My jeep is outside."

I watch the way her throat works as she swallows. The rapid way her pulse thrums against her flesh.

She's not the one I want.

But she'll do.

For now.

Chapter 10

Aspen

I turn my focus back to my locker when I see them saunter down the hallway, hoping like hell they stroll past me without stopping.

No such luck though, because a moment later the sounds of their heels clicking on the terrazzo floor come to a halt.

"Hey, Aspen."

Dammit.

Nothing good ever comes from my exchanges with Traci and Staci—two popular cheerleaders with chips on their shoulders the size of Texas.

Refusing to make eye contact, I switch my history textbook out for my biology one.

"Traci." I try to clear the bitterness out of my throat but fail, "Staci."

I can practically feel their eyes boring holes into me, and I brace myself to be insulted.

Only to my surprise, it doesn't happen.

"What are you doing tonight?" Traci asks instead.

It's a trick question. I know damn well the second I tell them I'm either studying or working, they'll make some dumb quip about me being a nerd who doesn't have any friends.

Bitches.

I go with the safer of the two options. "Working."

"Well, do you think you can take the night off?" Staci chimes in. That's…odd.

Curious, I tilt my head to look at them. "Why?"

Traci flips her long blonde hair over her shoulder. Seconds later, Staci does the same.

Even though they aren't related, they somehow look like clones of one another. Perfect, silky blonde hair, bright blue eyes, tall with mile-long legs, and *of course* they're both a willowy size zero.

Not that there's anything wrong with being a size zero…

Unless you're a cunt who likes to make those who aren't feel inferior like these two do.

A trickle of jealousy washes over me because I wish I were as pretty—and skinny—as they are.

That said, I'd rather look like me than ever act like them.

Yet—I'd be lying if I said there wasn't still a small part of me that wishes I were popular and fit in.

Sometimes it gets lonely being an outcast.

"We want to hang out."

It's all I can do not to drop the stack of books in my arms.

I blink in disbelief, effectively thrown. "With me?"

Staci laughs. "Yeah, silly."

"Why?"

It's a legitimate question, given they're so much higher on the food chain than I am. Not to mention the little jabs they've both thrown my way over the years.

"Well," Traci begins, "senior year will be over soon, and we realized that we haven't been very nice to you."

Staci nods in agreement. "We don't want that kind of bad karma on our conscience, so we were hoping to make amends."

Yeah, this conversation just went from odd to super fucking weird.

Since when do Traci and Staci have a conscience or give a shit about karma?

On the other hand, who the hell am I to snub either of them for trying to be a better person?

"It's fine," I tell them, slamming my locker shut. "We're cool."

Staci takes her compact out of her purse. "Does that mean you'll come chill after school?"

"Can't," I mutter. "I have to work."

I'm about to walk away, but then Traci says, "Well, if you can't hang out tonight, then what are you doing this weekend?"

"There's a bonfire party at Devil's Bluff Lake," Staci adds.

I've heard all about the parties at Devil's Bluff, but until now I've never been invited to one.

It's on the tip of my tongue to decline, but then Traci utters, "Come on, Aspen. Don't be such a loser. Come with."

Staci smirks. "We can even do your hair and makeup beforehand."

Traci chews on her bottom lip as if she's pondering something. "Maybe you can tell Knox and he can come, too?"

There it is. They're not being nice to me to make amends. They're being nice because they're hoping it will get them closer to Knox.

Which is strange because everyone at Black Mountain is terrified of him.

Then again, I've caught Traci and Staci talking about how hot he is while applying their lipstick in the girls' room more than once. *Gross.*

Knox would rather swallow nails than go to that party. He might be a homicidal freak, but his disdain for the bullshit social hierarchy around here is something I can respect.

I shake my head. "Sorry—"

"Ken Ruckman will be there," Staci chirps.

Traci grins. "Word on the street is that he *really* wants you to come."

If that were the case, he'd ask me himself.

Not that it would matter because my crush on Ken is ancient history, and I have a boyfriend.

Well, not a *boyfriend* on account he's definitely not a *boy.*

Not to mention…married.

Maybe that's why I find myself saying yes.

Not because of Ken…

But because for *once* it would be nice to fit in, act like an eighteen-year-old, and have a sense of normalcy in my life for a night.

"Ginger, I need you out on stage in five," Freddie says from the doorway.

Seriously? I just got off stage twenty minutes ago.

Hand propped on my hip, I turn to look at him. "Again?"

As much as I hate being on stage, I need to make some money tonight. And the only way to do that is to book private rooms.

Freddie sighs. "Violet took the night off and Candi never showed up for her shift, so we're short."

That's weird.

I look at Heather, or should I say—*Bambi*. "I can't believe Candi didn't show up."

Lord knows I can't stand her, but it's not like her to ghost on a shift. Hell, I'm pretty sure she spends more time here than she does her actual apartment.

Bambi waves a dismissive hand. "She probably overslept." Picking up a tube of mascara, she rolls her eyes. "Or she's too busy screwing her latest train wreck of a guy and lost track of time."

That definitely sounds like her.

After reapplying my lip gloss, I place the black and green masquerade mask over my face. "Yeah, you're probably right."

However, I can't shake the weird feeling snaking up my spine as I walk out of the dressing room.

What if she's not?

Chapter 11

Aspen

*A*fter applying some winged eyeliner, I take a step back and examine myself in the mirror.

I never wear this much makeup—except at work. I run my hand down the bones of the tight black corset I paired with an even tighter pair of jeans. And I *definitely* never dress like this.

Which is exactly why I chose to.

Tonight, I get to have fun.

I study myself for another long beat before deciding my hair could use some curls and volume.

Too bad I left my curling iron at work.

Fortunately, my mother has damn near every beauty product known to man.

"Mom," I call out as I walk out of my bedroom, "can I borrow your curling iron?"

No response.

Stifling my huff of annoyance because Traci and Staci will be here in a half hour to pick me up, I stomp down the stairs in search of her. "Mom."

When I still hear crickets, I walk into the living room and stride over to the large window facing the driveway. Her car is still parked, so she's obviously home.

I'm walking back up to my room when I pass the bathroom and

hear the shower running. Since I'm in a rush, I quickly knock before charging inside.

"Sorry to bother you, I just—"

My sentence jams in my throat when I realize it's not my mother standing in the steam.

It's Knox.

I'm about to walk out, but it's too late. He's already wrapping a towel around his waist and stalking toward me like an animal approaching their prey.

I quickly back up and turn around. "What the hell is your problem?"

My hand is already on the doorknob when Knox extends his arm past my head and slams it shut, trapping me.

His warm breath tickles the side of my neck when he speaks, "You look like a whore."

Screw him.

I know he's only saying that to get under my skin and to make me feel like shit.

Because that's what bullies do.

I turn around to face him. "No, I don't."

He braces his arms on either side of my head, caging me in. "You're right." A smug smile curls his lips. "Whores are attractive... you're not."

It's obvious he wants a reaction from me, but I refuse to give him one.

"Is that supposed to hurt my feelings?" I laugh, but there's not an ounce of humor. "Do I run off and cry now because a worthless asshole like you deems me ugly?" I poke his bare, wet chest with my finger. "Sorry, but—"

Words die in my throat when I feel the ridge of his cock dig into my stomach, hard and demanding.

He can deny it all he wants, but the body doesn't lie.

Knox might hate me as much as I hate him...but he also wants me.

And that knowledge fills me with an almost lethal dose of satisfaction.

It's my turn to smirk. "That's funny. It sure doesn't *feel* like you find me unattractive."

The cruel way his face twists makes it clear I'm provoking the beast. To my surprise, he doesn't argue with me.

What he does next is so much worse.

My lungs freeze when the tip of his finger trails down the column of my neck. The movement is gentle but calculated. I swallow thickly when he traces the tops of my breasts, which are sitting high, thanks to the strapless push-up bra I'm wearing under my corset.

"Knox."

It's meant as a warning, but it almost sounds like a plea.

And I hate myself for it.

His touch should feel like razor blades beneath my skin. Yet it feels like tiny little sparks lighting every nerve ending of mine on fire.

I reach behind me for the doorknob again, but he leans in so close it almost hurts.

Those piercing orbs of his darken. "Get on your knees."

Jesus Christ. It's all I can do not to laugh because he's out of his damn mind.

The murderous look in his eye warns me not to protest.

I do anyway.

"Not a chance in hell—"

I yelp when he dips his head and his teeth sink into my neck hard enough to puncture my skin. He's like a venomous snake digging its fangs into their victim…injecting me with his poison.

A small drop of blood trickles down my cleavage and he runs the tip of his tongue along the crimson liquid, lapping it up. "On your knees, Stray. *Now*." I loathe the way my nipple pebbles when he pinches it. "I won't tell you again."

When I don't move, his mouth hovers over my jugular, threatening.

He's a killer—I remind myself.

You're trapped in a room with a goddamn killer.

And if someone could murder their own mother, they wouldn't hesitate to kill their stepsister, whom they despise.

It's that stark realization that makes me concede.

The moment my knees hit the floor, he drops his towel.

Despite overhearing Shadow's proclamations about his size, I'm still stunned to find out just how right she was.

Knox's dick is thick, veiny, and every bit as angry as he is.

It's also exceedingly big.

So big you'd definitely feel the ache when he stretches you.

Bile surges up my throat because I shouldn't be having those thoughts right now—or *ever*—about Knox.

He's a vicious psychopath. And I refuse to be his pawn.

Therefore, I won't make this easy for him.

If he wants this, and it's obvious he does, he'll literally have to force me to get it.

I clamp my mouth shut when he grips the base of my neck.

His gruff voice vibrates through me, "Open."

Peering up, I tell him to go to hell with my eyes.

That only makes him chuckle, like this is all a game to him.

A knock on the door makes me jump.

"Aspen, did you need something?" my mother chirps from the other side.

Realizing it's my chance at freedom, I speak up, "Y—"

Knox takes the opportunity to shove his dick inside my open mouth.

I'm too shocked to move for a few seconds.

His grip on my hair tightens, and he thrusts his hips, forcing his cock so far down my throat, I can't help but gag as my eyes begin to water. "You shouldn't talk with your mouth full, *sis*."

"Is everything okay?" my mother questions, sounding confused. "What's going on?"

As if sensing I'm about to bite the damn thing off, the asshole withdraws his dick.

"Everything's fine," I tell her, my stomach churning with indignation. "I'm just looking for a curling iron."

"Oh. It's on the fourth shelf in the closet." She makes a sound of irritation in her throat. "I have to go, I'm late for my meeting with the caterers."

A second later, I hear her footsteps fade away.

I should get up and leave because it's evident this disgusting altercation is over now.

But then he'll know he won, and he'll assume he's the one with all the control.

Fuck that.

Before I can talk myself out of it, I part my lips and slide my mouth down his thick length, sucking him as deep as I can.

Briefly, I see a flicker of surprise flash in his eyes before they squeeze shut, and he groans, almost like he's in pain. "Fuck."

He braces one hand on the sink and clutches the side of my face with his free one. "Good girl."

Fighting the sudden rush of arousal that hits me, I scrape my teeth along his shaft, expecting to hear him squeal and push me away.

But he doesn't.

"More." He grunts, his grip on my face tightening.

I bite down harder, but that only makes him grind out, "Is that all you got?"

The tendons in his neck flex as a sheen of sweat dots his forehead. It's obvious I'm hurting him.

Yet, he's also enjoying it.

Almost like he's the one controlling the pain—controlling *me*—instead of the other way around.

"Come on, Stray," he growls, his face tensing as he glares up at the ceiling. "Make me fucking bleed."

Holy shit. He's crazier than I thought.

"Jesus," I exclaim, wiping my mouth with the back of my hand. "What the *fuck* is wrong with you?"

He doesn't say a word as I push to my feet, and that only makes me more irate.

"You're such an asshole." I glare at him. "Pull that shit again and I'll tell your dad."

He holds my stare. "Do it."

Animosity flows like ice through my veins. "I hate you."

He picks his towel up off the floor and slings it around his waist. "I hate you more." The corner of his lip curls. "And for the record, you give a shitty blow job."

I should let it go and walk away, but I can't. My dad used to always tease me about needing to have the last word, and well, he wasn't wrong.

"Trust me, it wasn't like I was actually trying to please you. Hell, you *forced*—"

"The moment you got on your knees, I let go of the door. You could have left whenever you wanted. But you didn't."

Wow. He's delusional. "That's because my mother was standing right outside—"

"So you'd rather suck your stepbrother's dick than have mommy dearest come to your rescue?" He rubs his chin. "Interesting."

It's all I can do not to reach over and throttle him. "Fuck off. I didn't want—"

"Then you should have left." Smirking, he inches closer. "But here you are." His heated stare holds me frozen. "Christ, you're pathetic."

I open my mouth to speak, but he brushes past me. "I know what you want…but it will never fucking happen."

"I don't want a damn thing from you, asshole," I hiss before the door slams shut.

But even as the words leave my lips, I know it's a lie.

Because buried deep down…beyond all the hurt and pain.

Beyond all the lies I've convinced myself are the truth and all the truths I've forced myself to believe are lies…

I want to know why something inside me comes alive whenever he's near.

I want to know what makes him tick and what makes him so evil.

I wanted a battle…but he gave me a war.

Chapter 12

Aspen

*T*he earthy smell of smoke from the large bonfire fills my nostrils as I step out of Traci's Volvo.

Staci says something to me, but I can't hear what due to the rap music bumping from the large speaker someone set up near a tree stump.

I've been to Devil's Bluff lake once before, but never while there was a party going on.

I turn my head to ask Staci to repeat herself, but she links arms with Traci and they both rush ahead of me to be with the sizeable crowd of people gathered around the fire.

Not only do I feel totally out of my element, I'm seriously regretting not bringing a sweatshirt because it's chilly up here in the mountains.

Dirt and branches crunch under my shoes as I take a tentative step. Sucking in a breath, I look around. There's a freshwater lake peeking out of the cleft between two enormous mountains, which are surrounded by trees and moss.

It's serene and tranquil. Like a scene a talented artist would create.

Well, except for the large keg, various bottles of liquor being passed around, the red solo cups littering the ground, and the half-dressed teenagers grinding against each other.

I side-step the partygoers and wander over to a hollow log that sits overlooking the lake. I feel stupid for coming here, and regret sits heavy on my chest. I've been excluded for so long, I just wanted to know what it was like to fit in.

However, I should have known better. You don't need to experience a root canal to know it will suck, and the same applies here.

"Hey," a deep voice says behind me.

When I cock my head, I see Ken Ruckman standing there.

"Hey."

Taking a step forward, he gestures to the log I'm sitting on with the beer bottle in his hand. "Can I sit?"

I move over a little to give him and his broad shoulders some room.

Although I probably should have given him more, because he sits a little closer than I expected.

Eyes trained on the lake, he takes a swig out of his beer bottle. "I guess this isn't really your scene, huh?"

I wouldn't know. I've never been invited here before. But so far? It blows.

"That obvious?" I mutter instead, wishing I had something more clever or interesting to say.

Not that I'm looking to impress Ken. Even though he is impossibly cute with his wavy light brown hair, honey eyes, and the red and black varsity football jacket he's sporting.

"Kind of." He shrugs his big shoulders. "Then again, you've never been one to follow the crowd."

It's on the tip of my tongue to remark that *the crowd* never wanted me around, but then he adds, "It's something I've always admired about you."

I can't help but laugh, because while Ken might not be the nucleus of the popular clique, he's definitely a part of it.

"Wow. That's…" I shake my head, letting my words fall by the wayside.

"What?" he prompts, turning those honey eyes on me.

I decide to be honest. "It's just kind of weird you'd admire *me* for not fitting in when it's blatant that you do."

If my statement offended him, he doesn't show it. "Survival of the fittest."

When I give him a look, he adds, "It's easier to adapt to your environment instead of going against it." He motions to me with his beer and a ghost of a grin touches his lips. "Doesn't mean I don't appreciate a girl who can fight, though."

A gust of wind rustles through the trees and I fight back a shiver, the tiny hairs on my arms standing on end.

Ken shucks off his jacket and hands it to me. "Here."

Glancing around, I mock gasp. "Are you sure? Letting me wear your jacket might ruin your probability of survival and all."

At that, he laughs. "I'll take my chances."

I sling his jacket around my shoulders and immediately the potent scent of Axe body spray invades my nostrils.

Generic teenage boy odor aside, I'd be lying if I said I wasn't enjoying our little exchange.

I care about Leo, but we don't get to attend high school parties or sit close and flirt in the public eye. Not only because of our age difference, but the fact that he's married.

What we have will always be behind closed doors.

Concealed from the world.

And even though every adult I've met always remarks that I'm wise and mature beyond my years—which is probably a big part of why Leo and I *do* work—it's kind of nice talking to someone who doesn't make me feel guilty or like I have to look over my shoulder constantly because what we're doing is wrong.

It's nice feeling *normal* for once.

"So, what colleges have you applied to?" I question, not wanting the conversation to turn stale.

Ken grins. "I actually just found out I'm getting a full ride to play football at Notre Dame." He takes another swig from his beer bottle. "You?"

I fight the rush of jealousy flickering in my chest. I've applied to tons of colleges, but I haven't had any responses.

It's the end of January, so I figured it was still too early to receive an acceptance letter.

Evidently not.

"I haven't heard back from any yet," I mumble, fighting the flush of embarrassment. "But congrats on getting into Notre Dame. That's awesome."

"Thanks." He pins me with a reassuring look. "Don't worry.

There's still plenty of time." He smiles. "Besides, I'm pretty sure I only got in because it's my dad's alma mater and he's a football legend there."

I know he's only saying this to make me feel better, but it has the opposite effect.

"Right."

He moves closer. So close our thighs brush. "They'd be stupid not to accept you. You're smart and determined…" His voice dips ever so slightly, "Beautiful."

If I had any doubt Ken was flirting with me before, I don't now.

"But let's not talk about school anymore." He points his beer at me, gesturing for me to take a sip. "Tonight should be about letting loose and having fun, yeah?"

I fight the urge to tell him I don't drink, but I don't want to come off as a party pooper—or a prude—so I take a tentative sip. "Yeah."

He smiles. "Atta, girl—"

Whatever he was going to say next is cut short when Staci and Traci stride over.

"Well, don't you two look cozy," Staci chirps.

Ken slings an arm around my shoulders. "Aspen's decided to have some fun tonight."

Traci's face lights up. "Finally." After taking a sip from her red solo cup, she hands it to me. "You have to try this. It's *so* good."

A big part of me wants to decline—because I've never been one to give in to any kind of peer pressure—but I also want to let loose and have a good time.

The drink is so strong it burns going down my throat.

"What is this?" I ask, trying to suppress the impulse to cough.

Staci waggles her perfect eyebrows. "Jungle juice."

I go to hand it back to her, but she declines. "Nope. That one is all yours." She tilts her head in the direction of the bonfire. "I'm gonna go grab another cup."

Before I can utter another word, she grabs Traci's hand and they wander off.

"Is it good?" Ken questions.

"It's…strong." I slip off his jacket because I'm feeling pretty warm now. "Want some?"

He shakes his head. "Nah. I'm drinking beer. Can't mix the two."

"Oh." That's when it occurs to me. "But I just took a sip of your beer before. Will—"

He places his finger to my lips, silencing me. "Aspen."

"Yeah?" I answer, my head suddenly feeling ten times lighter than it did a moment ago.

"Just relax."

Everything is so fuzzy—almost like I'm floating.

"Where—" I try to speak, but another wave of exhaustion sweeps over me.

Faintly, I feel someone fumbling with the zipper on my jeans.

Despite shaking my head and trying to push their hand away, they tug it down.

It's like I'm stuck in a movie or a bad dream where everything is happening around me, but I'm utterly powerless to stop it. I don't know what's going on or who's touching me.

"Dude, she's *totally* trashed," I hear someone who sounds a lot like Staci say before she laughs.

"How much did you give her?" another female voice—my guess is Traci—asks.

A flash of panic spirals through my system and I try to open my eyes, but they feel weighed down by bricks.

"I don't know. A lot since she's fat."

They both share a laugh, until a male voice cuts them off, "I can't get her jeans off. They're too tight and the bitch keeps fighting me."

Someone sighs.

"Well, then make her do something else," Traci suggests.

"Like what?" the guy questions.

Another irritated sigh. "Seriously? Come on, Ken. You can't be *that* dumb. I'm sure her mouth still works."

A second later, I'm hoisted up and then shifted so my head is positioned in his lap.

"Hold on," Staci says. "Let me press record on my phone."

A firm hand grips the back of my neck. "You like sucking this big cock, don't you, Aspen?"

My insides churn when I feel smooth skin followed by the ridge of his dick brush against my lips.

"Open."

Bile surges up my throat and I gag when two thick fingers are shoved into my mouth.

"Yeah, that's it," Ken says as the two girls laugh.

"God, Aspen. Who knew you were such a whore?"

Nausea rolls through me in one giant wave and a rush of liquid leaves my mouth.

"What the fuck?" Ken barks.

"Ewe," Staci squeals.

"That shit better come out," Traci whines. "Or I swear to God, I'll kill her."

Ken pushes my head away. "Fuck. I can't believe she puked all over me."

"Well, what the hell do we do now?" Staci questions. "Should we leave her on the side of the road or something?"

"Nah. Her stepdad is an FBI agent, remember? Everyone saw her leave the party with us, so if something bad happens to her, it's on us."

"That's true," Traci agrees. "I'll just drop her off at her house, I guess."

Another wave of exhaustion—much stronger than before—washes over me.

I vaguely register the sound of a car door opening and the sharp thud of my body hitting something hard before everything goes black.

Chapter 13

Knox

*R*ain splatters against my windshield so hard it sounds like rocks hitting pavement as I pull into the driveway.

My shoulders sag as I cut the engine, a potent mixture of anger and resentment swirling through my system.

Clenching my hand into a fist, I punch the steering wheel and scream into the darkness.

"Fuck!"

I punch it again for good measure, enjoying the flicker of pain that runs up my hand and forearm.

With a grunt, I hop out of my jeep and into the pouring rain. I'm about to walk inside, but a figure lying in the street in front of the house snags my attention.

Trepidation sparks through me as I cautiously approach the body.

What the fuck…

The muscles in my chest draw tight and I freeze when I see Aspen lying there motionless, the hard rain beating down on her limp frame.

Kneeling, I grab her wrist, ignoring the surge of relief that spirals through me when I feel her pulse.

"Aspen," I bite out, shaking her shoulders. "Wake the fuck up."

No response.

Goddammit.

I should leave her here to teach her a lesson about going to parties and getting so loaded she passes out…but then it dawns on me that this shit isn't like Aspen.

And she didn't go to that party alone.

It's only then I register the faint smell of puke wafting off her and notice the button and zipper on her jeans are undone.

It doesn't take a fucking genius to figure out that something isn't right.

I shake her again, harder this time. "Dammit, Stray. Wake the fuck up."

Nothing.

Muttering a curse, I haul her into my arms. She makes a gagging sound when I stand, and I manage to push her head to the other side just in time for her to puke.

Fucking hell.

Her eyes flutter open and the confusion swirling in them quickly turns to sheer terror when she looks up and sees me.

A violent shiver wracks her body and I faintly hear her mumble, "Please, don't kill me," before her head lolls to the side and she passes out again.

I trek up the pathway to the house, intending to take her to her bedroom, but I find myself walking around back, entering through the side entrance that leads to the basement where I sleep.

Even though she's still unconscious, a tremble runs through her and her teeth start chattering. If I don't get her out of these wet clothes soon, she'll probably get sick.

Good.

Gritting my teeth, I drop her on the floor beside my bed. Wincing, she curls her arms around her midsection, almost like she's trying to protect herself from the boogeyman.

She looks so fucking pathetic it's all I can do not to laugh.

"You fucking owe me," I tell her as I yank her off the floor and put her on my bed.

Her back bows as I place her in a sitting position and work to get her top off.

"Dammit. Stay still," I growl, realizing it's fucking pointless because it's not like the bitch can comprehend anything right now.

When she hunches forward, I take the opportunity to undo the zipper located in the back and toss the damp corset on my floor. Then I shove her so she's lying on the mattress and attempt to take her jeans off. They're soaked too, though, making the task that much harder. Kneeling in front of her, I shove my hands under her ass and wrench the tight, wet denim down her legs.

Along with her little black panties.

Fuck.

I clench my jaw, opposing the way my cock twitches before it starts to thicken.

Most girls shave or wax everything until they look prepubescent—because society tells them that's what men prefer—but not Aspen.

While most of her cunt is smooth and bare, she intentionally left a neat, tiny strip of pubic hair...as if silently proclaiming a big fuck you to anyone who might doubt the validity of her natural hair color.

Instinctively, I lean forward, smelling her scent and getting a better view. Her lips are every bit as pouty and plump as the ones on her face. Impulsively, my hand reaches out to touch her, but I swiftly come to my senses and yank my hand back.

Aspen stirs, her thighs parting ever so slightly as her chest heaves, causing one pale pink nipple to pop out of her bra.

I groan, my cock swelling painfully in my jeans.

I could unzip my pants, whip it out, and give her no fucking choice but to take every inch of me.

But then she'd know the truth.

That as much as I loathe her with every fucking fiber of my being...

I'm also completely fucking drawn to her.

And I know deep down she feels the same.

We're like two magnets...the electrical currents running through us simultaneously repel and attract one another.

I fucking hate it.

Hate her.

Disgusted, I haul her underwear back up her thighs, pull a dirty t-shirt out of my hamper and slip it over her head.

After shoving her to the other side of my king-sized bed, I decide to do some digging.

I know Aspen went to the party with Staci and Traci, two

popular—and annoying as fuck—cheerleaders. But while that explains how she arrived at the party, it does fuck all to explain how she ended up unconscious on the street in front of our house.

Grabbing my phone, I pull up Instagram. The only reason I have the app is to keep tabs on Aspen. Since her profile is private and I knew she'd never accept a request from her nemesis, I had to create a sock puppet account.

Lighting a cigarette, I click on her profile. She rarely posts updates—and when she does, it's just stupid bullshit like nature, coffee, and baked goods. However, Staci and Traci are insta-attention-whores and like to tag people in everything.

Sure enough, when I click on the icon to see the posts Aspen's tagged in, there's a new one posted by Staci.

Traci is at the wheel of her car, giving the camera the finger while Staci's arm is wrapped around her. In the backseat is Aspen… awkwardly smiling like she'd rather be anywhere else. The caption states—*party time with my bitches*, followed by a million dumb tags.

Blowing out a puff of smoke, I click on Staci's thumbnail because there's no way in hell her page is private. However, instead of bringing me straight to her profile, it forces me to see a reel of *stories*. There's a brief video of her pouring some beer into a red solo cup, a picture of her making a kissy face at the camera, one of her and Traci dancing near the bonfire, and another fucking kissy face photo. I'm about to exit out of the app, because looking at this shit is making me lose brain cells, but then another video pops up on my screen.

It's dark and grainy, but it looks like the back of a car based on the view of the rear window. The camera suddenly shifts downward and what I see next has my blood boiling.

A guy is grabbing the back of Aspen's neck, even though it's obvious by the way her head is hanging limp in his lap that she's out of it.

"You like sucking this big cock don't you, Aspen?" a familiar voice taunts, but I can't quite place it.

The video cuts off, but another one immediately gears up.

"Open," the guy instructs.

The camera juts up slightly. Not enough to show his face, but enough that I can see the black and red letterman jacket he's wearing.

A second later, a gagging sound infiltrates my ears.

"Yeah, that's it," the guy says, followed by the sound of laughter.

"God, Aspen," someone who sounds a lot like Staci chirps. "Who knew you were such a whore?"

The video cuts out after that, but it doesn't fucking matter.

The damage is already done.

I stomp out my cigarette in an ashtray. "Jesus Christ." I look over at Aspen, who's still passed out in my bed. "You're fucked."

The kids at Black Mountain Academy are vultures, always looking for the next victim to target.

Unfortunately for my new stepsister…they just found their latest one.

Chapter 14

Knox

Past...

I closed my eyes, forcing my body to go slack as I waited for the throbbing pain to subside to something more manageable.

I used to think there was only one type of pain.

But it turned out there were different levels of it.

The sharp sting that stole your breath because it took you by surprise.

The hurt that you prayed passed quickly...because it constantly taunted you and you knew it was only a matter of time before it would rear its ugly head again.

And the agony that you knew would be permanent...because it seeped into your soul and became scar tissue.

At that moment, I was experiencing the first one...

While hiding from the monsters as I huddled in the basement... waiting for the second.

I flinched, the tiny hairs on my neck prickling with fear when I heard footsteps coming down the staircase.

"Trent."

My mother's voice was soft and velvety—like a blanket wrapped around you during a snowstorm.

The kind of voice that made you want to forgive her for all her transgressions.

Even though you knew better.

Part of me wanted to stay silent so she'd go back upstairs…but I knew if I did, that would only make it worse.

Squinting in the darkness, I found her form. "I'm over here."

She reached up for the string on the ceiling fan, flooding the basement with light.

My mother was beautiful. So much so, people always commented on her appearance.

She was tall and slim, with skin so pale it was almost translucent, and blue eyes so bright the sky and ocean paled in comparison.

But my favorite feature of hers was her hair.

Long, silky red locks that fell down her back in soft waves.

My mom once told me she was made fun of for her red hair while growing up, but I never understood why.

It made her different…*unique.*

She looked like a princess out of a storybook…

But our lives were the farthest thing from a fairytale.

I winced when she kneeled and palmed my cheek. "I'm sorry."

She was always *sorry*.

But sorry wasn't enough.

Not when the same thing kept happening over and over…like a record skipping while playing one of the worst songs you ever heard.

"Close your eyes," she whispered, but I shook my head.

That's the thing about permanent pain…

It made it hard to trust.

Not only others, but yourself.

"Please."

I knew better than to refuse, so I obliged.

"I got you a present."

I wasn't surprised.

Presents always came after the pain…like a rainbow after a storm.

Only the storms were becoming too powerful and occurring far too often.

And there was no more shelter.

"Put out your hands."

When I did, I felt something dry and scaly against my skin.

Confusion flooded through me when I opened my eyes and looked down at the lizard with the blue belly.

I had seen him earlier when my mom took me out on a walk. I begged and pleaded to keep him, but she said we couldn't.

My father had a strict rule against pets. My mother said it was because he was allergic to both dogs and cats, however he didn't want birds or reptiles around either.

"I got a small tank from the pet store down the street that we can keep him in. As long as you promise to feed and look after him."

I nodded so hard I'm surprised my head didn't come off. "I promise."

I ran a finger down his back, then paused. "What about dad?"

She gave me one of her gorgeous smiles. "Well, we'll have to keep it a secret from him. Think you can do that?"

I nodded again. I was so used to keeping secrets, it was second nature.

"What do you want to name him?"

I shrugged. I'd never been allowed to have a pet before, so I never took the time to think of what I would name one if I got the chance.

"He's green," I noted. "And scaly." I laughed when his long tongue came out. "And kind of cute."

"Kermit," I declared because he was green like the frog on my favorite TV show.

He obviously wasn't a frog, but it was close enough.

My mother patted his tiny head with her finger. "Kermit it is."

I shifted uncomfortably, trying to gather the courage to ask. "Mom?"

Her blue eyes softened. "Yeah?"

I needed to know why.

Why did it hurt so much?

Why did she let it happen?

Why did I deserve it?

The sound of the front door opening upstairs made me jump, and I lost my nerve.

"Nothing."

She ran up the staircase while I went off in search of a safe place to keep Kermit.

Too bad I could never find one for myself.

Chapter 15

Aspen

"Mom," a deep voice calls out, stirring me awake.

I open my eyes and glance up at an unfamiliar ceiling. It suddenly dawns on me I'm not in my bedroom.

And I'm not alone.

My brain pounds against my skull, like a hammer thumping a wall.

I jolt when I take in my surroundings and realize I'm in the basement.

What the...

Sheer horror surges through my bones when I notice I'm in *Knox's* bed.

Despite the migraine from hell and the exhaustion pummeling me, I lurch off the mattress.

"What the hell is going on?"

Shock roots me to the spot when I look down and see I'm wearing nothing but a black t-shirt.

One that smells just like him.

"Shut the fuck up," Knox's raspy voice grunts from under the covers.

Is he freaking serious?

Walking over to his side of the bed, I rip the pillow he's sleeping on away and hit him with it. "Why am I in your bedroom, asshole?"

An irritated rumble escapes him as he rolls over, and if looks could kill I'd no longer have a pulse. "Because it's where I put you."

With that, he snatches the pillow out of my hands and rolls back over like it's no big deal.

Where he put me? What the hell does that mean?

I poke his naked back with my finger. "Knox."

"Go *away*," he snaps.

I poke him harder. "I need answers."

He pounds the mattress with his fist. "And I need sleep."

Rolling my eyes, I flick my gaze to the alarm clock on the nightstand. "No, you don't. It's two—"

Holy shit. It's two in the afternoon.

I never sleep this late.

I snatch his pillow away again.

"Goddammit," he roars, sitting up in bed. "Why the fuck are you extra annoying today?"

"Gee, I don't know," I start. "Maybe because I woke up in *your* bed wearing *your* t-shirt and I have absolutely no idea how I got here."

With a huff, he reaches for his cigarettes on the nightstand and brings one to his mouth. "You seriously don't remember anything from last night?"

Folding my arms around myself, I shake my head. "No. I mean, I know I went to a party with Traci and Staci, but after that…"

"After that, *what?*" he prompts, bringing a lighter to the end of his cigarette.

"Everything is kind of fuzzy, and then it just goes blank."

Like there's a glitch in my memory.

I have no idea what to make of the look on his face.

I take an awkward step back, hoping like hell that the worst didn't happen. "Please tell me we didn't sleep together."

I know people do stupid things when they drink, but I never thought *I'd* be one of them.

My worst fears are confirmed, when Knox laughs callously under his breath.

I can feel every ounce of color drain from my face. "Oh, my God."

"Technically, we did sleep together," he states through a cloud of smoke. "But I didn't fuck you." He snickers. "You couldn't pay me enough to do that."

Relief flows through me. For once, we're on the same page.

I notice my jeans, heels, and corset on the floor and I'm about to pick them up, but Knox halts me. "What's the last thing you remember?"

Normally I'd tell him to go fuck himself, but a flicker of concern slashes across his face, rendering me speechless.

"Dammit, Stray," he gripes. "Quit standing there gaping at me like a fucking idiot and answer me."

I chew on my thumbnail, trying my hardest to think. "I uh...I was talking to Ken Ruckman by the lake. He was telling me how he got into Notre Dame on a football scholarship."

Knox takes a long drag of his cigarette. "Was he wearing his letterman jacket by any chance?"

"How do you—"

"Answer the question."

"Yeah." My mind flits back to the events of last night. "He gave it to me when I got cold."

I'm not prepared for his next inquiry.

"Did he force you to drink anything?"

"No, Ken didn't *force* me, but I had a sip of his beer." Realizing where he's going with this, I quickly add, "The same beer I saw him drinking out of."

Surely if he slipped something into my drink, he wouldn't drink out of it himself before *and* after.

Same goes for Traci and Staci and their *jungle juice*.

Although, Staci did get herself another cup after she handed it to me, but I thought she was just being nice.

Then again...I can't seem to recall *anything* after that.

It's like my memory is a database that's been wiped clean.

"Aspen," Knox grits out, pulling me from my thoughts. "Tell me you're not that dumb."

"I thought they wanted to be friends," I whisper, feeling so stupid I could cry. "Why would—"

"Who?" Knox growls, making me jump.

"Staci and Traci." I look down at my feet. "They gave me something to drink at the party—"

"Jesus," he interjects, bringing the cigarette to his mouth. "I know your mom is a space cadet, but I didn't think she passed the dumbass gene on to you. Don't you know not to take a drink from any—"

"Yes, I do," I yell because it's hard enough realizing I screwed up without having him rub it in my face. "However, I didn't think it was a big deal because I saw Staci take a sip before she gave it to me. Everyone was drinking at the party and I just wanted to…" my voice cracks and I stop talking.

Knox stabs his cigarette out in a nearby ashtray. "Wanted to what?"

"I wanted to have fun and fit in, okay?" I swallow the tears prickling the back of my throat. "I wanted to see what it was like to be popular and—"

A sardonic snort cuts me off. "Well, congrats. You're definitely popular now."

I raise a brow. "What's that supposed to mean?"

Getting out of bed, he swipes his phone off the nightstand. "Here's some advice, Stray. When two bitches who have always been cunts to you invite you to hang out…don't fucking do it."

I start to speak, but he twists his phone around and what I see and hear next nearly brings me to my knees.

"*You like sucking this big cock, don't you, Aspen?*" someone who sounds exactly like Ken Ruckman says.

I close my eyes when the sounds of me gagging fill the room, and I want to scream at him to shut it off because I don't think I can take anymore.

"Good news is it will only be up for a few more hours," Knox states dryly as I hear Staci and Traci laugh on the video. "Bad news is, I'm pretty sure everyone at school has already seen it."

"Thank you, captain obvious," I choke out, trying my hardest to keep my impending tears at bay because I refuse to give him the satisfaction of watching me break.

Because he'd enjoy it too much.

Another horrifying thought hits me, and it takes every ounce of self-control not to curl up into a ball on the floor.

I woke up in his bed.

If there's one thing I know about Knox, it's that he not only enjoys tormenting me…he loves teasing and enticing me first—drawing me in like a moth to a flame.

Only so he can watch me burn.

"Let me guess," I say, my voice a painful rasp. "This is where you open the closet door, hold my underwear up, and tell a bunch of guys I smell like tuna?"

He raises a brow. "Wh—"

"This is where you confess it was all your idea?" I interject. "That you convinced Staci, Traci, and Ken to go along with your plan to set me up?" I take a step forward, so disgusted I could puke. "God, you've really done some sick, horrible shit to me before, but this takes the cake."

If I didn't know any better, I'd say the bastard almost looks offended. *Almost.*

"You think I had something to do with this shit?"

"No, I don't think," I say, closing the space between us. "I know." I hold his stare, mustering up the bravado I don't quite feel yet…but I will.

"You've fucked with me for the last time." Rising on my tiptoes, I brush my mouth against his ear, because I want him to hear this. "And now? I'm going to fucking *ruin* you."

His hand wraps around my wrist, and he walks forward until my spine meets the wall behind me. "Go ahead and try…I dare you." He grips my chin with his free hand. "Maybe then you'll learn not to make threats you can't carry out."

"Oh, it's not a threat, Knox. It's a fucking promise." I'm positive the smile on my face looks downright psychotic, but I don't care. "First, I'm gonna tell your daddy all about what you did to me. Then, I'm going to file a police report." I run my finger down his cheek. "And finally, I'm going to stand in a courtroom and make sure justice is served." I point to my mouth. "And the smile on my face right now? Take a good, hard look at it. Because you're going to see it again when they send you back to the goddamn asylum where you belong."

He tugs my hair so hard, I yelp. "You're gonna try to destroy me, huh?"

I pierce him with a wicked glare. "Not try…I *will.*"

Just like he destroyed me.

His grip on my hair tightens, and he dips his head, skimming his nose along the column of my throat. "You're forgetting something, Stray."

"What's that?"

"Your little plan will take some time." His teeth sink into my neck and I cry out in pain. "But mine will only take a few minutes." I close my eyes when his fingers hover over my throat, threatening to squeeze. "I thought you'd be smart enough not to threaten to ruin someone's life. Especially someone who's very capable of *ending* yours."

I struggle and thrash against him, scratching him with my nails so the police will be able to gather evidence later…but he's bigger. *Stronger.*

He pins me against the wall with the strength of his body. A moment later, his fingers begin to close around my throat.

This is it.

He's finally going to kill me.

If he's expecting me to beg him not to, he'd have better odds of watching pigs fly.

I hold his stare as he slowly, *meticulously* wrings the air from my lungs, like he's done this a hundred times before.

Hell, maybe he has.

For a brief moment, I let myself give into the fear. There are so many things I wanted to do with my life.

I wanted to go to college.

I wanted to open a bakery one day—a pipe dream really, because it's not very practical, but still…I wanted it.

Suddenly, he releases his hold on me. "Someone who went out of his way to help you."

I open my mouth to ask what the hell he's talking about, but he takes a step back and grunts, "I found you in the street last night."

I blink in confusion. "What? Where?"

He walks over to the nightstand and takes a cigarette from the pack. "In front of the house." He brings a lighter to the end of it and inhales. "It was raining pretty hard, and you had been out there for a while by the looks of it. I tried to wake you, but you were knocked out cold. The moment I picked you up, you puked, so I didn't think it was a good idea to leave you alone." He pins me with a menacing look. "I brought you here so I could keep an eye on you."

I look down at the t-shirt I'm wearing. "And took off my clothes."

"You were soaked and shivering. Trust me, it wasn't like I wanted to see your hairy little snatch."

Mortified, my cheeks flame, but I quickly recover. "Well, if you're expecting a thank—"

"I'm not."

I gather my clothes off the floor. "You swear you had nothing to do with this?"

"Aspen." He waits for me to look at him before he says, "If I wanted to set you up, I'd do it myself. I wouldn't enlist other people to do my dirty work for me."

As fucked up as that might be, he has a point.

I'm heading for the staircase when it hits me.

It's two in the afternoon.

"I missed breakfast."

Knox's dad is strict about eating our meals together like one big happy family. He probably wasn't thrilled about my disappearance.

"I covered for you."

I shuffle my feet. "What did you tell them?"

He flicks the ash from his cigarette and shrugs. "That you were sick in bed."

I raise a brow. "And my mom—" my sentence falls by the wayside when I realize that she wouldn't check up on me.

Because she doesn't care.

No one does.

"Right."

With that, I head up the stairs, but not before I hear Knox bark, "This isn't over, Stray."

I have no idea what he's talking about.

I turn. "Wha—"

"You threatened me." He takes a long drag from his cigarette and exhales, blowing the smoke in my direction. "And every action has a consequence."

Chapter 16

Aspen

*I*t's Monday morning, and while Mondays notoriously suck…this one is particularly bad.

There's no doubt in my mind that nearly everyone saw that video.

I rub my sweaty palms on my plaid skirt as Knox pulls into the school parking lot.

I expect him to tease me, especially after the warning he issued a couple days ago, but he remains silent…something I'm thankful for right now.

My stomach rolls when he cuts the engine. I want nothing more than to run far away from this hellhole and forget everyone and everything.

Knox stalls, twirling his keys around his finger, as if waiting for me to make the first move.

But I can't.

I sit frozen in the passenger seat of his jeep, unwilling to get out.

Because I know the second I do, all hell will break loose.

A single tear rolls down my cheek, and I'm so humiliated I close my eyes, clutching the pearls my dad gave me.

God, I wish he were here right now.

"You're gonna be late," Knox says after another minute passes.

"Fine by me."

His jaw clenches. "Stray—"

"You don't fucking get it," I snap, bile rising in my throat. "I was fine being a loser. Yeah, sometimes it sucked, and I got lonely, but for the most part I flew under the radar. No one paid attention to me or gave a fuck about what I did." I clutch my pearls harder. "But now? I'll never be able to blend in with the wall. I'll never be able to walk into a classroom and not think the whispers I hear are about me. When people look at me now…they won't see an uptight nerd who wears pearls and gets good grades. They'll only see me with a dick in my mouth. They'll think that's all I'm worth."

He leans over the seat. "You're right." His voice is a low rumble in my ear. "Now, what are you gonna do about it?"

I don't understand what he's implying. "What do you mean what am I gonna do about it? There *isn't* anything I—"

"Exactly," he snaps, cutting me off. "There isn't a damn thing you can do about what happened." He opens the door and gets out. "Might as well walk in there and own it."

Jesus. He's insane. "Own being a whore?"

"Ninety-nine percent of the girls walking around school have had a cock in their mouth, Stray. You're not fucking special."

"That may be true, but they weren't drugged and taped without their—"

"Boo fucking hoo," he taunts before his voice evens out. "Just because their perception of you has shifted, doesn't mean yours has to."

With that, he slams the door and treks over to Shadow's car.

Even though Knox is a rude asshole, he kind of has a point.

I can't change what happened, or how people will think of me now.

But I can change how I react to it.

I can still be the nerd who wears her pearls and gets good grades.

Besides, there's only a few months left before we graduate. I never have to see these people again.

I climb out of the jeep with my head held high, ignoring all the whispers and pointed fingers as I walk to my locker.

"Are you okay?" Brie questions as I transfer some books into my bag.

"I'm fine."
And even though it's not true…I pretend it is.

Because projecting the image I want people to see is something I've always been good at.

Chapter 17

Knox

"*H*ave a nice nap?"

Confusion mars Ken Ruckman's face when he opens his eyes and looks around the empty football field.

He tries to move, but he won't get very far.

Given he's handcuffed to the scoreboard.

"What the fuck?" He struggles against the cuffs, but he's still out of it so he doesn't have much strength behind the movements. "What the hell are you doing, freak?"

Picking up my father's police baton, I slap the end of it against my open palm. "I like to call it—giving you a taste of your own medicine."

The drowsiness from all the Thorazine I slipped into his water bottle before school ended makes his words slur. I thought about slipping him a roofie like they did to Aspen, but I want him to remember every moment of this.

"What are you talking about?"

Halting my movements, I inspect the baton. "I heard you had a little fun with my stepsister this weekend."

He snorts. "More like she had a little fun with me, if you know what I mean—"

I thump the side of his face with the baton, grinning when I see a stream of blood trickle out of his mouth.

"Why do you care?" he spits, his features twisting in pain.

"Everyone knows you hate Aspen. Hell, if anything, I did you a favor, freak."

Leaning down, I get close to his face. "I don't need your *favors*."

The confusion is back on his face. "Okay. Duly noted. I still don't get why you're defending her."

I bitch smack his other cheek with my open palm, because someone like him doesn't deserve my fists.

"I heard you got into Notre Dame."

He quirks up a brow. "Yeah…yeah, I did. But what the fuck does that have to do with anything?"

A shrill howl cuts through the air when I bash the baton against his right knee, enjoying the crack it makes.

"Congrats, man. It's a shame you won't be playing football for them."

Or anyone else.

A tremble runs through his large frame. "I'm sorry, Knox. Is that what you want to hear?"

Nah. It's too late to apologize.

What's done is done.

"Please," he begs when I raise the baton above my head again. "I'll do anything you want, Knox. *Anything*."

I pause, deciding to have a little fun with him.

"Anything?"

He nods emphatically. "Anything, man. Just don't end my career over some bitch that neither of us like."

I sigh. "I mean, you'll be off the field for a while, but I only hit you once in your right knee so chances are good that you'll make a full recovery."

He breathes a sigh of relief. "Yeah."

"But since you're offering to give me whatever I want…I should probably take you up on it, huh?" Stepping between his legs, I stroke my chin. "Decisions, decisions."

He swallows thickly. "Whatever it is, I got you." He starts rattling off a stream of suggestions. "Need me to fuck someone up for you? I'll do it. Want me to wash your jeep? I'll make it happen. Buy you lunch every day for the rest of the year? You got it, bro. Hell, I'll even rub your feet—"

"I want you to suck my dick."

Disgust twists his features. "What the fuck? I'm not a faggot."

I hold his stare. "Why not? It's the same thing you made Aspen do to you after those bitches drugged her." Shrugging, I motion to the baton. "But since you refuse, I'll just have to finish what I started."

He eyes me warily. "Okay."

I cup my ear. "What's that?"

Deflated, he drops his head. "I'll do it."

Undoing my zipper with my free hand, I move closer. "You gonna swallow my load like a good boy, too?"

He looks like he's about to gag. "Jesus."

"Are you?" I bite out, taking my cock out of my pants.

His eyes snap shut. "Whatever you want."

I take out my phone and press the record button. "You're gonna like sucking this big cock, aren't you?"

When he doesn't answer, I grab the back of his head. "Tell me how much you're gonna like sucking it."

"I'm gonna like sucking your big cock," he grits through his teeth. "Now can we get this shit over with?"

"Open," I instruct.

Begrudgingly, his mouth parts.

"God, Ken," I grind out, stepping closer. "Who knew you were such a whore?"

Shooting him a malicious grin, I unleash a stream of urine into his mouth.

He sputters and gags before dry heaving.

And that's when I whack the baton against his other knee over and over, crushing it until it's nothing but a flab of loose skin.

I clasp his chin, forcing him to look at me through his tear-filled eyes and wet face. "If anyone asks, you were jumped by two men wearing ski masks, so you couldn't see their faces."

"Fuck you," he seethes. "I'm telling the police it was you."

"And I'll make sure my dad—Aspen's stepfather and a member of the FBI—knows what you did to *her*." Motioning to my phone, I shoot him an icy glare. "I'll also release the video I took. The one that makes it look like *you* were the cocksucker this time."

I pat his cheek. "You might not have a football career now, but you can still have your reputation. Not to mention, I've just saved you the embarrassment of trying to make it into the NFL and not being successful—which let's face it, was bound to happen. Now people will look at you with pity and think of you as a could have been, instead of a failure. However, if you tell anyone the truth…you'll just be a loser who enjoys sucking cock in his spare time and got his ass kicked for taking advantage of someone's sister."

I can see I've made my point when he bows his head. "Fine."

Whistling, I hike the baton over my shoulder and start walking down the field.

"Oh, and Ken?" I call out.

He narrows his eyes. "What?"

"To answer your question from earlier, you don't get to fuck with Aspen because she's *mine*."

Which means the only one who gets to hurt her is *me*.

The next day news of Ken's unfortunate *accident* with the two men who jumped him while he was working out on the football field last night has spread through school like wildfire.

Now there's just one more thing left for me to handle so I can restore order.

I find Staci and Traci standing at their lockers after lunch.

Gritting my teeth, I stride over to them.

No doubt bewildered by my presence; they exchange an inquisitive glance.

"Can we help you with something?" Traci questions.

Leaning against a locker, I cross my arms. "I heard you two were the ones behind the video."

Staci bats her eyelashes innocently. "What video?"

Traci shares a grin with her friend. "We have no idea what you're talking about."

"Too bad," I say dismissively as I turn to walk away. "I thought it was pretty badass, but if it wasn't you—"

"Wait," Staci chirps.

Traci's voice drops to a whisper. "It was us."

Staci giggles. "I mean, *obviously*. I posted it on my Instagram story."

"Knox doesn't have Instagram," Traci informs her with a crinkle of her nose. "He's too cool for it."

I take out my phone, making it appear like I can't be bothered with this conversation any longer because I know it will only entice them into my web that much more.

"Duces. I gotta go take care of some shit."

"Hold on," Staci utters.

"For what?"

She exchanges a nervous glance with Traci before she speaks. "It's just…you never come over and talk to us."

No shit. They're both annoying cunts who hide behind their makeup and filters and think their shit doesn't stink when it fucking reeks.

Irritated, I shoot her a pointed look. "And? What's your fucking point?"

"We were just curious why you did today is all," Traci mumbles, looking away.

Staci chews her lower lip. "You really think what we did was bad ass?"

Traci nudges her in the ribs, no doubt issuing a warning about how desperate she's acting.

I shrug. "Maybe."

"Aspen's so annoying," Traci says with a roll of her eyes. "Always walking around with her nose in the air like she's better than everyone else."

Pot meet kettle.

"Plus, she's fat," Staci adds.

Aspen isn't fat. Then again, standing next to these two would make a skeleton look chubby, but that's irrelevant.

"Right." I type a text out on my phone, letting Shadow know I have plans after school. "Gotta go."

"Wait," Staci says when I start to leave again.

"What?"

She licks her lower lip. She probably thinks the move is sexy, but it's not. "We should hang out sometime."

Traci glares daggers at her friend. Whether it's because her desperation is embarrassing, or because she's jealous Staci made the move before she could, I'm not sure…but I'm willing to take the gamble.

Slowly, I drag my gaze up and down her petite form. "What are you doing after school?"

She looks caught off guard before she answers. "Nothing."

"We were supposed to go to the mall," Traci mutters.

I turn my stare on her, giving her a cocky grin. "Too bad. I was thinking maybe the *three* of us could chill."

Because the two of them played a part in what happened that night…

Which means I'm going to fuck them both.

Traci—who looked checked out of the discussion a moment ago—suddenly perks up. "Oh." She looks at Staci. "I mean, my parents are in Bora Bora for the week. I have the entire house to myself."

I lean in closer. "That so?"

She blushes. "Yeah."

"Meet me at my jeep after school. Both of you."

With that, I turn and walk down the hall.

I notice Aspen standing at her own locker a few feet away. Judging by the pissed off expression on her face, she obviously overheard our little exchange.

"I can't give you a ride home today," I state as I stroll past her.

She looks like I plunged a knife into her heart.

Good.

Chapter 18

Aspen

Leo: How's my girl doing?

I quickly type my response.

Aspen: Fine.

 $\mathcal{P}$ lacing my phone on the lunchroom table, I stab at my salad with my fork, wishing it were Knox's eyeballs. It's been two days since I caught him making plans to hang out with Staci and Traci.

And while I didn't think we were suddenly friends, nor did I expect him to defend me at school, I didn't think he'd go out of his way to start hanging out with the two bitches who drugged me at a party and set me up to get raped.

And to think for a moment, I actually thought Knox was the one who beat the crap out of Ken instead of two random muggers like he claims.

I should have known better, though.

Knox is an evil, vindictive killer.

And I will hate him with every piece of my heart and soul until my very last breath.

My phone vibrates with another incoming text and it's all I can do not to throw the damn thing across the room.

Leo: Is everything okay?

Gritting my teeth, I type out my response.

Aspen: Everything is fine.

I slam my phone on the table.
Well, aside from a certain asshole who deserves to have his balls chopped off with a chainsaw.
Grabbing my fork, I stab my salad again.
I hope Staci and Traci give him warts.
My phone lights up with yet another text.

Leo: Can we see each other later? I bet I can make you feel better.

Aspen: I'm studying with Violet tonight.

Guilt prickles my chest, because I know Leo's only trying to put a smile on my face and it's not his fault that his nephew is Satan.
I quickly send another text.

Aspen: I should be free after, though.

Leo: It's a date. I'll pick you up after my brother goes to bed.

Aspen: Sounds good.

Leo: Chin up, honey. Whatever has you down will work itself out. I'm sure of it.

Leo's positive outlook on things is something I usually admire about him, but right now it's just pissing me off.
And it's not like I can tell him the truth about what happened at the party. He'll lose his shit, get my stepfather involved, tell my

mother who will blow a gasket like the drama queen she is, and my life will only get worse.

I just want to move on and forget it ever happened.

Something the entire school is unwilling to do because it's still all everyone is talking about.

"Aspen," Brie whispers from across the table.

"What?" I snap, but immediately regret it when I see her cower.

Brie doesn't deserve my wrath. In fact, she and Violet are the only people in this hellhole who don't treat me like I have leprosy and bring up what happened, which is something I'm grateful for.

She looks down at her half-eaten plate of food. "Nothing. It's just…you're doing more stabbing than eating today."

She's right. But I just don't have the appetite.

I open my mouth to apologize for biting her head off, but my phone buzzes with *another* text.

I'm about to lose my shit on Leo, but then I see everyone else in the cafeteria check their phones, too.

My stomach drops because when the whole school receives a mass text message, it's never a good thing.

"I really hope it's not a shooter," Brie whispers, whipping out her phone.

"Me too—" I start to say, until I see a text from an unknown number.

Or should I say…*video*.

I'm torn as to whether or not I should press play because it could be some kind of virus.

Then again, Leo purchased the protection plan when he bought me my phone, so I take my chances and click on it.

My mouth drops open when I see Staci and Traci sitting on a bed wearing nothing but their bras and panties.

"If you want this dick," a deep, familiar voice says, "then touch each other and make out."

What in the actual fuck?

The girls exchange a nervous glance before giggling and pressing their lips together.

The camera zooms in on them.

"Atta girls," someone who sounds exactly like my stepbrother says as their tongues tangle in a sloppy kiss. "Now take off her bra and suck on her nipple."

Traci does exactly as she's told.

Snickers emit around the cafeteria.

"Holy shit," someone calls out. "This dude is my fucking hero."

Poor Brie looks like a tomato, but just like the rest of us, she's unable to peel her gaze from her phone screen.

Knox's voice drops. "Now tell her thank you by taking off her panties and giving her cunt a kiss."

The girls freeze, hesitation flickering in their eyes.

"Seriously?" Staci says after a minute, her bare breasts now on display.

"Come on, ladies," a guy at the next table yells and everyone chortles. "Don't stop now."

"I thought you two wanted to have some fun?" Knox questions.

"We do but…" Staci pauses, looking at her friend. "Even if we agreed, we wouldn't let you film it."

"But I thought you liked filming things?" Knox taunts and I can't help but notice the shadow on the wall. It looks like he's stroking himself. "Do you want this cock or not?"

"Come on, Staci," Traci urges. "It's not like you haven't done it before. Remember Paris?"

"Oh shit," someone calls out. "What the hell happened in Paris?"

"Some carpet munching by the sounds of it," another guy answers and the cafeteria fills with laughter.

"I always knew they were more than friends," Vivian—a member of the cheerleading squad—jeers from another table.

Rolling her eyes, Staci urges Traci onto her back and takes off her underwear.

A moment later, her head disappears between her friend's legs and the video cuts off.

"What the hell?" a group of guys yell. "Party foul."

Brie's eyes lock with mine from across the table. "It's safe to say everyone will talk about *that* video now."

"Yeah—" my sentence jams in my throat when I see Knox enter the cafeteria.

He folds his arms over his chest, his dark stare zeroing in on me as my phone vibrates with another text. This time from him.

Knox: You're welcome.

When I look up, he's already gone.

———

I have no idea what I'm supposed to say as I trek over to Knox's jeep after school lets out.

Am I supposed to thank him for being morally twisted and serving them the same dish they served me?

Even though they deserved it, I just can't bring myself to revel in it.

Uploading sexual videos of *anyone* is wrong, and two wrongs never make a right.

My lips twitch ever so slightly. *But God, it felt good witnessing those bitches get their karma.*

The sound of arguing tears me from my thoughts.

My eyes widen when I see Knox and Shadow fighting in front of his jeep.

"I know your voice, asshole," Shadow shrieks, jabbing a black fingernail into his chest. "You told me you were busy."

Knox looks more annoyed than angry as he takes a drag of his cigarette. "I was."

"Yeah. Busy getting your dick sucked and fucked by those two ditzes." Without warning, she slaps his cheek. "I can't believe you cheated on me."

At that, Knox laughs, like getting reamed out by his girlfriend is hysterical. "How can it be cheating when we're not together?"

Oh, boy.

Shadow slaps him again, so hard it knocks the cigarette out of his mouth. "Bastard."

My feet move on their own accord as I take a step in their direction. "Okay, that's enough. Some of us need a ride home."

Shadow turns her furious stare on me. "Fuck off."

I open the passenger door of the jeep. "Don't get mad at me

because your non-boyfriend fucked someone else." I dig the knife a little deeper since I've never been a fan of her. "Actually…make that *two* someone's."

"You cock-sucking bitch."

She lunges for me, but Knox grabs her. "Go home, Shadow."

"We're so over." She points a shaky finger at him. "I mean it."

His harsh stare fills with pity, and that only serves to deepen the cut he issues next. "Over? We never fucking began."

Shadow's lower lip trembles and I actually feel bad for her as she runs off to her car.

"Jesus," I whisper as he climbs into the driver's seat. "She's *really* upset."

It's obvious her feelings for Knox are light-years beyond whatever feelings he doesn't have for her.

"She'll get over it." Starting the engine, he brings a fresh cigarette to his lips. "She always fucking does."

"So, you make it a habit to cheat on her?"

His hand tightens around the steering wheel. "She gets my dick wet, but that doesn't mean she owns it. I can fuck whoever I want."

I was only trying to ruffle his feathers, but then I realize,

"You *did* fuck them?"

His lips curve as he pulls out of the parking lot. "You don't own my dick either, Stray."

"Trust me." I avert my gaze out the window. "I want nothing to do with you or your dick."

Chapter 19

Aspen

"So," my mother announces, clasping her hands together. "I've decided it will be a dinner party."

Despite no one looking up from their plates, she continues to prattle on.

"I'm going to rent a few long tables and set them up outside on the patio. I've hired an excellent catering company, as well as a company that's going to transform the backyard into a beautiful extravagant oasis while we dine. We'll even have a dance floor and a DJ after dinner is finished."

"Sounds boring," Trent says as he shoves another piece of steak into his mouth. "And expensive."

She tries hard not to show it, but it's clear his comment struck a nerve.

"I think it sounds nice," I mumble, throwing her a bone. "I'll be around that day if you need any help."

Ignoring me, she turns to Knox. "Knox, what do you think about the party?"

He shrugs, not looking the least bit interested. "Whatever." He looks at his father. "Do I have to go?"

Not missing a beat, Trent wipes his mouth with a napkin and answers. "Yes."

He looks at my mom. "Well, in that case, I think it sucks."

"Watch your mouth, young man," his dad scolds.

"May I be excused?"

Trent takes a sip of his drink. "Excused for what?"

"I'm hanging out with Shadow."

Seriously? It's barely been twenty-four hours since she declared they were over.

"You've been spending a lot of time with her lately," his dad notes. "What exactly do you two do while you're together?"

It takes everything in me not to cover my ears.

Knox pushes some food around his plate. "Study, watch movies…"

Fuck and fight.

Trent clutches his fork so hard I'm surprised it doesn't bend in half. "Well, all this *supposed* studying isn't paying off since you only received a C on your last math test."

In all fairness, that test was hard. Even I got two questions wrong and Math is my best subject. It's like Mrs. Monsen specifically went out of her way to choose the hardest problems known to man. The fact Knox got a C when most people bombed is awesome.

"No one did well on that test," I mutter, scooping some mashed potatoes on my fork.

He turns his irritated glare on me. "What grade did you receive?"

"Ninety-four."

Trent slams his hand on the table, startling my mother. "See? If your sister can manage to get an A, why can't you?"

"She's not my sister." Knox gets out of his chair with so much force it tips backward. "But she is a brainiac who can solve math problems in her sleep."

"Where do you think you're going, young man?" Trent sneers when Knox stalks out of the kitchen.

"Out," is his only response before the front door slams shut.

My mother looks around anxiously. "I need to make a phone call."

An uncomfortable silence falls over the room after she leaves.

I quickly grab my dish and head for the sink.

"I know you probably think I'm too hard on him," Trent begins.

I scrape the remaining food off my plate into the garbage bin before putting it in the sink. "Your relationship with your son is really none of my business." I can't help but add, "That test was difficult, though. Only five people in the class passed, and he was one of them."

Heaving a sigh, he rises from the table and walks over to me. "I don't know if you've noticed, but my son isn't right in the head." His nostrils flare on an indrawn breath. "Ever since his mother's death he's been battling with a lot of mental issues, and it's my job to keep him in line and make sure they don't…get out of hand."

I don't like the weird turn this conversation has taken, so I shoot my gaze to the clock on the wall behind him. "I'm supposed to meet Violet."

His eyes narrow. "You've been studying with her a lot."

"Studying got me a ninety-four on that exam," I point out.

He laughs, but it's devoid of humor. "Right."

I start to leave, but he grabs my wrist. "My brother tells me Trenton has been bothering you."

Fucking hell. I told Leo not to say anything.

"That's not true."

He tenses and I can practically see the indignation rippling through him. "Are you calling my brother a liar?"

"No," I state, because I'm now caught in a catch twenty-two and I have no idea how to get out of it.

"So my son *is* bothering you?"

"It's nothing I can't handle," I settle on.

I motion for him to let go of my wrist, but he doesn't.

"I want you to come straight to me when that happens so I can take care of it. I don't like the thought of you feeling uncomfortable while you're here."

I want to point out that I'm feeling pretty *uncomfortable* right now, but my brain snags on the other half of his statement.

While I'm here.

Like my stay will be temporary.

"Sure thing," I grit through my teeth because I just want this conversation to be over.

I nearly jump out of my skin when he runs his free hand down my cheek. "Good girl."

A rush of uneasiness wells up inside me, but I can't focus on that because someone clears their throat.

When I turn my head, I see Knox standing there.

Briefly, his gaze flicks to his dad's hand on my cheek before he walks over to the counter.

"Sorry to interrupt." He plucks his keys off the counter. "Forgot my keys."

With that, he storms back out.

"Can I go now?" I ask, motioning to the wrist that my stepfather's hand is still tightly wrapped around.

The wrist that wasn't visible to Knox.

"Of course," Trent says, finally releasing his hold.

I'm so exhausted after my shift at the Bashful Beaver, I can barely see straight. If it weren't for Leo pressing me to meet him for a quick screw in his car, I would have gone straight home and into bed.

I try to suppress my yawn as he drives down my block, but it slips out anyway.

"Maybe you should stop studying with Violet so late," he remarks, pulling to a stop in front of the house.

"I can't." *I need the money.* "You know how important getting into a good college is to me and the only way I can pay for it is to get a scholarship."

Or take my clothes off for men twice my age.

A resigned sigh leaves him as he turns toward me. "I told you I'd help pay for college."

Shaking my head, I reach for my school bag containing my stripper shoes. "I don't want your money."

"I know. You don't want my money. You don't want my help. And as of late, you don't even want to text me words containing more than one syllable." His jaw works. "So apart from the thing in my pants, what exactly *do* you want from me?"

I'm not sure what he means. "I don't—"

"Goddammit, Aspen. Don't play dumb."

"I'm not," I snap. "Just stop skirting around whatever your problem is and spit it out."

"Why have you been acting so distant?" His brows furrow. "Is it someone else? Is that who you've been sneaking off to see instead of this *Violet* girl?"

It's all I can do not to roll my eyes. "Are you serious? I barely have time to see you, let alone another guy."

His expression softens. "Well, if it's not someone else, then why the sudden distance?"

Oh, for fuck's sake. He literally came inside me ten minutes ago.

"There's no distance, Leo," I assure him. "I've just been busy."

Blowing out a breath, he hangs his head. It's clear my response didn't satisfy him. "Where is this thing going between us?"

Oh, boy. This is so not the conversation I want to be having at two in the morning when I'm so exhausted I can barely stand and my head is pounding thanks to the music at the club.

"I like things the way they are," I whisper, hoping that puts an end to it.

Another sigh. "Well, I don't."

It's on the tip of my tongue to tell him to man up and end it then, but then he says, "I want more."

"More...meaning—"

"Just *more.*" He pounds the steering wheel with his fist. "I want you to want me to leave my wife. I want you to ask me how my day is going because you care about me. I want you to let me take care of you." His voice lowers a fraction. "I'm in love with you, Aspen."

I feel many things for Leo, but love will never be one of them.

Love is bullshit.

Love is nothing but lies and hurt concealed in the notion of a fairytale we're all forced to believe is vital to our wellbeing.

Love always leads to pain.

However, it's still nice to hear that someone is capable of feeling that for me.

Leaning over the center console, I press my lips to his. I might not be able to tell him the same, but I can still make him feel good.

Leo groans when I brush my tongue against his and climb over the console to straddle him.

Reaching between us, I tug his zipper down and move my underwear to the side.

"Honey," he whispers between short, frenzied kisses. "Sweetheart, I can't."

I rub him through his pants, hoping he'll get nice and hard for me. "It'll be quick. You can go back home to your wife right after."

"It's not that." His eyes squeeze shut, and he groans. "I'm tapped out, honey."

Disappointment blooms in my chest. "Oh."

Talk about a buzzkill.

Trying to conceal my frustration, I climb off his lap. "It's late. I should probably head inside."

His forehead creases. "Yeah."

I gather my things, intending to get out, but then I remember. "Why did you tell Trent that Knox was bothering me?"

He looks like a deer caught in headlights before his expression turns serious. "Because I don't want him anywhere near you. I told you, he's dangerous."

That may be true, but I still don't like him talking to his brother about me. Especially when I asked him not to.

"I can handle Knox myself."

He snorts. "Honey, no one can handle Knox. My nephew is a psychopath. I'm ashamed we share the same blood." Reaching over, he tips my chin. "Promise me you'll stay out of his path."

"I promise," I utter, not because I take orders from him, but because I'm so tired of arguing about this.

He gives me a quick peck on the lips. "Good girl."

Normally I love when he says that, but a weird sensation crawls up my spine.

I open the door and step out of the car. "Goodnight."

He starts the engine. "I'll call you tomorrow."

Rubbing my temples, I amble up the walkway to the house.

I seriously hate that Leo went behind my back like that. I get that he's worried about me, but I can't help but think that Knox…

My thoughts flitter away when a tiny figure with bright blue hair flies past me before collapsing on the lawn in a fit of tears.

What the hell?

Upon closer inspection, I realize it's Shadow.

I approach her as one would approach a bomb. "Are you okay?"

She whips her head around to look at me, and the fear in her tear-stained eyes steals my breath. I assumed she and Knox had another fight, but I've seen them argue before.

Shadow's usually the instigator, and Knox doesn't care enough to fight back.

However, right now…she looks utterly petrified. Like a kid who finally saw the monster lurking under their bed.

And I can only think of one reason that might be.

I look at the red mark around her neck. "Did Knox hurt you?"

Without warning, she staggers to her feet and runs off to her car that's parked across the street.

Shit.

Despite the alarm bells going off in my head telling me not to get involved, I walk around to the back of the house, swing open the basement door, and march down the stairs.

I find Knox sitting shirtless on his bed, smoking a cigarette in the dimly lit room.

"What the fuck did you do to Shadow?"

For a fraction of a second he looks confused, but then he scowls and stands. My eyes take in the fresh scratch marks on his chest and abs.

She must have been fighting him off.

He walks toward me with a resolve that's akin to a vulture circling its prey. "What the fuck are *you* doing in my room uninvited?"

I don't want to make things worse for Shadow, but I don't want Knox thinking he can get away with this shit either.

Someone has to put him in his place.

"Shadow ran past me when I came home. She was crying and clearly upset." I swallow hard. "She also had a red mark around her neck." I fold my arms across my chest. "You obviously hurt her."

His eyes narrow as he studies me, an unreadable expression on his face.

Suddenly, he moves, closing in on me like an eclipse as he backs me into the wall, caging me in with his body.

Those piercing eyes of his are harsher than I've ever seen before as he brings his fingers up to my nose.

Embarrassment mixed with fury floods my cheeks when I inhale.

"I didn't do anything she didn't ask for."

I want to wipe the smug smirk off his face more than I want to take my next breath.

Instead, I bring my knee up, striking him in the balls so I can get away. "Touch me again and I'll tell your dad."

He lets out a deep grunt as he bends over.

I'm aware that I sound like a five-year-old, but it's the only thing that seems to get a rise out of him.

I'm almost to the staircase when his arms wrap around me from behind. "What did I tell you about threatening me, Stray?"

I struggle against him. "Go to hell, asshole."

"I warned you there would be consequences for your actions." His teeth scrape the nape of my neck and he inhales me. "And since you can't keep your nose out of my business, you've given me no choice but to return the favor."

With that, he releases his hold on me. I dash up the stairs and to my room.

Chapter 20

Aspen

I point to the plush brown leather chair. "What about this one?"

Leo looks at the price tag and makes a face. "Too expensive."

I gesture to the black imitation leather chair next to it. "Okay. How about this one then?"

He crinkles his nose. "Too cheap."

I honestly don't know why he insisted on me accompanying him to shop for new furniture for his office when he doesn't seem to like anything I pick out.

"Maybe we should look at desks instead."

Truth be told, I don't see why he needs new furniture to begin with. Then again, he did just get a promotion at his firm, so I guess he wants new stuff for when he switches offices.

Personally, I think it's a gigantic waste of money. As long as there's a functioning desk and chair, that's really all you need.

"Good idea."

He takes my hand, but swiftly drops it when he remembers we're in public and someone might spot us.

I walk over to the large U-shaped mahogany desk on the other end of the store.

"This one is nice," I say, running my hand along the shiny wood.

He rubs his chin, inspecting it. "Actually, it's not half bad. You have good taste."

He flags down a sales associate who tries to talk him into getting a more expensive one, but Leo stands firm.

People really shouldn't argue with lawyers.

"So, I was thinking," Leo begins as the salesperson walks into the back room. "I should hire an assistant."

I quirk a brow. "Do you need help picking out one of those, too?"

He chuckles. "No…well, kind of. I was hoping that maybe *you* would take the job."

I'm about to remind him I'm still a full-time student, but he quickly adds, "You can work after school, of course. Hell, you can even do your homework and study while I'm in meetings."

As tempting as it is to take him up on his offer…there are too many things that have the potential to go wrong.

For starters, I'm already sleeping with my potential boss, and having sex with someone who signs your paychecks is a big no-no.

Plus, if we ever ended things, that could make things super awkward and I'd be unemployed.

The whole thing is a recipe for disaster.

Not to mention, I'm willing to bet I'd still make way more at the shit-hole Bashful Beaver than I would working for him.

I also have a sneaky suspicion as to what his real motivations behind this idea are.

He wants to give me money, but he knows I won't take it. However, if he can legally hire me… I'll have no choice but to accept it.

"Thanks, but no thanks."

He's visibly offended. "It sure didn't take long for you to turn that down."

"I appreciate it, Leo. Really, I do. It's just…things could get messy." I shrug. "Plus, I'm going off to college in a few months so it would be temporary, and you'd end up having to train someone else to take my place."

"No one can take your place, Aspen. Trust me."

His words are sweet and I can't help but smile. "I appreciate everything you do for me."

He scoffs. "I hardly do anything for you, honey."

"That's not true."

He's *here*.

Which is a lot more than I can say for my father.

Or my mother.

After paying for his new desk and arranging delivery, we leave the store and walk out to the parking lot.

"Have any plans this evening? I was hoping we could get a hotel for the night."

I frown because I hate disappointing him. "I can't. There's a huge chemistry test tomorrow that Violet and I have to study for."

I can tell he's upset by this, and I can only imagine how much more upset he'd be if he knew the truth.

"I see." He opens my car door for me. "Will you at least let me take you out to dinner before then?"

I tap my bottom lip with my finger, pretending to think. "I guess." I waggle my eyebrows. "But fast food and only something off the value menu."

Shaking his head, he laughs. "Anyone ever tell you you're stubborn?"

It's my turn to laugh as he climbs into the driver's seat. "Yeah…*you*."

He palms my cheek, his expression going serious. "I love you, Aspen."

Well, shit.

I guess that's going to be a *thing* now.

"Fine, you twisted my arm. You can buy me *two* things off the value menu now." Tilting my head, I kiss his thumb. "Thank you."

His brows draw together. "For what?"

For being here when no one else is.

———————

Gripping the pole, I shake my ass as the song comes to an end, my movements slow and exaggerated.

A couple of men in the audience throw a few bills on stage and I sashay a little, giving them a silent thank you before collecting the money in a bag and walking off so the next girl can come on.

Whipping off my green and black mask, I walk down the empty hallway and into the dressing room.

"Well, that blew," I tell Violet and Heather. "It's dead tonight."

"Tell me about it," Heather remarks as she applies her lipstick in the mirror. "I'm starting to think Candi Kane took all the clients with her when she ran off."

"I can't believe she still hasn't shown up."

Granted, being a stripper isn't exactly a job you need to hand in your notice for or anything, but it's been over two weeks since she's been gone.

"Maybe she's going through some shit," Violet offers with a shrug as she fiddles with her phone.

Heather laughs. "Or maybe she realized she's too old to be shaking her ass next to a bunch of eighteen-year-olds."

Yeah, I'm pretty sure that's not it. Candi was popular around here and made just as much money as we do on any given night… sometimes more.

"She had a few loyal regulars." Fetching my water bottle, I take a sip. "Maybe one of them knows something we don't."

Violet thinks about this for a minute. "Maybe."

Heather rolls her eyes. "To be honest, I'm not sure I even care enough to find out what she's up to."

Heather has a point. It's not like any of us were close to her, and God knows she wasn't nice to any of us.

But still…she was one of us.

And now she's gone.

"Anyone up for ordering food?" Heather asks. "It's dead and I'm starving."

I'm about to tell her I could go for some pizza, but the door swings open and Freddie pops his head in.

"Ginger, you have a private room."

The girls and I exchange a confused glance. The only way to book a room is when a dancer offers one while talking to you on the floor.

Well, usually. It's not unheard of for a client to book a room when he walks in, it's just more expensive and the patrons here are cheap as hell until you hustle it out of them.

However, it's been so empty here tonight, I've barely been doing any networking. I'm pretty sure there's been a mistake and it's for Violet, because she's been booking *a lot* of private rooms lately.

I raise a brow. "Are you sure it's with me?"

Because I don't really have *regulars*. Sure, I have guys who come in and tell me how sexy I am, and say they'll be back to see me again, and sometimes they do, but not enough that they'd ask for a private room before even talking to me on the floor.

Freddie looks annoyed with my questioning. "Yes. He specifically requested a redhead."

Well, okay then.

Heather waves her hands. "Girl, what are you waiting for? It's been a shitshow tonight. Go make that money."

She's right. When there's money on the table, you don't leave it there.

I slip my mask on and touch up my lip gloss before heading down the hallway.

"Room five," Freddie tells me before he walks off.

My heels clack on the floor as I amble to the very last room at the end of the hall.

I'm not usually nervous about private dances anymore, but my stomach flutters like I swallowed a jar of bees.

I take a deep breath when I reach the black door, then apprehensively turn the knob.

The lights are dim when I walk in, so all I see is the profile of a shadowy figure sitting on the couch. The smoke from the lit cigarette hanging out of his mouth wafts through the air.

But then he turns his head…

And those intense, menacing eyes lock on me.

My stomach twists, my insides welling with dread.

How does he know?

Why is he here?

The second question is easy to answer. He's here to terrorize me…because that's all Knox is capable of.

I'm about to tell him off, but then I remember I have my mask on.

There's a chance—albeit a very slim one—that Knox just came here looking for a lap dance from a random redhead.

God, that sounds stupid even to my own ears.

He's here because of me.

I back up, intending to make a run for the changing room.

He's caught me off guard and I need time to figure out a plan for how to deal with my nemesis knowing my secret.

"Come closer, Aspen." His voice is a rumble of smoke and ashes. "Or should I say…*Ginger*."

I don't move a muscle.

"What are you doing here?" I whisper, defeat rushing through me.

He brings his cigarette to his mouth. "I told you there would be consequences."

I'd assumed those consequences would be him tormenting me even more than usual…not digging up my dirty little secret.

He crooks a finger. "Come here."

I don't want to, but I have no choice.

I'm now his unwilling pawn.

"Monster" by Meg Myers plays through the speakers as I make my way over to where he is.

I'm about to sit down on the other end of the couch, but he shakes his head. "By the pole."

If he thinks I'm going to dance and strip for him, he's out of his damn mind.

"No."

He stares me down in challenge, but I refuse.

When it's clear I'm not going to budge, he cocks his head and smirks. Almost like he expected me to snub his request.

"I guess I'll have to tell your mom and my dad about your after-school job then." Veiled in his threatening tone, there's also a hint of amusement. Like this is funny to him. "See how aggravating it is when someone threatens you?"

My heart lodges in my throat as I stand in front of the pole. "How long have you known?"

His face hardens as he snuffs out his cigarette. "Since the first night you started."

I want to ask how he found out, but I'm too distracted by the fact that he's known about this for so long.

Yet, he hasn't told me or presumably anyone else about it.

Which means he was either saving this little bomb in his back pocket so he can fuck with me at the time of his choosing…

Or he wants something in exchange for his silence.

A smug smile curves his lips. "Shouldn't you be dancing?"

I look him right in the eyes. "I don't dance for douchebags."

Fear skitters up my spine when he stands, eyeing me like a serial killer eyes his next victim.

The room feels smaller, the air growing thin as he approaches. The pole digs into my back the closer he gets.

Instinctively, my hand flies up to protect my throat.

Knox dips his head, his lips ghosting over my ear before he speaks. "You'll do anything I want you to, Stray."

I ignore the goosebumps breaking out along my flesh and steel myself, unwilling to give in to the fear pumping through me, because that's exactly what he wants. "So that's how this is gonna work now? You're gonna blackmail me by telling people about my job?"

A job I desperately need.

I wince when he grips my chin between his fingers. "Blackmail would imply that I want something." His gaze drops down, his features twisting with disgust as he takes in my sparkly black bikini top and booty shorts. "But you have nothing that I want."

We both know that's a lie.

There's a thin line between hate and lust…and he walks across it like a tightrope master.

But even the greatest ones can lose their balance.

I press a hand to his chest, ushering him toward the couch.

He steps back without protest, a glint of intrigue in his harsh features.

When he sits, I step between his parted legs. "I'm pretty sure I have something you've always wanted."

He sits like a stone, his expression giving nothing away as I slowly begin moving to the music.

I hook my thumbs into the sides of my shorts, lowering them enough to reveal the top of my G-string.

There's a flash of challenge in his eyes now, daring me to make my next move.

Holding his stare, I slip them down my legs and step out of them. Then I spin around, giving him a deliberate roll of my ass and sway of my hips before I plant myself in his lap.

Knox might have all the power right now, but I'll be damned if I'm not going to fuck with him a little.

"What if I let you take me right here?"

He doesn't say a word, but I feel the hard ridge of his cock between my legs, so I taunt him more, grazing the length of him with my ass as I dance.

"Or would you like it better if I begged for it like a good girl?"

I'm about to end this little tease, but he grabs my hips. A deep grunt leaves him as he thrusts upward, grinding his hard dick into me.

My skin tightens, and my stomach dips as everything around me starts to spin.

He fists my hair, yanking my head back before running his nose up the side of my neck. "Don't start something you can't finish."

I open my mouth to tell him to fuck off, but his hand clamps around my jaw, tilting my head so his lips can capture mine.

His mouth is savage and hungry. *A reward and a punishment.*

My heart picks up speed as his fingers tighten around my jaw and he feeds me his tongue in greedy strokes, giving me no choice but to take it. He runs the metal barbell against the roof of my mouth and I fight back a shiver from the sensation.

One hand drops to my neck while the other slides down the length of my torso. To my horror, a moan escapes me. I dig my nails into his thigh, warning him to stop, but that only makes him deepen the torture by skimming his thumb along the edge of my panties, teasing me.

Coming to my senses, I clamp down on his tongue until I taste the hint of copper.

His fingers twist the sides of my G-string as he edges away and bares his teeth, looking like a feral animal.

"You're disgusting." Reaching down, I bend his fingers until they're about to break and the automatic reflex to let go takes over so I can move freely again. "I hate you."

"I paid for a private room and a dance," he snarls as I get off his lap.

I glare at him. "So, enjoy it…by yourself."

I'm almost out the door when he comes up behind me and places his arms on either side of the frame, holding it shut. "Do you want me to tell your mom and stepdad where you work? All the kids at school?"

Jesus. He's a fucking monster.

"Of course, I don't," I spit, stating the obvious.

He sweeps my hair to the side and I can feel the heat of his breath on the nape of my neck when he speaks. "Then this isn't over."

"God, you're pathetic." Closing my eyes, I shake my head. "If you want to fuck me so bad, just man up and admit it so we can get it over with already."

This way it takes all the power he's holding over me away.

"I *do* want to fuck you, Stray." His hand comes around and he squeezes my tit. "Just not the way you secretly wish I would."

Feeling helpless, I swallow my pride. "I'll stay out of your business, okay? And I won't ever threaten to go to the cops and have you thrown in an institution again. Promise."

"It's too late for that." His teeth nip at my shoulder blade. "Like I told you, every action has a consequence." His thumb skates down the length of my spine. "Every sin has a punishment."

He's unbelievable. "If that's the case…what's yours?"

I feel him tense behind me. "You."

I have no idea what that means.

Pushing me aside, he opens the door. "But your secret is safe with me…for now." An arrogant smirk plays on his lips as he walks out. "See you later, sis."

Chapter 21

Aspen

I clutch my mug of coffee, watching the steam rise as the sun fights with the clouds outside the window, battling to see who will win for the day.

I feel his presence behind me as I bring my cup to my lips and take a sip. I wanted to enjoy a few moments of peace before everyone came down for breakfast, but I should have known better.

There is no peace when he's around. Especially now that he's holding my job over my head.

Wearing nothing but a pair of gray sweatpants that hang dangerously low on his hips, Knox makes a beeline for the coffeepot on the counter. I can't help but notice he likes his black…just like his soul.

Glaring, I reach for the French vanilla creamer on the island and pour more into my mug.

I swear I see a hint of a smirk on his face as he turns and places a bagel into the toaster.

I peel my gaze away when I realize I'm staring at his back and the way his broad shoulders and sculpted muscles tense and coil.

I look around the kitchen, noticing my mother hasn't come down yet. She usually has breakfast made for everyone, as per her husband's request.

As if reading my mind, Knox says, "My father got called into work early this morning. We're on our own for breakfast."

I breathe a sigh of relief. It's nice not having to deal with the bullshit.

Twisting back around, Knox picks up his cup of coffee. "Be ready in twenty."

I hear him talking, but my brain is having a hard time comprehending what he's saying because all I can focus on are the severe v-cuts running down his lower abdomen and the lewd outline of his cock peeking through his sweatpants.

"Stray," he snaps, forcing my gaze up.

"What?"

He grabs one half of his bagel from the toaster. "Stop staring at my dick like you want it for breakfast."

I open my mouth to tell him I'd rather dine on rat poisoning, but he's already walking away.

The hallway is full of boisterous chatter as I head toward my locker. I assume it's about the usual—Staci and Traci's video…or mine.

However, Brie rushes over to me the second I begin turning the dial on my lock. Given we don't really talk outside of lunch, it's a little unusual for her to seek me out.

"Did you hear what happened?"

It's even more unusual for Brie to come to me with gossip.

But one look at the startled expression on her face tells me something bad happened.

I close my eyes, silently praying Knox didn't make good on his threat to tell everyone at school that I moonlight as a stripper.

"Aspen," Brie whispers, concern lacing her tone.

I focus my attention back on her.

"Sorry." Shaking my head, I take a few books out of my locker. "Yeah, no. I didn't hear anything. Why, what's up?"

"They found a body at Devil's Bluff last night."

That's…alarming. Black Mountain is a relatively safe place. Sure, we have the occasional murder, but not often.

"Really? Who?"

"A young woman. I didn't know her, but it's all over the news."

She worries her lower lip between her teeth. "Kind of scary that it happened so close to home, you know?"

She's not wrong about that. "Yeah."

She looks down at her shoes. "I just wanted to make sure you're okay."

"Thanks," I tell her as I take out my phone.

I only have a few more minutes before class starts, so I quickly pull up a news article.

Sure enough, there was a female body found at Devil's Bluff by someone walking their dog.

The police don't have any leads yet, but the victim was a thirty-year-old woman named Sheri Garside, daughter of prestigious heart surgeon, Dr. Phillip Garside.

However, it's the photo in the article that nearly brings me to my knees.

For a moment I think I'm seeing things, because the picture is a dated one that looks like it was taken out of a yearbook.

But upon closer inspection, there's no mistaking it's definitely Candi Kane.

My stomach churns as I brush past Brie. "I have to go."

"Are you okay?" she calls out after me, but I keep trudging down the hallway.

My heart's in my throat as I race down the halls of the school, searching for Violet.

I can't believe Candi's dead.

I can't believe she was *murdered*.

I find Violet by her locker talking to *Big Mike*, a notorious school player. I want to warn her he's bad news, but it's really none of my business. Plus, there are way more pressing issues at hand.

"Hey, can I talk to you for a minute?" I flick my gaze to Big Mike, who looks thoroughly annoyed I'm interrupting their conversation. "Alone."

Violet's eyes widen in surprise when she sees me. We rarely speak during school because, well…neither of us like talking to people, so we stick to ourselves.

Turning to Big Mike, she clears her throat. Reluctantly he takes the hint, but not before telling her, "I'll see you later."

The second he leaves, she looks at me. "What's up?"

Taking her hand, I lead her to the nearest restroom. After we're inside, I check all the stalls to make sure it's empty and no one can overhear us.

"Okay, you're kind of starting to freak me out. What's going on?"

"Did you hear about the body found at Devil's Bluff?"

She nods. "Yeah, someone stumbled on it while walking their dog. I know it's scary, but try not to freak—"

"It was Candi Kane."

I can tell this is news to her because her eyebrows shoot up to the ceiling and she blows out a heavy breath. "Shit."

Shit is right.

"I know." I rub my temples as I recall the rest of the article. "Apparently, her father is a renowned heart surgeon." My heart clenches. "And her real name was Sheri."

"That's…damn. I never would have guessed."

That makes two of us. Typically, people don't become strippers when they have a stellar home life and rich parents.

Then again, I have no idea how her home life was. Maybe we were more alike than I thought.

But I'll never know…because she's dead.

Violet frowns. "As sad as it is, there's really nothing we can do about it. We have no clue what Candi was into when she wasn't at work. For all we know, she could have been involved with the wrong crowd." Reaching over, she gives my shoulder a squeeze. "We're late for class, though. I'll see you at work later, okay?"

"Yeah."

She's almost to the door when the bad feeling brewing in my gut grows. "Violet?"

"Yeah?"

"Just…stay safe."

She gives me a warm smile. "Everything will be fine, Aspen. Sometimes bad shit happens. I'm sure the police will figure out who did it and lock them up soon."

Yeah, she's probably right.

But just to make sure, I know exactly who I can ask.

If given the choice between being bit by a thousand fire ants while lying on a bed of hot coals or striking up a conversation with my stepfather, I'd happily choose the former.

Unfortunately, I don't really have a choice but to involve him. I want to make sure Candi gets the justice she deserves. And since Trent had no problem swooping in to help with the investigation regarding the death of my father, he should have no problem lending a hand with the death of Candi.

Getting to the bottom of this is so important to me, I end up calling into work just so I can talk to him.

I find Trent typing something on the computer in his office later that night.

Swallowing my pride, I knock on the door.

Surprise crosses his features when he sees me. "Aspen, come in."

"Remember how you said I could come to you if I had a problem?"

He pinches the bridge of his nose. "Christ. What did my piece of shit son do now?"

"Nothing," I quickly say. "This isn't about Knox. This is about Ca—" I catch myself and clear my throat. "Catching a murderer. There was a woman's body found at Devil's Bluff yesterday."

"I'm aware." He scrubs a hand down his face. "Evidently, the victim's father is a big wig with connections and he insisted the FBI be brought in." Leaning back in his chair, he rolls his eyes. "Waste of time if you ask me."

I raise a brow. "Why do you say that?"

He exhales sharply. "Because the victim was a stripper at a *classy* joint across town called The Bashful Beaver."

I try my best to keep my expression neutral. "Oh." Confused, I rub my forehead. "Why would that be a waste of time?"

It's clear by his expression that he isn't enjoying my line of questioning.

"Well," he drawls slowly, like I'm an infant who can't comprehend anything. "In my experience, girls like that reap what they sow. Most of the time they're involved in prostitution and drugs. It's no wonder most of them end up dead. Not to mention, it's a complete waste of tax dollars and resources to run around trying to track down the pimp, dealer, or john who offed them."

His harsh words cut like a knife.

That might be his experience, but it's not mine. Most of my colleagues are trying to put themselves through school or put food on the table for their kids.

Plus, whether or not she was a stripper should have no bearing on conducting an investigation.

"But she was murdered," I whisper, my chest caving in. "Right here in Black Mountain. Doesn't that—"

"Aspen," he interjects, concern crossing his features. "You have nothing to worry about. Your father is an FBI agent who sleeps with a loaded gun next to his bed every night. I'd never let anyone hurt you. You're safe here."

"Stepfather," I correct, bile working up my throat. "And it's hard to believe I'm safe now when the people who *should* be taking murders seriously aren't."

With that, I turn on my heel, so infuriated I could scream.

I pace the floors of my bedroom. *I need to do something.*

Part of me wants to call Leo and convince him to talk some sense into his brother, but I know he'll only have a bunch of questions for me.

Questions I can't answer without outing myself.

I stop pacing when another thought occurs to me.

There *is* someone who knows my secret. Knox and his father might not get along, but maybe if Knox speaks to him, Trent'll have a change of heart.

Feeling a new surge of energy, I exit my room and trudge to the staircase leading down to the basement.

Only to find the door locked.

I knock a few times, but there's no answer.

Huffing, I walk over to the window. Knox's jeep is in the driveway, so he's definitely home.

I walk around the house to the outside entrance of the basement.

Exasperated, I knock a few times on that door, but I still don't get a response.

I'm peeved that he's intentionally ignoring me. I'm about to trek back into the house, but a soft crying sound snags my attention.

When I shoot my gaze out toward the backyard, I see something small, white, and furry.

I approach and quickly realize it's a kitten. Judging by its tiny size and very weak cry, the poor thing is starving.

Starving and alone.

I brush my hand along his fur, hoping I don't startle it away. However, the kitty is so tired, it makes no protest about being touched. "Hey, buddy. Where's your mama?"

Because a kitten this small is definitely still nursing.

I glance around the yard, hoping to find a larger cat somewhere…but there's no sign of her.

"What are you doing?"

I jump at the sound of Knox's voice behind me.

Turning my head, I look up at him. "Did you know there was a kitten in the backyard?"

His face scrunches as he glances down. "No."

He starts to walk inside, but I halt him. "Where were you? I knocked on your door."

He gestures to the sweatpants and damp t-shirt he's wearing. "I went for a run." His eyes narrow. "What do you want?"

Telling him about Candi is going to have to wait because I need to get some food into this kitten.

"Right now? A can of tuna."

His lips curl. "You shouldn't feed strays."

"If I don't, he'll die, asshole," I shoot back, glaring at him.

Visibly annoyed, he rubs the back of his head. "Fine."

I pet the kitten, trying my best to console him. "Hang on, little guy. You're gonna get food soon."

A few minutes later, Knox returns with an open can of tuna. "Here."

I place it in front of the kitten, but he's so lethargic, he doesn't move. Not even when I place some on my finger.

"Come on, baby," I urge. "Take one little bite."

"Maybe he wants to be left the fuck alone."

"He'll die if I leave him alone. Something must have happened to his mother." Swallowing my pride for the second time tonight, I utter, "There's an emergency vet hospital twenty minutes away. Do you think you can give me…us…a ride?"

He looks like I just invited him to a tea party. "Fuck no."

Frustration courses through me. "I'll do whatever you want, okay? I just really don't want him to die."

Lord knows I've had enough death for one day.

Gripping his neck, he looks up at the night sky and mutters a curse. "Fine, but you're leaving him at the vet. My father's allergic to cats and he'll lose his shit if we bring that thing in the house."

"I won't bring him inside the house. Promise."

Chapter 22

Aspen

*T*hree hours later, I have the kitten—who's evidently a female—swaddled in a blanket in my arms as I feed her formula from a dropper.

While sitting on the floor of Knox's bedroom.

Smoking his cigarette, he glares at me from across the room.

"It will only be for a few days," I assure him. "As soon as Whiskers is healthy, she'll go back to being an outdoor cat."

But I'll make sure to stock up on cat food and sneak her some every day after school so she doesn't go hungry.

He glowers. "Whiskers?"

I stroke Whisker's fur. "I figured she should have a name during her stay." I smile as her tiny whiskers tickle my fingers. "Whiskers is cute. Just like she is."

He grunts.

After Whiskers is done eating, she curls up into the blanket on the floor.

"She's only three weeks old, so she'll need to eat every three to four hours."

He glances at his watch. "Guess your ass will be back down here at two a.m. then."

I should have expected nothing less from him. Knox doesn't have a nice bone in his body...not even when it comes to poor, innocent animals.

Although, he did give me a ride to the vet and albeit, *reluctantly*—agreed to let Whisker's stay down here for a few days.

"For what it's worth, I appreciate you doing this."

Another grunt.

After I'm sure Whiskers is comfortable and fast sleep, I decide to broach the topic of Candi.

"I don't know if you heard, but there was a body found at Devil's Bluff."

He tenses, reaching for another cigarette as he leans against the headboard of his bed. "I heard."

Blowing out a breath, I walk over to him. "The victim was a girl from my job."

He says nothing, so I continue, "I tried asking your dad if he could help with the investigation—"

"You asked my father for help?"

I nod. "Yeah…but it didn't go well. He pretty much said she was a whore and got what she deserved."

Knox snorts. "No surprise there."

Biting my lip, I shove my hands in the pockets of my jeans. "I was kind of hoping that maybe you'd talk to him for me. You're his son, so perhaps you can convince—"

"Are you out of your fucking mind?" he snarls. "If he won't listen to you, what the fuck makes you think he'd listen to me?"

I guess he has a point. "I don't know." Looking down, I wring my hands. "She was murdered, Knox…then left out in the woods to rot like a piece of garbage. And the people who can help figure out who did it don't seem to give a shit just because she took off her clothes for a living." My arms curl around my frame. "I know what it feels like to know that no one in the world gives a fuck about you. And the more I think about it, I'm realizing that it could have easily been me who was murdered instead of her." I shrug. "I guess I'd just like to know someone would still fight for me if it was."

Knox doesn't say a word as he takes a long drag of his cigarette.

I feel so stupid for confiding in him. I should have known better. "Forget it. I don't expect someone like you to understand."

"Aspen," he barks when I head for the staircase.

"What?"

When I turn to look at him, I see he's already charging toward me.

I take a step back, but he takes a step forward, cornering me into the wall.

His dark gaze lingers on my mouth as he trails a finger down my cheek. I flinch because the gesture is so gentle and I'm not used to that from him.

"What are you doing?" I question.

"You told me I could have whatever I wanted earlier."

My pulse quickens when he fists my hair, drawing me closer.

His breath brushes my lips. It's a teasing whisper of a caress that has my nipples pebbling under my t-shirt.

My eyes flutter closed and I part my lips...waiting for him to kiss me.

But he doesn't.

And for reasons I can't explain...I almost *need* him to.

"That right there." His voice is gruff. Taunting. "That's exactly what I wanted."

I shove at his chest. "You're an asshole."

He laughs as I march toward the stairs, but then it comes to an abrupt halt and his tone goes serious.

"Stray?"

"What?"

"Leave my father alone. The less you piss him off, the better. For everyone."

Chapter 23

Aspen

A little over a week has passed since they found Candi's body and apparently people are over it, because no one is talking about it anymore.

She's officially forgotten.

I stab at my mac and cheese as the clatter in the lunchroom picks up.

"Are you okay?" Brie asks, looking equally down.

"I'm fine." *Stab. Stab. Stab.* "Okay. Not really."

"Want to talk about it?"

Not really, but I find myself doing so anyway.

"Where do I begin?" I start ticking things off with my fingers. "The fact that no one cares about the girl who was murdered? Or that I *still* haven't heard back from any colleges…including Stanford, which I have my heart set on."

She winces, and it's enough to let me know that she most likely heard back from *tons* of colleges already, and I'm screwed.

I place my fork down since I'm probably starting to resemble a homicidal maniac and I don't want to scare her. "I'm also supposed to put together a stupid prom committee and—" I stop talking and eye her hopefully. "Do you want to be on it?"

She shakes her head profusely. "No, thanks."

Yeah, I didn't think so, but still. Can't blame a girl for trying.

"I don't want to be on it either. Hell, I'm not sure if I'm even going to prom."

"Well, if you're running the committee, I think you kind of *have* to," she points out.

Yeah…she's right.

Which means I have to get a dress and shoes.

I place my palm to my forehead and groan when I realize.

Brie's eyes widen. "What?"

"Nothing."

Except…I can't even bring my boyfriend to prom because he's forty-eight years old and married.

"Ever wish you could press reset on your life and have a do-over?"

She snorts. "I *used* to all the time."

The bell rings and she stands. "I gotta go. My next class is all the way on the other side of the building and I still have to stop at my locker."

I smile as she walks off. Brie's been more talkative lately and coming out of her shell a little. If I had to guess why, I'd say it might have something to do with her boyfriend, Colton.

At least it's *something* positive.

Well, aside from Whiskers.

According to Knox, she's overstaying her welcome, but I think he kind of enjoys having her around, too.

The other day I noticed a small litter box next to her blanket and since I didn't buy it for her, it must have been him.

Grabbing my lunch tray so I can throw it in the trash, I get up from the table.

My next class is History, and it's my favorite…mostly because I get to stare at Mr. Donati and his gorgeous blue eyes for forty whole minutes.

I do a quick sweep of the classroom as I walk in. My stomach drops when I pass by Shadow's desk and notice she's still absent.

The last time I saw her was when she was hysterically crying on my front lawn.

I've tried bringing it up to Knox, but he said it wasn't his responsibility to keep tabs on the bitches he screws.

He's a real class act.

Shoulders sagging, I take a seat at my desk and whip out my history textbook.

I pull up the Uber app on my phone and tip the driver before I step out of the car. I normally try to save my money, but Knox came up to my locker after school ended and said he had something to do so he couldn't give me a ride home today.

Given he looked like he was in a rush, I didn't press him about it.

The house is quiet when I walk inside and place my knapsack down in the mudroom.

"Trent, is that you?" my mother calls out from upstairs.

"Nope. It's me."

Your daughter who you couldn't care less about if you tried.

My eyes land on the half-empty bottle of wine on the island in the kitchen.

Surprise, surprise.

I bet if I turned myself into a bottle of merlot, she'd finally pay attention to me.

Stuffing those feelings down, I pick up the pile of mail on the counter and shuffle through it.

I freeze when I see one addressed to me. From Stanford.

It's thick. Thick is good, right?

My hands are shaking so badly, I almost drop the envelope on the floor as I open it.

I close my eyes, silently praying to whatever God exists that I got in, because I've wanted this for so long.

I feel like I'm going to faint the moment I see the words, *congratulations* and *scholarship*.

I did it.

I worked my ass off for years, trying to reach this one goal, and it finally happened.

My heart squeezes. *I miss my dad.*

Despite his mistakes, I know how much he wanted this for me, too.

I wish he were here to share this moment with me.

I sprint up the stairs and run into my mother's bedroom. She's lying on the bed with a glass of wine in her hand, her eyes looking bleary as she stares at the television.

Hopefully, this news will snap her out of it because who wouldn't be proud of their kid getting into a prestigious school?

"Mom." I frantically wave the envelope in the air. "I got into Stanford!"

"Okay." She tips her glass, causing her wine to slosh over a little. "Shoot. I just washed these sheets. Trent's gonna kill me."

"Mom," I repeat, because it's clear she didn't hear me the first time. "I got into Stanford."

She blinks. "What's Stanford? Is that a club or something?"

"No. It's a college. A fantastic college."

The college of my dreams.

She nods, not looking at all impressed. "Well, congrats—wait a minute. What's the catch? How much is this going to cost, because Trent—"

"Trent can go fuck himself because he doesn't have to pay for a goddamn thing." I slap my chest. "I got a scholarship."

I earned it on my own. Without anyone else's help.

And with the money I saved up from stripping, I'll have enough to pay for books, clothes, food, and whatever else I'll need.

And if I keep dancing until the summer ends, I could earn enough that I won't even have to work for the first couple of semesters. I can focus on studying full time.

"Watch your mouth, Aspen." She holds up her glass. "And get me another refill."

Disgust rolls through me as I stalk out of her room and back down the stairs. I honestly don't even know why I bother anymore. It's the same story with the same tragic ending.

I only do it to myself.

Fishing my phone out of my purse, I call someone who does give a shit.

But Leo's phone goes straight to voicemail.

He once told me I could call his office if there was ever an emergency and I couldn't reach him.

Getting into Stanford seems like a pretty big deal to me.

"Leo Knox's office," a chipper female voice answers. "This is Tiffany speaking. How may I help you?"

I cradle the phone between my shoulder and cheek. "Hi, is Leo there? This is…" I stall because I didn't think this part through. "Aspen…his niece."

Ugh. I hate myself.

"Leo's in an important meeting right now, but I'm his new assistant. Can I take a message?"

New assistant, huh? That's news to me.

"Um, I guess just tell him I called."

"Sure thing, hon."

Sadness fills my chest as I hang up and grab a bottle of water from the fridge.

I have the best news and no one to share it with.

A smile touches my lips. *On second thought, that's not true.*

Placing the water on the counter, I rush outside and run around to the basement entrance. Knox said he'd leave it unlocked for me so I can take care of Whiskers, and I'm glad he stayed true to his word.

"Hey, you." I pick the little kitty up from her blanket and cuddle her. "Guess who got into Stanford?"

Whisker's purrs a little, nuzzling her head under my chin.

I run my fingers through her fur, which is much softer and healthier than it was when I found her. "At least you're here for me."

Maybe I can convince Knox to let me keep her hidden in the basement for the next few months and save up for an apartment near campus that allows pets. "Would you like to live with me and be my college study buddy?"

She purrs again, and my heart does a little flip. "And people say cats have attitudes."

Not Whiskers. She loves to be loved up on.

I'm so into our little cuddle sesh, I don't even realize Knox is home until he's downstairs.

"Hey." Picking up Whisker's paw so she can wave, I turn around. "Look who—" My mouth drops when I see his puffy eye and bloody lip. "What the fuck happened to you?"

For once, he's the one who looks caught off guard. "Nothing."

I place Whiskers back on her blanket. "You look like you got into a fight with Mike Tyson…and lost."

He walks over to his mini fridge and takes out some kind of protein drink. "Trust me…I *wouldn't* lose."

"Right, well…something obviously happened to you." I wave my hand, gesturing for him to fill in the gap, but he doesn't.

Turning around, he whips off his shirt and throws it into the hamper. I notice a nasty bruise forming on the side of his stomach.

"Seriously, Knox. What the fuck happened?"

He rolls his shoulders and groans, making it clear I'm irritating him.

However, I won't let up. "Kno—"

"You really want to hear about my hookup?"

I blink, not understanding. "Your hookup?"

"The girl I fucked." His tongue finds his cheek. "She likes it rough."

So rough you need to put aside money for a copay afterward?

"Jesus. That's…" I shake my head because I don't even have the words to express how fucked-up that is.

Knox's eyes narrow into tiny slits. "Don't ask questions you don't want to know the answers to." Bringing his arm up, he sniffs. "I'm gonna go grab a shower."

"I got into Stanford," I blurt out as he walks up the stairs.

I hear him come to a full stop. "Great. How long until you and that furball get the fuck out?"

I raise my middle finger. "Dick."

Chapter 24

Aspen

I mix the ingredients together in a large bowl, watching them blend before I add my favorite ingredient for optimal moistness—vanilla pudding.

Tonight is the dinner party my mother's hosting, and while I have no inkling to help her after our exchange about Stanford last week, I really love to bake.

The party gives me a perfect excuse to do it.

After spooning the batter into cupcake foils, I place the tray on top of the stove. A moment later, the timer buzzes, letting me know another batch is done.

"What are you doing?" Knox questions as I switch out the trays.

Taking out some tongs, I place the new cupcakes on a cooling rack, so they don't overcook.

"Making cupcakes for the party."

His face scrunches and I notice the bruises from his *sexcapades* have started to fade. "Did you get permission to do that?"

Now I'm the one who makes a face. "Permission? To bake cupcakes?"

Hell, if anything, I might actually get a thank you out of my mother for helping.

Turning to the island, I pick up the pastry bag filled with homemade icing and start frosting a different batch that's had time to cool.

147

I can feel Knox's stare on me the entire time…watching me. After I'm done frosting, I sprinkle some coconut shreds on top.

"Do you like chocolate cupcakes?"

It's probably a dumb question, because almost everyone I know likes chocolate. However, Knox is usually the exception to the rule, so I figured I'd ask before offering him one.

I'm not prepared for his response.

"Don't know. Never had one before."

I'm about to laugh because he's obviously joking, but his earnest expression tells me he's not.

"You've never had chocolate cupcakes before?" I'm about to point out that technically these are chocolate caramel coconut, but the next words out of his mouth are even more bizarre.

"I've never had a cupcake, period."

"Not a big fan of sweets, I guess?"

Turning to the fridge, he takes a bottle of water out. "Don't know. Never had any."

I do a double take. "Are you fucking with me right now?"

"No," he deadpans. "My father loathes baked goods and never wanted them in the house, so my mom never made them."

My jaw drops a little because that's fucking tragic. Part of the reason I love baking so much is because my dad surprised me with an easy bake oven when I was nine.

It was love at first sight.

Even when we didn't have money for sweets, I used to pretend I was baking something delicious to make me feel better.

The fact that Knox missed out on something so *normal* is…sad.

"You never had any outside the house?"

He shrugs, appearing annoyed. "Never really had the inkling."

"That's…" I let my sentence trail off and pick up a cupcake instead. "Well, you know what they say, there's a first time for everything."

His eyes scan my face, like he's trying to memorize every freckle on it as he walks toward me. My cheeks heat with every step he takes.

I expect him to snatch the cupcake from me so he can eat it, but he dips his head…then runs his tongue ring across my lower lip.

"It tastes sweeter than it looks," he murmurs before edging away.

I'm at a loss for words. There are times he can be so cruel it takes my breath away…

But then there are moments like this—ones where I can feel an electric current running between our bodies—that confuse me.

Entice me.

Like an evil magician who casts a spell you can't seem to break.

Clearing my throat, I hold up the cupcake. "Try—"

"What's all this?" my mother questions as she walks into the kitchen.

"I baked cupcakes for the party."

Surprise illuminates her face. "Oh—"

"You did *what?*" Trent snaps, stalking in behind her.

It's clear he isn't in the greatest mood.

"I baked cupcakes," I repeat. "For the party."

And while he might not be the biggest fan of sweets, the guests coming to his home tonight might be.

I watch as anger spreads across his face, twisting his already harsh features. "Throw them out."

Wait? *What?* Is he kidding?

I look at my mom, but she won't meet my eyes.

"No." I shake my head, trying my hardest not to laugh, but it slips out anyway. "I'm not throwing perfectly good cupcakes out just because you don't like them."

That's stupid.

Hell, this whole confrontation is stupid.

I gesture to the tray of frosted cupcakes. "If you don't want them at the party, fine. Don't serve them. I'll just—"

It happens so fast, I barely have time to process what's transpiring as Trent sweeps his hand over the island and the tray lands on the floor.

"I don't want that shit in my house. Get rid of it. *Now.*"

He's insane. The way he's acting is downright bizarre.

"Holy shit. You're crazy. What the hell is wrong with you?"

Next thing I know, his hand seizes my chin, gripping it so hard it hurts as my lower back digs into the counter.

"Watch your mouth, young lady."

He's out of his mind. There's no other explanation for it.

"Fuck you." I look at my mother, who's now peering down at the floor. "Are you really gonna let him speak to me that way?"

Because my dad would *never*.

"I will not tolerate disrespect in my house." Trent raises his hand. "It's time you learned—"

"Dad," Knox barks, wedging himself between us. "Aspen didn't know the rule."

The *rule*? Jesus. This place is becoming more like a prison every day.

The look he gives Knox sends a chill up my spine as he takes a step back and looks at my mother. "Handle your daughter, Eileen. Or so help me God, I will."

Finally coming out of her trance, my mother lifts her head. "Aspen, go to your room."

"Seriously?" I scoff. "I'm not twelve."

"Eileen," Trent warns.

Walking over to me, she takes hold of my elbow. "Room. *Now*."

I plant my feet. "No."

The sting of her palm slapping my cheek is so startling—and humiliating—I blink back tears.

I miss my dad.

It's the only thought I have as I run up the stairs and into my bedroom.

That and…*I want to leave.*

I turned eighteen at the beginning of January, so there isn't much my mother can do to stop me from moving out.

I can use the money I saved from dancing to find an apartment until college starts.

I don't know why I didn't think of this before.

Taking a suitcase out of my closet, I start filling it with clothes… but pause.

I need to come up with a plan first.

But in order to do that, I need to figure out exactly how much money I'm working with. Then I can budget some out for a hotel and food while I look for an apartment.

I walk over to my desk and boot up my laptop. After typing in my password, I log into my bank.

My stomach drops.

I have fifty-seven dollars in my account…but there's no way that's possible. I should have *thousands*.

Heart in my throat, I study my activity.

I see the thousand-dollar vet bill for Whiskers and some miscellaneous things I remember purchasing, like pizza, an Uber ride, and the prom dress I bought a couple of days ago.

But there's been other activity. Large ATM withdrawals that I don't recognize.

The maximum amount has been withdrawn quite a few times over the past three weeks, sometimes multiple times a day. Or should I say…*night?*

Because it seems to always occur around four a.m. while I'm sleeping.

None of this makes any sense.

Picking up my phone, I call the bank. After waiting an ungodly amount of time to speak to a representative, I finally get ahold of one.

Only they aren't very helpful because they end up transferring me to the fraud department.

I pinch the bridge of my nose, waiting for the call to connect when there's a knock on my bedroom door.

When I don't respond, they knock again. Harder this time.

"Come in."

I'm surprised to find my mom on the other side of the door.

"Aspen—"

"Go away."

I want nothing to do with her.

She looks around the room, her stare landing on the half-packed suitcase on my bed. "Where do you think you're going?"

"None of your business."

She hasn't given a shit about me or what I do for as long as I can remember. Now she suddenly wants to start asking questions?

She sighs. "Trent will not like this."

I snort. "I don't give a shit what Trent likes."

I never did.

"Aspen, please."

"Please what, mom? Stop pretending like you actually care when we both know you don't. Trent just has this weird fantasy about wanting the perfect family and for reasons I'll never understand, you like feeding into it. I played along because you're my mom, and once upon a time I thought that meant something. But it doesn't. Not anymore."

Not when you choose your new husband over your daughter and physically assault her over cupcakes.

She sits down on my bed. "Trent lost his composure down there, but he didn't mean it."

I'm not surprised she's sticking up for him. "Then tell him to apologize."

Still won't make a difference, but it would sure be nice to see him tuck his tail between his legs.

She frowns, her lower lip trembling. "You can't leave, Aspen. I need you."

"Need me for what? To fetch you more merlot?"

She takes hold of my hand. "I married Trent so we could have a better life…which we have now. I did it for us. You walking out when he's made a very nice life for us here, is disrespectful."

"And him flipping out over cupcakes and you slapping me—"

"That was wrong. But sometimes people make mistakes." She ruffles my hair. "I know I haven't always been the best parent, but I'll try harder, okay? Just stay. Stay because I'm your mother. Because I gave you life and brought you into this world. That has to still count for something, right?"

Dramatics aside, she's never been so candid with me before.

Still doesn't mean I want to stay.

However, I'm in no position to leave anymore because…

Son of a bitch.

I opened my bank account shortly after my dad died at the beginning of my junior year.

However, I was only sixteen, so I needed a parent to come with me and co-sign. My mother agreed, but only because I told her I was getting a job and she needed help with the bills.

I hang up my phone. "I'm going to ask you this once and once only. Did you steal my ATM card and take money out of my account *multiple* times?"

She tries to play it off, but she looks guilty as hell. "No. Of course not."

"Mom," I press, ready to snap her neck like a twig.

She stands. "Okay, fine. I might have borrowed a little money, but it was only because Trent put me on a strict budget for the party and I couldn't work with that impossibly small number." Annoyed, she waves her hands. "He also cut down my weekly allowance. I'm trying to fit in with the other wives at the country club and make some friends, but Trent makes doing that impossible with his penny-pinching ways."

"Mom." It takes everything in me not to wrap my hands around her throat and squeeze. "You *stole* money from me."

"Borrowed," she amends. "And I'll give it back." Her lips purse. "Besides, what exactly are *you* involved in that you had so much money in your account, anyway? There was over seven grand in there, Aspen."

I know. Because *I* fucking earned it. Not her.

The only thing she did was fuck and marry an asshole.

"I've been saving."

She quirks up a brow. "Saving how? By doing what?"

"Babysitting," I blurt out. "And dog walking."

She still looks skeptical. "Well, if I knew *dog walking* paid that much, I would have married one of those."

I wouldn't put it past her.

"It beats stealing from your own kid."

She ambles over to my door. "I already told you I'd give you the money back."

I want to ask her how she plans to do that when she doesn't have a job and she spends her allowance on booze and parties, but then she says, "I know you don't think so, but we're a team."

Yeah…and the price of my mother's love was only seven grand.

She opens my door, but hesitates. "You should put your hair up in a bun and wear that long black dress in your closet tonight. It's classy."

With that, she walks out.

Chapter 25

Knox

*A*fter cleaning the floors and counters in the kitchen, I haul the trays of cupcakes Aspen made to the garbage outside.

Rage simmers in my gut as I toss everything into the bin.

I turn to walk away...but stop.

Reaching back into the bin, I pick up one of the cupcakes and bring it to my mouth.

The moist sweetness hits my tongue and all I can think is...

Fuck him.

Reaching into my pocket for my keys, I walk out to my jeep.

I need something to clear my head.

Something to tame the beast.

Something to make me forget.

Something to dull the pain.

"You should keep a better eye on your sister," my father's voice calls out behind me. "Make sure she follows the rules."

I snort. "Sure thing."

Convincing Aspen to follow his rules is like trying to tame a wild horse.

Sure, they can *eventually* be trained...but it takes a hell of a lot of time and effort.

"Excuse me?"

I turn to face him. "Yes, *sir*."

He scratches his chin, chuckling to himself. "She's got quite a mouth on her." His smile falters and his dark eyes sharpen. "I don't like it."

"Right."

He eyes the keys in my hand. "Going somewhere?"

I tuck them back into the pocket of my jeans. "No."

Whistling, he walks to his car. "I have to run a few errands before the party tonight. You're welcome to join me."

Ice flows through my veins. "No. Thank you. Sir."

When he reaches his car, he stills, holding my stare. "It's the strangest thing. I've been sneezing a lot lately and I have no idea why."

I grit my teeth as he gets into the driver's seat, starts the engine, and backs out.

After he's gone, I trek to the back of the house.

A metallic smell hits my nostrils the second I enter the basement.

My stomach sours and the tiny hairs on the back of my neck stand at attention as I take in the trail of blood on the floor.

No.

Acid works up my throat as I round the small corner to my bed.

I inhale a sharp breath when I find Whiskers on the floor in front of my bed.

With her throat slashed.

I clench my fists, my chest recoiling as I stare at the mutilated kitten.

This was a warning.

And if she's not careful…it will only get worse.

Chapter 26

Knox

Past...

"Kermit?"

Reptiles didn't typically respond to humans like dogs did, but I was just a kid, so I didn't know any better.

In my defense, I had taught him a few things, like how to eat from my hand, so maybe he'd come when called, too...but no such luck.

Worried, I checked every nook and cranny in the basement.

Every hiding spot I could think of for a lizard.

But he was nowhere to be found.

It didn't make sense because I always made sure to put him back in his cage after I played with him.

I asked my mom if she'd seen him earlier, but she said she hadn't.

Dad would be home from work any minute now, so the sooner I found him, the better.

He'd be angry if he stumbled upon Kermit, and I shuddered to think of what he would do.

"*Every action has a consequence.*"

Although I suppose I could play dumb and let him think Kermit just wandered into the house.

But then he'd blame my mother for not keeping things tidy and Kermit would be out on the street.

"Trenton," my dad bellowed from upstairs. "Get upstairs. Now."

Shoot.

I quickly straightened my spine and marched up the staircase.

"Go wash your hands for dinner," my mother instructed when I wandered into the kitchen.

I watched in confusion as she grabbed a few plates and dishes from the cabinet.

I expected my mother to be cooking dinner because she always did, but my father was pulling what looked like takeout from a paper bag.

We rarely had takeout, so I was excited.

After doing as I was told, I sat down at the table.

Like one big happy family.

Just the way he wanted it.

I made a face when I looked down at my plate. I expected Chinese food or Pizza. But this was something I didn't recognize.

My mother nudged me with her foot under the table.

"Is there a problem?" my father barked, those dark eyes narrowing.

I quickly shook my head. "No."

"No...*what?*"

"No, Sir."

"I figured we could all try something new for a change," my father declared. "Dig in."

I grabbed my fork, hoping it tasted good because it didn't look that appetizing.

The last time I refused dinner...the consequences were...

Suppressing a shudder, I closed my eyes and brought my fork to my mouth.

It was weird. Kind of crunchy with a strange aftertaste.

"What is it?" I asked.

My father smiled, his teeth flashing white before his expression hardened.

"Barbeque lizard."

Chapter 27

Aspen

"*W*hiskers?"

The party starts in an hour and I need to feed her before people start arriving. However, she's not in her blanket like she usually is.

Huffing, I walk over to Knox's bed. She's grown more brazen, so maybe she wandered over there.

I just hope she didn't leave him any *presents* on his mattress or pillow because then I'll never hear the end of it.

When it's clear she didn't snuggle up on his bed, I decide to check under it. "Come on, baby. Where are you?"

Dropping to my knees, I extend my arm as far as it can go, hoping to feel some fur, but no dice.

There's not a lot of space between the frame and the floor, but she's still tiny. Maybe she's stuck in a corner under there.

Using the flashlight on my phone, I search under the bed. The only thing I find are cobwebs and lint.

I'm about to stand up and search elsewhere, but something sparkly catches my eye.

Edging forward, I grab the object with my fingers.

My blood runs cold as I take in the Swarovski crystal candy cane necklace.

The same necklace Candi Kane always wore.

My heartbeat drums in my ears as I stare down at it.

159

Why would he have this?

I close my eyes, sucking in a heavy breath. My brain knows the truth, but the organ in my chest keeps trying to look for a loophole.

The room blurs as my mind tries to put the pieces together…but fails.

I startle when I hear the door open and Knox walks in.

My expression must give me away because he eyes me warily.

"I—"

I hold up the necklace. "Why do you have this?" I quickly get to my feet. "Why the *hell* do you have her necklace, Knox?"

His jaw locks, and he takes a step closer. It feels like an eternity before he speaks.

"Why do you think I have it?"

My stomach drops.

Don't be an idiot, Aspen. There's only one reason he would have it.

I move, but so does he. It's like a terrible game of Simon Says.

I open my mouth, but no words escape. I feel like I'm choking on them.

My palms sweat and everything around me starts to spin.

"Did you kill her?" I croak after another minute passes.

I feel like I'm going to pass out as I wait for him to answer.

I expect him to deny it. I *want* him to deny it. However, the next words out of his mouth only leave me more conflicted.

"What do you think?"

That's a loaded question.

I know what I should think.

I know what the evidence points to.

I know about his past.

I know what my mind is telling me.

I just don't want to believe it.

I want to hold on to the hate I feel for him…

Because that's when I trust my instincts and keep my guard up.

And something's telling me that's the only way I'm going to survive these next few months.

I avert my gaze. "Where is Whiskers?"

Taking a step back, he shrugs. "No idea."

"What do you mean, you have no idea? No one else stays down here with her."

He reaches for his cigarettes on the nightstand. "I don't know where your stupid cat is, okay? Now fuck off."

I clench my hands until they become fists. "Where is Whiskers, Knox?"

There's no way he doesn't know. He's the only one who's always here with her.

He lights his cigarette, takes a drag, and proceeds to blow the smoke in my face. "The bitch was overstaying her welcome. Kind of like someone else I know." His lips curve into a menacing smirk. "But I think she got the hint when I left the door open on my way out earlier."

It's like a knife lodged in my heart. He knows how much I care about her.

So of course he'd use that to hurt me.

Because that's what he does.

Every reward is followed by a much harsher punishment.

Stepping closer, I spit in his face. "I hate you."

He drags his thumb over the wet spot on his jaw and brings it to his mouth. "Don't worry, I'm sure she'll come back." His eyes sharpen as he delivers his next words. "Strays always do."

Chapter 28

Aspen

$\mathcal{I}$ shake my hair out of the clip and smooth my hands down my short silky white dress. So short it stops mid-thigh.

Peering into the mirror, I run my nude lipstick across my lips, then put on another coat of mascara.

Smirking, I take out some black eyeliner and draw a dramatic cat eye on my top lids…just like I do when I'm at the club.

My mother wanted me to look *classy* tonight for all her ritzy friends.

But she stole my hard-earned money, so fuck her.

Payback is a bitch.

And tonight? So am I.

The *party* is in full swing by the time I trot down the stairs and out to the patio, which, as promised, has been transformed into a beautiful oasis.

Apparently, the guests have a choice between surf and turf and lobster ravioli to go along with their elegant *ambiance*.

Thanks to all my goddamn money.

By the looks of things, dinner has already been served and everyone's nearly done with their meal…so I'm right on time.

"Aspen," my mother utters when I approach, and wearing this dress was so worth it for the horrified look on her face. "You're here. Finally."

"Sorry, mom. I was busy getting ready. Wanted to make sure I looked my best."

Trent—who doesn't appear pleased one bit by my appearance, or my extreme tardiness—gestures to the only open seat on the other side of the never-ending table. "Have a seat. *Now*."

Shooting him a fuck-you smile, I take my place at the table.

Unfortunately, it's next to Knox.

However, I notice that Leo is seated directly across from me. He'll make this dinner *much* more bearable.

"Hi, Aspen," Leo says. "How have you been?"

"Great," I answer, playing right along with his pseudo small talk. "How's work? I heard you got a promotion."

"I didn't know slutty nightgowns were suitable dinner attire," Knox hisses.

A few people around the table exchange a glance, and my mother's cheeks turn red.

"Oh, you know brothers," my mother jokes tersely. "Always teasing their sisters."

"Knox," Trent says in warning as a server places a plate in front of me. "Stop teasing your sister." His angry glare swivels to me next. "And Aspen…"

I can tell he wants to ream me out, but he can't because we're surrounded by people. Such a shame.

"Be good," he settles on before going back to his lobster.

I bat my eyelashes at my stepfather. He wants the perfect family? Well, I'm gonna give it to him.

"Sure, daddy," I state with a mock pout. "I'll do *whatever* you want tonight."

Beside me, Knox chokes on his drink.

Trent's eyebrows shoot up to the sky.

My mother looks like it's taking every ounce of willpower not to reach over and strangle me.

And Leo looks at me like I've lost my damn mind.

Mission accomplished.

"So," Leo says, attempting to change the subject. "I heard you got into Stanford." He raises his glass and I see the pride shining in his eyes. "Beautiful *and* smart…that's a winning combination."

"How's Aunt Lenora?" Knox interjects. "It's a real shame you didn't bring her tonight. I would have loved to see her."

The smile falls from Leo's face. "Yes, well. I'm sure she would have loved to be here, but she hasn't been feeling well and needed to catch up on some rest."

Instantly, guilt snakes its way up my spine.

"Is everything all right?" a woman sitting next to him asks.

"Yes." His mouth turns down in a frown. "But my wife has amyotrophic lateral sclerosis."

Underneath the table, I feel Knox's hand graze my thigh.

I shoot him a threatening look, but as usual, Knox doesn't give a fuck.

"She's in a wheelchair and can't speak," my mother unhelpfully adds.

I try clamping my thighs together when I feel him moving closer, but Knox is stronger and pries them apart. Then, lifting my leg, he drags it over one of his and secures my calf with his free hand, ensuring I stay put.

"Oh, the poor thing," the woman says with a sympathetic expression. "That's so sad. You're such a great husband for taking care of her."

"He really is," my mother concurs with a smile. "Then again, the Knox men are excellent when it comes to taking care of their women."

I jolt when his finger brushes the crotch of my panties.

He is not doing this. Especially here. *Now.*

I give Knox's arm a sharp pinch, but it's no use. He's determined to make me uncomfortable.

However, *I* refuse to give him the power to do that.

He can do whatever he wants…but I don't have to respond to it.

I'm the one in complete control over *my* body. Not him.

And the second he realizes that, he'll stop and move on to something else.

Taking a deep breath, I relax against the chair and force my body to go slack. Kind of like an animal who plays dead when they sense their enemy's approach.

Besides, Leo—the man I care about—can't even make me

orgasm. Therefore, I *highly* doubt the guy I loathe will ever be able to.

"We're excellent at *all* things," my stepfather cuts in and everyone laughs.

Except me, because Knox pushes my thong to the side, exposing me. Then he begins skimming my pussy with the pad of his finger... tracing the outline of my lips...before running his knuckle along the length of my slit.

His touch is gentle...teasing. *Torture*.

"But still," the woman from earlier says with a sigh. "I can't imagine how hard it must be for you. I mean, of course she's still your wife, but...you know." Her eyes get misty. "It's just so tragic."

I tense when, ever so slowly, he slips his long finger inside me.

I swallow hard as my pussy stretches around the invasion.

"Aspen, you're not eating," my mother notes with a crinkle of her nose.

Seriously? The woman never pays attention to me, but she decides to start now?

"Is everything okay?" Leo says, concern lacing his voice.

Knox slides his finger out, wiping the wetness on my inner thigh... intentionally mocking me. "Everything is f—" Without warning, he pushes two digits inside me. "Fine."

I pick up my fork as he begins methodically thrusting his fingers, trying my hardest to focus on the lobster ravioli on my plate instead of what he's doing to me.

Bringing the ravioli to my mouth, I take a bite.

The heel of his palm grinds against my clit, and unexpected white-hot pleasure blazes through me like a firework.

"Oh, God." My face heats when everyone stops talking and looks at me. Thinking quick, I point to the dish and blurt, "This is so *good*."

This is so bad. *Very bad*.

I steal a glance at Knox and there's a sly smirk on his face as he continues working me.

"Yes. Dinner is divine," the woman sitting next to Leo agrees. "You must give me the caterer's number, Eileen."

I really wish she'd shut the fuck up because she's annoying, but she's also distracting everyone.

Mom smiles. "Absolutely."

I reach for my glass of water, but Knox massages my clit with his thumb in a slow, torturous way that has me shuddering with the movement.

"Are you okay, Aspen?" Leo suddenly inquires. "You don't look well."

Shit.

"I'm a little—" Knox begins fucking me with his fingers. Pleasure jolts through me, hot and sharp. I can't help but edge forward on the chair, causing him to penetrate me deeper. *Faster.* "Cold."

"Maybe you should have worn something more appropriate," Trent remarks.

"Do you want my jacket?" Leo offers.

I shake my head, my nipples puckering as I fight to keep my breathing in check. "No. Thank you."

The woman turns to him again. "What is it you do for a living?"

I'm thankful for her nosiness, because Knox curls his fingers and an orgasm tears through me so fast my head spins as I clutch the chair for dear life.

That's when I feel a sharp pull on my panties. I'm in no position to protest, so I don't as he wrenches my thong off before tucking the silky material into his pocket.

I'm still wrapping my mind around what happened when Knox finally removes his hand from between my legs.

His harsh stare shoots across the table, resting on Leo. A smug smile tugs at his lips as brings his fingers to his mouth and sucks them. "Can you pass the salt, Uncle Leo?"

I swear my jaw nearly falls to the floor.

Visibly annoyed at being interrupted, Leo pushes the saltshaker toward Knox as the woman asks him another question about his job.

I'm grateful when my mother declares dinner is over and the servers come in to clear everything away before quickly transforming the patio into a makeshift dancefloor.

I look around for Knox, so I can tell him off, but he's nowhere to be found.

Leo sidles up beside me once everyone starts dancing.

"Interesting choice of dress," he whispers in my ear.

I glance across the dancefloor at my mom, who's still playing the perfect hostess. "My mother pissed me off."

"Well, she should do it more often." His voice dips. "My cock has been hard for you all night." He looks around before uttering his next words. "Meet you upstairs in five?"

It's on the tip of my tongue to decline because I don't feel right having sex with him after Knox...did what he did.

However, I don't want Leo to think something is wrong, so I nod. "I'll head up to my room first."

His hand briefly skims my lower back. "Can't wait."

After I'm sure no one is paying attention to me, I walk inside the house and up the staircase leading to my bedroom.

I nearly jump out of my skin when I enter and see Knox lying on my bed.

"What the hell are you doing here?"

Sitting up on his elbows, he drags his gaze around the room. "This used to be my bedroom."

I hike my thumb toward the door. "Great. Get the hell out."

He curls his lip. "Nah. I think I'll stay." Those intense orbs darken. "Unless you're planning on having company."

A surge of uneasiness floods my stomach.

No. There's no way he knows about Leo and me.

He can't.

I brush off his suggestion with a laugh. "Trust me. There's no one down there I want to spend time with."

And no one in here that I want to see, either.

His gaze drops to my breasts before meeting my eyes. "Then lock the door."

"No."

"Stray." The warning is clear in his tone.

Having no choice, I flick the lock on the door. "Happy?"

"Not yet." Narrowing his stare, he crooks one long finger at me. "Come here."

I want to protest, but he's got me right where he wants me.

Folding my arms over my chest, I take a few steps toward the bed.

"What do you want?"

My chest heaves when he tugs down his zipper, reaches inside his pants…and pulls out his cock.

It's even veinier and bigger than I remember.

Angrier, too.

My eyebrows rise when he licks his hand—the same one he fingered me with—and wraps it around his length. "I got you off." I watch the tendons in his wrist flex as he strokes himself. "It's time for you to return the favor."

"Go to hell."

I turn on my heel, but then he threatens, "I'll tell everyone down there that you take your clothes off for money. And I mean…*everyone.*"

I close my eyes.

Telling my mother and Trent is one thing.

But telling Leo?

He'll never look at me the same way again. He'll be so upset…so hurt…that not only have I been stripping for other men, but I've been lying to him about it for all these months.

I'll lose the only person left who ever gave a fuck about me.

I turn around to face him. "I won't fuck you—"

"Suck me," he says gruffly, his Adam's apple bobbing in his throat. "Now."

I hate him.

I approach the bed, ready to kneel…but he halts me.

"I want to see your tits."

Glaring, I lower the spaghetti straps of my gown. I didn't wear a bra, so they practically bounce out of my dress.

Still touching himself, Knox sits up on the bed. "Take it off."

But then I'll be naked. *Vulnerable.*

Just like he wants.

Swallowing my nerves, I let my dress fall to the floor.

I utter a gasp of shock when he edges forward and flicks his tongue over my nipple. "The better you suck my dick…the faster it will go." I hiss when his teeth clamp down on my nipple. "Get on your knees."

Kneeling, I close my eyes.

And that's when there's a tap on the door.

Leaning over, Knox grips the back of my head and brings his lips to my ear. "Who is that?"

"I don't know," I whisper, even though I know damn well who it is.

"Aspen," Leo says softly from the other side. "It's me."

Knox leans his forehead against mine, his eyes boring into me. "Is there something you're hiding from me?"

I keep my expression neutral. "No."

I've barely uttered the word when my phone rings.

Fisting his dick, he holds it out to me. "Prove it."

When I don't move, he runs the shiny head against my mouth, painting my lips with his pre-cum. "Put my cock in your mouth."

I dart my tongue out, tasting the salty tip as I hear Leo's footsteps fade away.

"More."

Glaring, I wrap my lips around his cock and slide down his length. My jaw begins to ache because of how big he is, but I don't let up.

The sooner I get this over with, the better.

With a low grunt, Knox grabs my hair, pulling and twisting as he shoves his cock down as far as it can go.

I gag, tears springing to my eyes as he pokes the back of my throat.

"Good girl." He juts his hips, causing me to gag again. "You look so pretty with a mouthful of cock."

Pure hunger fills his gaze, almost like this is as torturous for him as it is for me.

I can't help but wonder what it would be like to see him lose control.

To watch him fall apart...knowing the girl he hates is the one responsible for his pleasure.

Humming, I flick my tongue along the underside of his cock before taking him as deep as I can.

His jaw clenches as his eyes flutter closed.

Gripping his base, I suck him slow and gentle, wanting to drive him crazy like he did to me earlier.

It works because he tightens his grip on my hair and growls, "Stop moving. I want to fuck your face."

I still, my jaw going slack as he thrusts so hard it almost hurts. But

I force myself to hold his gaze, daring him to give me more, even as slobber runs down my chin and my eyes water and burn. His movements pick up, fucking my face so forcefully it throbs as his balls slap my neck.

"Fuck." He groans low and deep, his breaths leaving him in quick short pants as his face strains. "Take my cum like a good girl."

That's the only warning I get before a hot spurt of salty liquid fills my mouth.

He gives me a look like he's expecting me to gag again, but I theatrically swallow him, smiling as I do it for good measure.

I can take whatever he throws at me. And now that he's gotten what he came here for, he can leave.

"Get out."

Smirking, he scoops some leftover cum from my chin with his thumb, then pushes it into my mouth. "For a moment I believed you were enjoying sucking my dick...almost as much as you enjoyed the way I made you come at dinner."

I reach around the floor for my dress. "Don't flatter yourself."

"Don't lie to yourself," he counters.

Anger races over my skin and I point to the door. "Leave."

He slips his cock inside his pants. "Lock your door tonight."

I'm about to ask why, but he gets off the bed and walks out.

Leo was understandably upset when I called him later on, so I told him I accidentally locked the door and fell asleep waiting for him.

I'm not sure if he bought it, but at least he didn't press me about it after that.

I'm beginning to drift off to sleep for real when I hear the doorknob of my room jiggle.

What the hell?

It happens again, and I sprint out of bed, ready to tell Knox off.

But then I realize...*he's* the one who told me to lock the door before he left.

Which means it can only be my stepfather.

My heart hammers in my chest as I hear something enter the lock...as if he's trying to pick it open.

Thinking quick, I sprint into the closet, closing the door at the same time the one to my bedroom opens.

What the fuck is he doing here?

Better question…what the fuck does he want?

I hear a huff of irritation escape him when he enters my room and realizes I'm not there.

I squeeze my eyes shut, cowering in the corner of my closet as I recall the words I said to him at dinner.

"Sure, daddy. I'll do whatever you want tonight."

Oh, God. I feel sick.

Obviously, I didn't mean it…but what if he's here to cash in on that?

My stomach churns as I lean my forehead against the wall of the pitch-black closet.

Only, it's not smooth like it's supposed to be. Running my fingers over it, I realize something's been carved into it.

Almost like a secret message.

Tracing the wall, I make out the letter H easily. The next letter is more difficult, but I think it's an A. Following that one is a T…and I'm pretty sure the next is an E. Underneath it are two more letters.

An M and an E.

Hate Me.

That doesn't make any sense.

I hear the faint click of my bedroom door closing, but I don't trust him not to come back, so I make no move to leave.

I do, however, make a mental note to buy a deadbolt lock for my bedroom, and open up a new bank account tomorrow as my eyes close and I fall asleep.

I wake to my alarm clock going off a few hours later. I push open the closet door, letting the sunlight stream in.

Angling my head, I look at the carving etched in the wall.

My heart sinks.

It doesn't say Hate Me like I originally thought.

It says…

Help Me.

Chapter 29

Aspen

I try not to make eye contact with Trent over breakfast, but it's hard because he keeps trying to talk to me.

Even going as far as to offer to take me car shopping again, which I, of course, decline.

I just want to save up money and get the hell away from all of them.

I'm pouring myself a second cup of coffee when my mother announces, "Trent and I will be taking a weekend trip soon."

Knox and I exchange a curious glance. Clearly, this trip is news to him, too.

"When?" Knox asks at the same time I utter, "Where?"

Trent wipes his mouth with a napkin. "Not this weekend, but next." His eyes narrow on his son. "I expect you to be on your best behavior while we're gone." They swivel to me next. "Both of you."

"We're going to a beach house a few hours away," my mom says with a smile. "Given our wedding was so close to Christmas, we didn't really get a proper honeymoon."

Whatever. It will be nice to have them both out of my hair for a weekend.

I glance at the clock on the wall. "We should leave before we're late for school."

Knox pushes his chair back. "Let's go."

After leaving the table, I grab my knapsack off the floor of the mudroom and follow him out to his jeep.

I wait until we're buckled in and he's peeling out of the driveway to speak. "Thanks for the warning about locking my door."

The muscles in his forearm flex as he clenches the steering wheel. "You should get a deadbolt for your bedroom."

"I was planning on it."

His nostrils flare on an indrawn breath. "You should also keep your fucking mouth shut around him and quit pissing him off."

I want to ask him why he's defending a creeper, but I clamp my mouth closed for the rest of the ride.

Knox will take his dad's side. Just like he always does.

Besides, a horny old man looking for a piece of teenage ass for the night is something I'm used to fighting off at the club.

I can handle myself.

The school is up ahead on the left, but Knox speeds past it.

"Where are you going?"

He brings a cigarette to his mouth and lights it. "I have to run an errand."

I glance at the clock on his dashboard. "Well, you better do it fast. School starts in five minutes."

I'm expecting him to pull up to a gas station or a store, but he drives past those, too.

"What kind of errand?"

He doesn't answer, but instead makes a right-hand turn onto a residential street.

The same street Leo lives on.

My stomach dips. "Where are we going?"

Knox stays silent as he pulls up to his uncle's house…

And I hear the locks on his doors click.

The weird flutter in my stomach turns to full-on dread when he latches onto my seatbelt, preventing me from undoing it.

"Last chance to tell me the truth, Stray. Are you fucking my uncle?"

I adamantly shake my head. There's no way I'll let that secret leave my lips. Not only because it's none of his business, but it will ruin Leo's reputation.

And mine.

"Are you crazy? Of course not."

He makes a low growly sound in his throat before he opens the driver's side door and gets out. I attempt to climb out too, but he comes around to my side, blocking me from escaping.

After undoing my seatbelt, he grips my wrist…so hard I wince. "Well, if you won't tell me, perhaps you'll tell her."

Her?

I stop breathing when I realize what he's implying.

Oh, God. *No.*

My chest twists, everything going blurry as he yanks me out of the vehicle.

"Knox, please," I plead as he drags me up the walkway like I'm nothing more than a rag doll. "I'll do whatever you want, okay?"

I'll suck him off every day. I'll humiliate myself on his command so he can point at me and laugh. I'll be his goddamn slave.

I'll do *anything*.

Because there's no way I can look that poor woman in the eyes and tell her I'm sleeping with her husband.

"I wanted you to tell me the *truth*."

"Fine," I admit, both my voice and resolve cracking like glass. "You're right. I'm sleeping with him."

"And there it is." I see the tendons in his neck coil before he goes still. "You have the nerve to stand there and judge me, but you're no angel. You're screwing a married man almost three times your age while his wife sits like a goddamned vegetable. You're just as fucked up as I am."

I inhale a shaky breath, hating that he's right. "I know." My throat feels like it's closing in. "I'm sorry. I'll end it—"

Lifting a finger, he presses the doorbell.

I try to run away, but his death-grip on my wrist tightens. "Every action has a consequence, Stray. This is yours."

God, I thought I hated him before, but that compared to the way I feel about him now.

I will never forgive him for this. *Ever.*

A woman dressed in scrubs answers the door. I'm assuming she's his wife's private nurse.

"Hello." Confusion crosses her face as she takes in our school uniforms. "Can I help you?"

Knox brushes past the woman, tugging me along. "I'm here to see my aunt."

"Oh," the nurse exclaims, trailing behind us. "I didn't realize she would be having visitors today. Can I get you something to drink?"

My heart flies to my throat when we round a corner and walk into the living room.

One look at the stoic, sad woman in her wheelchair is enough to make me want to fall to the floor and start crying.

With my free hand, I tug on Knox's sleeve like a child begging not to leave a toy store. "Please—"

"Shut up," he grits through his teeth, before walking over to his aunt.

Dropping down, he plants a kiss on her forehead. "Hi, Aunt Lenora."

Her eyes widen in recognition—and bewilderment—when she sees him.

Turning his head, Knox regards the nurse. "I need to speak with my aunt. *Alone.*"

She's clearly taken back by his austerity, but she gives him a nod, anyway. "I was just about to make her some breakfast. Holler if you need anything."

With that, she rushes toward the kitchen…leaving the three of us alone.

Knox wastes no time getting down to business. "Aunt Lenora, you remember Aspen Falcone, don't you? She's Mile's—Leo's dead friend's— daughter."

His words are the equivalent of a slap across the face.

Given she can't move or speak, there isn't much reaction to that. However, I notice her size me up with her big brown eyes.

I met her once when I was a kid…long before she was diagnosed with ALS.

She was beautiful and kind. She offered me chocolate chip cookies and complimented my hair.

Now she's stuck in a wheelchair.

And I'm the whore sleeping with her husband.

The guilt pummeling through me is so thick—so visceral—I'm choking on it.

Knox looks between us. "I brought Aspen by today because she has something very important to tell you."

Lenora blinks, no doubt expecting me to speak.

But I can't.

I look at Knox one last time, pleading with him not to make me do this.

But he doesn't fold. If anything, my desperation only pisses him off more.

"Tell her, Aspen." His grip is so tight I'm positive it's cutting off my blood supply. "Or I will."

I open my mouth, but the words don't come out. They're stuck inside of me...unwilling to break this poor woman's heart.

God, I'm such a slut.

Such a stupid, evil whore.

I'm no better than my swindler father.

No better than Knox.

"She's screwing your husband," Knox declares, and I swear the entire world stops spinning.

I drop to my knees, clutching my throat. I feel so sick.

So fucking disgusting.

When did I become this person?

This evil person who does bad things.

This vile person who steals other women's husbands.

This horrible person who hurts other people.

This person I hate.

I can't bring myself to look at her, so I study the carpet. It's soft and plush. A cream color that she most likely picked out because Leo is terrible when it comes to choosing furniture.

"I'm sorry," I choke out, my voice cracking like crystal. "I'm so sorry."

"You're probably wondering when it began, huh?" Knox questions before turning to me. "Tell her."

From my place on the floor, I glare up at him, wishing I could scratch his eyes out. Hell, I just might after this.

"The night of my father's funeral."

It was right after my exchange with Knox.

The one where he told me he came to see me because he knew I'd be in pain.

I ran back in crying and Leo ushered me into an empty room.

I had so many feelings coursing through me.

I was sad, alone…and missing my dad so much it physically hurt.

But I was also angry.

Angry that the only person who ever cared about me was gone… because he was a thief.

Leo hugged me, trying to console me…but that wasn't enough.

I needed to feel something more.

Something wrong and ugly and real.

So, I kissed him.

Five minutes later, I was losing my virginity.

And that was it.

Knox's next words punch through the air like a bullet. "She was only sixteen." His face twists. "Sorry to be the bearer of bad news, Aunt Lenora, but now you finally know what a sick piece of shit your husband really is."

But it wasn't all Leo's fault.

I was the one who kissed him.

Tears burn my throat. I try to push them down, but I can't.

They pool in my eyes, and before I can stop myself, I start crying so hard it hurts to breathe. "I'm sorry." I force myself to meet her gaze. "I'm so sorry."

I expect her to look at me with revulsion, because it's what I deserve, but she doesn't.

She's looking at me with pity…

And that only makes me cry harder.

Reaching down, Knox grabs my elbow. "Let's go."

Hot tears pour down my face like rain as he pulls me to my feet.

I wish I knew how to make them stop, but I don't. He's filleted me wide open, forcing me to confront all the ugly parts of myself before leaving me to bleed out.

It's the slowest, cruelest kind of death.

But the worst part is…I can't even blame him.

Because it was my fault.

Chapter 30

Knox

*A*spen's such a mess she can barely walk to the jeep without her legs buckling underneath her.

I wish she would have told me the truth when I asked, but she didn't.

Therefore, she had to learn her lesson the hard and painful way.

I open the passenger side door, but she plants her feet.

She's still sobbing, but the look she shoots me is so full of hatred, I feel it in my bones.

"Get in."

She tries to run away, but I catch her by the waist and tug her back to me. "Not so fast, Stray."

Her loathing for me is practically rolling off her in waves as she kicks her legs.

Grinding my molars, I grip the collar of her white button-down shirt and shove her against the jeep. "I gave you a choice."

I tried so fucking hard to get her to trust me enough to be honest with me.

But she failed. Ergo, that shit is on her, not me.

"I hate you." She spits in my face as another sob escapes her. "I *hate* you."

She doesn't hate me…she hates herself.

She hates what she did.

She hates what *he* did.

She hates that I held up a mirror and forced her to look at herself without the façade she likes to put on.

Because she isn't a perfect girl who gets perfect grades and lives a perfect life while wearing her perfect fucking pearls.

She's raw and real.

She's flawed and fucked up.

She's also angry as hell.

Reaching up, she scratches my cheek. For as long as I've known her, she's always kept herself in check. Always managing to compose herself right before she goes over the deep end…but right now, she's like a feral animal that's unhinged.

And fuck me if it doesn't make my blood boil and my dick hard.

I crush my mouth against hers, biting and sucking her lips so hard I'm positive they'll be bruised.

Her fingernails scrape my back and I grunt, the pain making my cock throb that much more as she opens her mouth wider so I can feed her my tongue.

"I hate you," she chokes out against my lips, her breathy voice still thick with tears as I explore and tease her mouth.

I bet I can make her hate me even more.

On a new mission now, I open the backseat door. Then, gripping her plump ass, I lift and toss her into the backseat.

I climb in after her, my hands tunneling under her skirt where I find her panties damp and warm before I peel them down her legs.

"Knox—"

Hauling her up, I shift us into a sitting position and make her straddle my lap. "This is the way you liked to fuck him, right?"

The fire is back in her eyes when she snarls, "Fuck *you*."

I thrust, rubbing myself against her pussy. She's so soaked she creates a wet spot on my pants.

One I'm gonna make her lick up.

Placing my hands under her armpits for leverage, I twist her around in my lap, then push on her lower back until she leans forward.

"What—"

In one fluid motion, I tug her legs, positioning her so her head is in my lap and her thighs are on either side of my face.

I push her skirt down. "You left a mess on my pants, Stray. Clean it up."

"No—"

I run the length of my nose along her slit, collecting her juices on my face as I inhale her. "You sure about that?"

With a whimper, her tongue glides along the fabric.

Gripping her hair, I tug down my zipper. "Good girl. Now take out my cock and lick that."

I suppress a groan when she pulls me out, then sheathes me with her hot little eager mouth.

I spread her pussy with my fingers, stretching it as far as it will go before I lower my mouth and thrust my tongue deep inside her, extending it as far as I can.

Liquid heat fills my mouth as she squirms below me.

"You know why Leo didn't know I made you come last night?" I flick my tongue ring against her swollen clit and she moans around my cock. "Because he's never done it before." I suckle the sensitive bud as she gags on my dick and the sounds of me eating her fill the jeep. "He doesn't have a clue how you look when you come."

I circle my tongue in steady little swirls around her clit. "He doesn't know how wet your pussy gets when you're so turned on but trying your hardest to fight it." I suck her pussy lips until I find her hole again and tease that with the tip of my tongue. "The way this pretty little cunt tightens around you like a vise before squeezing and riding your fingers."

Aspen shakes and trembles beneath me. She's so close to coming, I can taste it.

Anger mixed with envy races through my veins.

"Sit up."

When she does, I wrap my hand around her throat and bring my lips to her ear. "Now squat over my dick like you're gonna fuck it."

As soon as she rises up on her knees, I drag the head of my cock through her lips, gathering her wetness. "You wanna get fucked?"

Her shame is tangible right before she whispers, "Yes."

In one fell swoop, I push her forward and spread her ass cheeks.

"Knox," she breathes as I work my cockhead into her tight little hole. "I've never…oh, God. That hurts." Choking back another sob, she slaps the seat. "So fucking much."

That's the point.

"Isn't this how you like it, Stray?" I push in a little more and spill my cum inside her, ignoring my own pleasure. "Because that's how he does it, right?" Her soft cries cause something to thaw inside my chest. "He comes just as fast as he leaves you. Uses your body as his little fuck toy and takes advantage of you with his old, wrinkly dick."

While making her believe it's what *she* really wants.

She scrambles to the front seat of the jeep. "I hate you."

Aspen keeps saying that shit, but I'm the only one who sees her.

The only one who can help her.

After tucking my dick back in my pants, I leave the backseat and open the driver's side door.

Not finished making my point yet, I grab her jaw, forcing her to look at me. "But *he's* such a good guy, huh?"

"He's better than you."

I snort, fury swelling inside my chest.

She's so fucking wrong.

Because if she knew what I knew…she'd be looking at him like *he* was the monster instead of me.

Peeved, I stick my key in the engine. "I don't want you seeing him again. Understood? Feed him some bullshit about wanting to focus on school and graduating. Hell, tell him whatever the fuck you want. Just make sure you end it."

Pain etches across her face. "Why are you doing this to me?"

That's where she's wrong.

I'm not doing it to her…

I'm doing it for her.

Chapter 31

Knox

Past…

*M*y lungs burned as my body silently begged for air.

Air I wouldn't get until he permitted me to.

My father shouted something, but I couldn't hear what because my head was submerged under the water filling the bathtub.

One of his hands was wrapped around the back of my neck, forcing my head down, while the other held both my arms behind me…ensuring I couldn't fight back.

I wouldn't, though. *I never did.*

Fighting back would only give him what he wanted.

And I would rather die than let him think he was winning.

My body jerked and thrashed against him, desperate for air, but my mind refused to concede.

I was only eleven—but one day I'd be bigger, faster…stronger.

One day, I'd strike when he least expected it.

The sound of my mother's shrill, anguished scream broke through the haze.

"Trent, please," she begged through sobs. "You're going to kill him."

I loved my mother more than life itself, but I really wished she'd stay the hell out of this.

Because the only thing worse than him attacking me…

Was when he attacked her.

As if on cue, he released his grip and stood.

His face twisted into a menacing scowl as he turned every ounce of his fury on my mother.

The sharp slap of his palm against her cheek was so forceful she fell against the bathroom door.

"I thought I told you to mind your fucking business when I'm talking to my son."

His hand curled into a fist, no doubt getting ready to issue another punch.

That's when I leapt up and jumped on his back.

"Run," I told her as he wrangled me to the ground.

A minute later, severe cramping pain impaled my body and his taunting, dark laughter filled the air.

Every muscle in my body tensed and clenched as he continued to tase me.

He knew how much I hated that thing. It felt like being struck by lightning.

Only it didn't last seconds.

It lasted so long, I was positive that either my heart would give out or I would die from the torture.

"Every action has a consequence," he taunted, just like he always did.

The pain was so excruciating I barely registered when it finally stopped.

Dark eyes filled with venom stared down at me. "When are you gonna wise the fuck up and stop trying to be a hero?" His lips curled into a cruel smirk as he sent a sharp kick into my ribs. "You pissed yourself, boy."

With those parting words, he walked out.

I curled up in a puddle of my urine, wondering how someone who was supposed to love me could be so evil.

"You better clean that piss up off the floor," my father barked to my mother who was standing in the hallway.

I tilted my head so I could watch them.

"I will," my mom responded, her thin frame shaking like a leaf in a hurricane.

He gripped her chin so hard I had no doubt it would leave another mark. "You will, *what?*"

She casted her gaze down, no longer daring to look at him. "I will, sir."

"Damn right you will." He reached down and pinched her ass. "Now give me a kiss before I leave for work."

Nausea worked up my throat, and I closed my eyes. Desperate to feel better, I reached into my pocket. The silky material from the ribbon brushed against my fingers, taking me back to that moment on the playground, and the physical pain slowly subsided.

I survived.

After the front door slammed shut, my mother scurried back into the bathroom, looking so distraught my chest coiled.

"I'm so sorry, baby." She quickly helped me up off the floor. "I can't believe…" her sentence trailed off, and she gave her head a shake.

Try as she might, she could no longer deny it.

The man she fell in love with when she was sixteen no longer existed.

Somewhere along the way he turned into a cold, calculating, abusive piece of shit.

Sobbing, she wrapped her arms around me, clutching me to her chest.

"We're gonna get out of here soon," she promised, just like she always did.

I used to believe her…but not anymore.

Because while my mother's side of the family was well off—on account of owning an oil company—and she had the money to escape and start over...

My father—Special Agent Knox—had all the power.

And he made damn sure we both knew we had nowhere to run.

And nowhere to hide.

Because sooner or later…he'd find us.

And when he did…

He'd kill us.

Chapter 32

Aspen

I lie on my bed in the darkness, mustering up the courage to do what I know I have to do.

Not because Knox demanded it, but because deep down I know sleeping with another woman's husband is wrong.

Everything about my relationship with Leo is wrong…and not in the sexy, taboo way I once tried to convince myself it was.

I latched onto him…because I'm damaged. Screwed up in the head.

A fucked-up girl with daddy issues.

Because I feared being truly alone.

Chest aching, I dial Leo's number and bring the phone to my ear.

He answers after the second ring, his voice groggy from sleep. "Hello? Is everything okay?"

I hear the bed creak over the extension, and I can't help but wonder if he's lying next to her.

My throat burns and I close my eyes. *I hope she can find it in her heart to forgive me.*

"Can we talk?"

"Yeah. Give me one second."

A moment later, I hear what sounds like a door closing behind him.

"What's wrong, honey?" Leo questions, his voice filled with worry. "You sound upset."

There's no easy way to say it, so I just rip the Band-Aid off.

"I can't do this anymore."

"Can't do what anymore, honey?" There's a sharp intake of breath. "Look, whatever is going on, please, don't harm yourself. I'll be right—"

"I'm not going to harm myself," I assure him, and I honestly can't believe that's his first thought. It's like he doesn't know me at all. Either that, or he only wants to see me as a little broken bird who can't take care of herself.

But I'm not. And I don't need him to swoop in and save me.

He needs that.

"I'm just…it's over, Leo."

It feels like an eternity stretches between us before he finally speaks. "Why?"

Sitting up in bed, I draw my knees to my chest. "I want to focus on graduating. I'll be leaving for college in a couple of months, and I think it's best we end things before I go."

I might have gone with Knox's suggestion, but it's not entirely false. Stanford is three hours away, so it will be hard to see each other.

Plus, I want to have the full college experience, and being tied down to him won't give me one.

"I think you're making a mistake." Sadness fills his tone. "I love you, Aspen. You know that."

But does he?

Because if he did, he would understand why I'm ending things. Hell, he would *want* me to end things.

He'd want me to go off to college and date guys my own age.

He'd want me to be independent, so I know that life can exist without him before I try to build a life with him.

He'd want me to be free…because expecting a teenage girl to carry the weight of a secret relationship with a married, older man isn't fair.

What it takes out of me isn't fair.

"I know you do, Leo, but—"

"I *need* you," he pleads, like it's physically breaking his heart. "Aspen, don't leave me."

It's always about Leo.

What he wants.

What he needs.

It's never about me.

Nothing is *ever* about me.

"I'm sorry," I whisper, because I truly don't want to hurt him. I just want it to be over. "But I need to do what's best for me."

He starts to protest again, but I hang up the phone.

I feel like a giant weight has been lifted off my chest...like I can finally breathe again.

Not only because I cut ties with Leo.

But because Knox can no longer blackmail me.

He can no longer hold *anything* over my head.

That knowledge fills me with an almost toxic sense of power.

It would be nice to steal some control from him for once. Maybe even scare him a little in the process.

Make him experience everything he makes *me* feel.

After tiptoeing down the stairs, I walk into the kitchen and grab a large knife from the wooden block.

I almost talk myself out of it, because this is fucking crazy...but a tempting, almost euphoric feeling washes over me as I walk outside in nothing but my t-shirt, wielding my big knife.

My footsteps slow as I open the back door and enter the basement. I move slowly and carefully as I tiptoe toward his bed, ensuring I don't wake him.

It's dark down here, except for the light coming from the flat-screen television in the far corner of the room.

Knox is still out cold when I reach his bed. He's lying on his back shirtless, donning a pair of sweatpants. My heart hammers in my chest as I get closer, and I can't help but take in the sharp angles of his gorgeous face, the dark stubble lining his strong jaw, the toned, lean muscles of his arms and stomach, and the indents of his lower abs that lead to the heavy, powerful thing between his legs.

Who knew monsters could be so beautiful?

Then again...that's exactly what lures you in.

Beauty is an aphrodisiac that attracts everyone.

Steeling my spine, I place the knife to his throat.

His eyes pop open, but he doesn't look scared.

Hell, he doesn't even look surprised. Almost like he sleeps with one eye open.

Jesus.

His throat bobs against the knife as he swallows, yet he's completely calm.

"I'm not your pawn anymore," I inform him. "Your little black-mail bullshit is over."

A smirk curls his lips. "Okay." He looks down at the knife. "Is that all? Because I'm tired."

Goddammit. Even when I'm the one holding a knife to his throat, he's still the one in control.

I press the knife harder, hoping to scare him.

His lids lower, and his hand grazes my bare knee. "Why are you down here, Stray?" Ever so slowly, his calloused palm moves up my inner thigh. "What is it you really want?"

An electrifying tremble breaks free and I suck in a sharp breath when he cups me between my legs.

I hate how his touch feels like both damnation and deliverance.

Right and wrong.

Bad meets evil.

His free hand trails down his sculpted stomach until it disappears under his sweatpants.

My heart speeds up, pumping hard against my ribs when he pushes them down his hips and his weighty cock bobs out, slapping against his abdomen.

"Is this what you want?"

My response is visceral as I stare at it, need and desire tangling in my chest. I want it inside me, filling me…fucking me.

But I want it on *my* terms.

Not his.

"Take off my panties."

Slipping a finger into the waistband, he drags them down my legs…deliberately taking his time to taunt me.

When they reach my ankles, I step out of them and kick the fabric away.

Still holding the knife to his neck, I straddle him, lining myself up with his dick. However, since I can't take my eyes off him, I have to instruct him to do the next part.

"Put your cock inside me."

I expect him to oblige, but he fists himself with one hand and takes hold of my hip with the other, guiding me and making it easier for me to do it myself.

Rising on my knees, I slowly lower myself onto him. He's so big, so *thick*, it aches as I stretch around him. My eyes flutter closed when I sink down and he fills me to the hilt, my skin tingling and my nipples puckering as I relish the sensation.

Slowly, I start to ride him. I suck in a breath when his grip on my hip tightens, and he bites his lower lip and groans.

He looks so sexy…so *hungry*. Like he wants this even more than I do.

I see a small trickle of blood oozing from his neck. I must have nicked him at some point.

Instinctively, I still. "I—"

"Don't stop." He pumps his hips. "Don't you fucking stop. Keep riding my cock like a good girl."

Oh, God. His brazen, needy demands set my skin on fire.

I moan, arching my back as I move again. He meets my thrusts, giving it to me deeper, harder.

Fucking me so good I'm losing my goddamn mind.

So good…I drop the knife.

I freeze when he snatches it, realizing I just gave him the upper hand.

No, more than that…I just gave a murdering psycho the weapon of choice to kill me.

An uneasy breath shudders out of me as the knife comes closer, his expression feral.

He's going to kill me.

Thrusting deep, he holds the collar of my white t-shirt with one hand and glides the knife down it with the other, slicing it.

"Take it off."

Reaching for the ripped fabric, I tear it the rest of the way, exposing myself.

I gasp when the sharp tip of the knife pierces the top of my breast. "Knox—"

In one fluid movement, he wraps an arm around my lower back and shifts us into a sitting position.

Groaning, he inclines his head and licks the blood from the small cut he made. "Every part of you tastes good." Squeezing my tits in his big hands, he sucks a nipple into his hot, wet mouth. "So fucking good."

I tilt my head, arching my back and closing my eyes...getting lost in the feel of his warm lips on my skin and his cock pumping deep inside me.

I hold on to him for dear life as his thrusts pick up speed.

Oh, God.

He's fucking me so hard, I'm afraid the bed might break.

That *I* might break.

He shoves me onto my back and his hand wraps around my throat, pinning me to the mattress as he gives it to me deeper.

So deep I no longer know where I end and he begins.

I moan, sucking air between my teeth when he rubs my clit with his free hand. He knows exactly how I like to be touched.

"That's it. Cum on my cock like a good girl."

The dirty things I like to hear.

I moan, scratching his arms with my nails as the pleasure comes to a crest and an orgasm rocks through me.

However, it's those eyes...those intense, fiery eyes, watching me intently as I come that causes something inside me to unhinge.

"Fuck."

A violent, almost animalistic sound tears out of Knox as he slams into me. His grip on my throat tightens before I feel liquid heat fill my pussy and a ragged breath shudders out of him.

He flops on the bed beside me and reaches for his pack of cigarettes on the nightstand.

It's only then that I notice the knife is on the floor. *A draw.*

He brings a cigarette to his mouth and lights it. "That was a one-time thing."

His words don't have a harsh tone like they usually do.

They sound indifferent. Like the same line he feeds to every girl he hooks up with.

And even though it shouldn't bother me, because I was the one who came here looking to use him…it does.

I don't say a word as he smokes his cigarette down to the filter.

However, when I move to leave…he drapes an arm around my waist, drawing me closer to him before we fall asleep.

Chapter 33

Aspen

I expected things to be awkward between us. Hell, at this point, I'd almost prefer it over this cool, detached energy emanating from him.

I watch as he takes the key out of the ignition, waiting for him to say something.

Anything.

But he doesn't. He simply opens the door of his jeep and gets out without so much as a grunt or a spare glance my way.

Screw him.

Muttering a curse, I pick up my bag, hop out of the vehicle, and make my way inside the school building.

I will not play his stupid little games.

So we slept together this weekend…big deal. People have sex all the time.

It doesn't have to mean anything.

I refuse to be one of those girls who pine over an asshole just because he gave you good dick.

I make a beeline for my locker, ignoring the groups of people huddled together talking in hushed whispers. They're probably gossiping and spreading rumors like they always do, because that's all ninety-nine percent of the students here at Black Mountain are capable of.

God forbid they use their mouths and brains for the greater

good.

Out of the corner of my eye, I spy Brie darting straight toward my locker.

She's out of breath when she reaches me, and there's no mistaking the concern lacing her voice. "Are you okay?"

"Yeah." I give her a look. "Why wouldn't I be?"

She opens her mouth to speak, but then clamps it shut and shakes her head solemnly, almost like she loathes the next words she's about to say. "They, uh…they found another body at Devil's Bluff yesterday." She swallows. "The press haven't confirmed it yet, but people are saying it's Shadow."

A chill grips my spine, and my head feels heavy as I take a step back.

"What?"

"Another body was found at Devil's Bluff yesterday," she repeats softly.

I nod because I comprehend what Brie's saying…I just don't understand how or why Shadow ended up dead.

You'd think Knox would have mentioned it…

Unless he doesn't know.

Her eyes dart around nervously before she speaks. "Some people at school are saying Knox did it." Her voice lowers a fraction. "You know…since he's done it before."

It's on the tip of my tongue to defend him, but I quickly come to my senses.

Of course, it's Knox. Not only because he's killed previously and is the epitome of a psychopath…but Shadow was his ex.

I close my eyes as a flash of her crying flits through my mind.

The last time I saw her alive she was running out of the basement—looking so upset and frightened, I'll never be able to get the image out of my mind.

But what if it wasn't him? A tiny voice inside me probes.

"Aspen?" Brie whispers, tearing me from my thoughts. "I know we're not super close, but I'm here for you." Taking a step forward, she reaches for my hand and gives it a gentle squeeze. "If you need somewhere safe to stay…I've got you. Okay?"

I nod, tears prickling my throat.

Her offer is incredibly sweet, but I wouldn't even know how to forge a genuine friendship with her.

I'd like to believe Brie wouldn't judge me for stripping, or for being involved with a forty-eight-year-old man…or for sleeping with my stepbrother who happens to be a murderer.

But the truth is, I just don't know. We're complete opposites, with Brie being on the good end of the spectrum.

Trusting others is something that's never come easily to me.

"Thanks."

Her eyebrows pinch. "Promise me you'll reach out if you need anything?"

"I will," I assure her.

The bell rings, signaling that it's time for us to get to class.

Despite looking like she doesn't want to, she lets go of my hand. "Check in with me later?"

"Sure."

The moment she's gone, I set out to find Knox.

I need to see how he's reacting to the news.

To know if he had anything to do with it.

However, I'm stopped by a teacher walking down the hall. "You're late for class."

I want to argue, but I know it will only put me in hot water.

I'll just have to see Knox later.

Either he's been intentionally dodging me all day, or his schedule has changed, because when I finally manage to catch up with him, it isn't until after classes let out.

Clutching the strap of my bag, I walk over to his locker. "Hey—"

"You need to get another ride home."

I balk at his impassive expression, and his statement. "Okay. Can we talk about Shad—"

The locker slams shut, effectively cutting me off.

Next thing I know he's stalking down the hall, heading for the exit doors.

I know Knox well enough to know that if I chase after him, he'll only make me look stupid in front of everyone.

I'll just have to confront him at home.

Chapter 34

Aspen

*I*t's been five days since they found Shadow's body and the police aren't giving any details.

And that includes my stepfather, who claims it's out of his jurisdiction and he doesn't have any extra information to offer me.

Hell, they won't even release her name officially. However, the police must have *something*, though, because her wake is tonight… which means they obviously released her body to her parents.

As for Knox, he's barely been home.

But when he is, it's only in the wee hours of the morning and he keeps both doors to his basement locked up tight like it's some kind of fortress.

I've tried to grill him on the car rides to and from school this week, but he doesn't say a word.

Which is why I'm beyond shocked when I walk into the funeral home and see him standing stoic like a statue in the back of the room where Shadow's wake is being held.

A shiver travels up my spine.

I once watched a true crime show where some experts claimed that the killer always makes an appearance at the funeral.

Is that why he's here?

I look around for Brie, but she told me she and Colton wouldn't be here until later.

I freeze when I see what I can only assume must be Shadow's

parents standing by her coffin. Her father is shaking hands, thanking everyone for coming...but her mom.

Is a complete wreck.

She's so distraught, her thin frame shaking so badly, the woman can barely stand next to her husband.

I probably have no business being here since Shadow and I didn't like each other, but I feel compelled to pay my respects.

There are a decent number of kids from school in attendance tonight, but none I know well enough to approach and strike up a conversation with.

I can feel them staring at me and whispering things as I wait in line.

Like how I'm the stepsister of a killer.

That I might be next because he hates me.

The knot in my stomach tightens when it's my turn to go up to the casket.

Her coffin is beautiful...well, for a coffin. However, it's the framed picture sitting on top of the ivory casket that snags my attention as I kneel and make the sign of the cross.

The Shadow I knew had colorful hair, thick black eyeliner, and piercings. But the Shadow in *this* picture looks completely different. Her hair is blonde, her makeup is minimal, and there are no piercings to be found.

She doesn't look very happy, though. Almost like someone was forcing her to smile for the camera.

And now she's dead.

That thought has my eyes filling with tears as I stand.

She was only eighteen and had her whole life ahead of her...but just like Candi's, it was stolen. And then her body was discarded in the woods like trash.

My eyes lock with Knox's across the room.

The stupid organ in my chest tells me there's a chance he didn't do it.

But my brain is telling me the writing on the wall is so obvious it's practically written in their blood, and I'd be an idiot to think otherwise.

"Were you friends with June?" Shadow's father asks, bringing me out of my thoughts as he reaches for my hand.

June?

I quickly realize they weren't cool hippie parents who named their daughter Shadow after all.

I don't want to lie, but I don't think me telling them we couldn't stand one other would be appropriate either.

"We went to Black Mountain Academy," I settle on.

The father nods. "Well, thank you for attending—" he gestures for me to fill in the blank.

"Aspen," I chime in.

The mother suddenly perks up beside him. "You're *Aspen?*"

Oh, shit. I should have told her a different name. No doubt she's heard the rumors going around about Knox.

I back away slowly as not to upset them further, but she grabs my hand. "June used to talk about you all the time."

Fuck.

This woman is going to punch me, and I'm going to let her because her daughter was murdered, and God knows she could use the outlet.

However, the next words out of her mouth send me reeling.

"She said you gave her a position on student council." The mother smiles at her husband fondly. "You two were even in the same ballet class."

I fight the urge to tell her the only dancing I've ever done was on a pole while wearing a G-string.

Clearly, they have me confused with someone else.

"Thank you for not only making her student council secretary, but taking the time to study with her after school at your house. Her math grades improved greatly because of you." She gives my hand a squeeze. "Our June was lucky to have such a good friend."

Dammit, Shadow. Usually when you're using someone as a cover up, you give them a *heads up* about it.

"Right."

It doesn't take a genius to figure out that Shadow—or rather, *June* — told her parents she was hanging out with me whenever she was spending time with Knox.

"June was a great person. She'll be missed," I fib, because they need those little white lies.

With that, I give them a somber smile and walk away.

It's crazy how sometimes you really *don't* know a person after all.

How we all have our secrets.

I scan the back of the room for Knox so I can get to the bottom of this, but someone takes hold of my elbow.

When I look up, I see my mother. And Trent.

"What are you doing here?"

"We came to pay our respects," Trent answers.

"But we see you already have," my mother notes.

Trent juts his chin toward his son, who's just spotted us. Knox attempts to walk out, but Trent is hot on his heels. He swiftly reaches for his shoulder, ushering him out of the room.

"Where are you going, Aspen?" my mother hisses as I leave her side, but I ignore her.

I catch the tail end of their conversation as I walk out to the parking lot.

"Get your ass back in there," Trent sneers through gritted teeth.

Knox's jaw tics as he presses the unlock button on his key fob. "Can't. I have somewhere to be."

Trent jabs a finger in his face. "The only place you need to be is where I goddamn tell you to be. Understood—" He stops when he sees me standing there. "Do you mind? I'm talking to my son."

Thinking quick, I blurt, "I just wanted to tell you that I'm leaving to go to Violet's."

He glowers. "Not right now, you're not. We're going up to that casket as a family to pay our respects to June and her par—"

"Shadow," Knox grits out, his expression indecipherable. "She liked to be called Shadow. Not June."

Trent looks like it's taking every ounce of willpower not to lose his shit. "I don't give a fuck what she liked to be called. I came here tonight to do you a favor. Now get your ass in there." He glares at me next. "Both of you."

I cross my arms, returning his glare. "I'm not going up there twice."

I can tell he wants to argue, but a small group of people walk past us to their car. "Fine." He gestures to Knox. "Let's go."

. . .

I inhale a heavy breath as they head back inside the building.

Knox might not be emotional about Shadow's passing, but he scolded his father for calling her June.

That has to mean something…right?

Then again, he ran out of the funeral home like his ass was on fire, and he hasn't been home much this week.

I rub my temples, forcing myself to think.

There's no way these two murders aren't connected, because I found Candi's necklace under his bed.

Maybe he's going back to the crime scene to clean up?

Another horrifying thought hits me.

Both Candi and Shadow were missing for a couple of weeks before they were found.

What if he's holding girls hostage somewhere and *torturing* them before he kills them?

Or *maybe*…he's keeping the bodies somewhere else before depositing them in the woods.

And *that's* where he's been this week, visiting his latest victim before he dumps her.

My chest tightens. *There's only one way to find out.*

I look around the parking lot. It's empty for the time being, which means I have to do this now before either Knox or someone else sees me.

I say a silent prayer that he didn't press the button on his key fob again as I trek toward his jeep.

I breathe a sigh of relief to find it's still unlocked. Being as quiet as I can, I quickly open the door and crawl over the seats to the very back of the jeep. Then I hunker down so no one can see me.

I'm surprised Knox can't hear my heart beating frantically when the door clicks open and he starts the engine a few minutes later.

Remembering that Brie will be at the wake soon and will no doubt wonder why I'm not, I quickly reach into my purse and turn off my phone.

I try to pay attention to all the turns he makes, so I can tell the police how to get there, but I end up losing track because there are so many.

It feels like an eternity before the tires drive over what sounds like dirt and gravel before coming to a complete stop.

I hold my breath when the backseat door opens before slamming shut.

I force myself to stay put because I don't want to pop my head up or leave too soon after him, in case he doesn't go right inside, provided there's even an *inside* to go into.

When I'm positive I can't take anymore, I finally crop up and peer out the window. Just like I thought, it's a dirt road.

After climbing over the seats, I hop out of the car.

My palms begin sweating and there's a painful constriction in my chest as I take in what looks like an abandoned warehouse.

This must be where he kills them.

Only, that doesn't seem quite right because there are other cars in the makeshift lot.

Surely, he wouldn't kill with an audience around.

Not unless there are a bunch of men involved.

Nausea churns my stomach.

What if he's into some real sinister dark web shit where people pay to watch despicable acts being committed against women and children?

Oh, God. I'd like to consider myself a strong person, but even I have my limits.

Gravel crunches under my shoes and for a moment I honestly think my legs are going to buckle as I make my way toward the entrance of the warehouse.

I clutch my phone, feeling stupid for not bringing a weapon of some sort with me.

I'm debating texting Brie and telling her where I am—not that I know for sure—when the sound of cheering assaults my ears.

I'm confused when I open the heavy door and walk through it. I was prepared for bodies and the stench of death. Women tied up with chains while they were tortured. Perhaps a group of men in business suits urging Knox to rape and kill his latest victim while they threw money at him.

Not *this.*

There's a group all right, but it's more like a crowd circling around two men who are beating the crap out of each other.

Upon closer inspection, I realize one of those men is *Knox*.

I make my way through the crowd, convinced this is some kind of weird dream.

Why the hell is Knox fighting someone?

Although, *fighting* doesn't seem to be the appropriate word because he looks like he's literally killing the other guy with every punch he throws.

His opponent—who easily weighs a good thirty pounds more than he does—keeps swaying and spitting blood.

You'd think they'd put a stop to this, because there's no way that guy doesn't need an ambulance, but they all keep shouting for Knox.

Knox—who looks like a dangerous feral animal trapped inside a cage with rivers of sweat dripping down his toned arms and abs. Blood trickles from his mouth and one of his eyes is puffy, but that only serves to make him look even scarier.

He curls a finger at the guy and gives him a lethal smile, luring him to throw a punch. However, when his opponent takes a step and brings his arm back, Knox bashes the heel of his palm against his nose, causing blood to spray everywhere.

The crowd goes wild, urging Knox to finish him off.

Knox grabs the guy by the neck—and then to my utter confusion and surprise—kisses his forehead…

Right before landing a hard jab to his ribs.

The guy howls in pain and I swear I see his eyes cross before they close, and he drops to the floor.

A short, pudgy man runs over to Knox and raises his arm, declaring him the victor.

Knox is about to walk away, but something in the audience catches his attention.

I quickly realize it's *me* when his gaze cuts to mine.

To say he's pissed would be an understatement. The look he's shooting me is full of so much venom a lesser person would cry and slink away.

But I stand firm, even when he shoves through the crowd and wraps his hand around my wrist.

"What the fuck are you doing here?"

I'm about to answer, but he begins tugging me out of the warehouse.

We're almost to his jeep when I blurt out, "Did you kill Shadow?"

He drops my hand like it's made of lava. However, he remains silent. And that only pisses me off more. Because if he didn't do it, he needs to say he didn't.

Otherwise…the rumors are true.

And the feeling in my gut is right. Even though I don't want it to be because somewhere along the way, I developed feelings for him… feelings that aren't enveloped in hate.

Which is stupid because he's the *last* person in the world I should be falling for.

Unfortunately, you can't control who your heart wants to attach itself to.

No matter how much they hurt you…or how bad of a person they might be.

"I want to believe you didn't kill her," I whisper to his back. "But I need to hear you say it, Knox." I watch the muscles in his neck and shoulders tense as I continue speaking, laying everything on the line. "And if you can't look me in the eye and say the words I desperately need you to say…then I'm done. And whatever we might have had is over. For good."

My heart jumps to my throat when he finally turns around.

"Over?" he exclaims, his rough voice and sharp features devoid of any emotion. "We never even began."

His words are harsh on their own, but it's the realization that it's the very same thing he said to Shadow that causes a swell of pain to infiltrate my chest.

I'm not an exception. Nor am I special to him. And we definitely don't have an unexpected, strange connection like I thought… because I was the only one who ever felt it.

I'm just another girl he fucked, hurt, and threw away.

I take a step back, wanting to put as much distance between us as possible.

"Get in the car," he orders.

I shake my head. I don't want to be anywhere near him.

When he takes a step forward, I hold up my phone and say the one thing that I know will make him leave me the fuck alone.

"I'll call the police and tell them I found Candi's necklace under your bed. I'll tell them how upset Shadow was the last time I saw her alive at our house. I'll tell them everything I know."

Hell, maybe I should.

Problem is, it still won't do any good. Knox's dad will do whatever he can to cover it up for his son, and the police obviously don't care enough to figure out what really happened.

Knox's face twists and he looks at me like I betrayed him somehow.

Good.

Now we're both hurting.

Chapter 35

Aspen

"Trent left you some money for food," my mother tells me.

I look at the ten-dollar bill sitting on the counter. The fact he thinks *that* will feed two teenagers for three days while they're away is almost comical, but at least it's something.

As if on cue, my stepfather comes barreling down the staircase.

"No parties." His gaze bounces between Knox and I. "Either of you."

Neither of us utters a word to them or to each other, which isn't surprising because we haven't spoken since the other night at the warehouse.

Fortunately, Violet has given me rides to and from school since then, and I've been taking Ubers back and forth to work so I don't have to see him.

Violet tried probing, but thankfully dropped it after I said I didn't want to talk about it.

Maybe one day I'll be able to be honest with her, but right now I still feel like an open wound and the only way to make the pain stop and to turn it into a scab is to close myself off to everything and everyone.

Especially him.

Trent and my mother walk over to the mudroom where their suitcases are sitting.

"We'll call and check in," my mother promises as they haul them out the door.

It takes everything in me not to laugh because she's never given a fuck before, so why bother now?

"Stay out of trouble," Trent grumbles, and it's clear his statement was aimed at his son.

The front door closes a minute later, leaving Knox and me standing there.

For a moment, he looks like he wants to speak, but I don't give him the chance because I turn and walk up the stairs.

I'm not interested in anything he has to say.

The sooner I save up money and leave him and this stupid town, the better.

"I mean, at least the girl wasn't a stripper," Heather says as she applies blush to her cheeks. "That's good news."

"Yeah, but she was still *murdered*," I point out.

She shrugs. "That sucks, but awful shit happens every day. Just be thankful it didn't happen to you."

For now.

Although, I suppose Knox could have killed me the other night if he really wanted to. We were in the middle of nowhere and everyone else was inside the warehouse.

He had the perfect opportunity.

Which only confuses me the more I think about it, because why the hell won't he just tell me he's innocent?

Because he's not, you dummy.

"Right," I say, hating myself for once again thinking about my stepbrother.

I look at myself in the mirror as I tie my hair into a bun. *Get your shit together.*

Heather gives me a once over. "Are you gonna get changed? You're up next."

As if on cue, the door to the dressing room opens and Freddie sticks his head inside. "Ginger, you're on in three." He raises an eyebrow when he sees what I'm wearing. "Why aren't you dressed?"

I stand up. "I am dressed."

He opens his mouth to argue, but I cut him off.

"Trust me on this."

Graduation is only seven weeks away and I'm desperate to make some money so I can leave.

Which means I'm going to have to do something I've never done before.

Chapter 36

Knox

"What can I get you?" the busty girl behind the bar asks.

"Coke."

Pursing her shiny red lips, she gives me a flirty wink. "Are you sure you don't want something a little…*harder*."

I don't miss the obvious double entendre, but I'm not interested. There's only one person I came here to see tonight, and she sure as fuck isn't it.

"Just the Coke."

Disappointment illuminates her face as she slams a glass on the bar and fills it with soda.

I'm about to tell her to go ahead and spit in it because I have no intention of drinking it. I only bought it because the club recently instituted a bullshit two-drink minimum for guests.

As if the Bashful Beaver is some kind of upscale, sophisticated establishment.

This place is a goddamn shithole and Aspen shouldn't be working here.

The chick slides the glass toward me. "Enjoy the show."

Irritation catches the back of my throat as I take it and search for an empty seat.

I've only been here twice and both times it was damn near empty.

But not tonight. Tonight, there's only one open seat, and it's all the way in the back, which suits me just fine.

The fluorescent lights dim and the hip-hop music that was playing comes to a stop before the DJ's voice emanates over the speakers. "Gentlemen, please give it up for Ms. Ginger."

I grit my teeth as I plop down in a chair and the chatter around me comes to a halt. Everyone's attention turns to the stage that's illuminated with a dark purple haze as the first few bars of "Hurt" the Nine-Inch-Nails version begins to play.

A second later, *Ginger* saunters out on stage.

Only it isn't Ginger…it's Aspen.

I've been to a few strip clubs before and the girls always come out in some sexy get up aimed to entice us.

But Aspen isn't wearing a sexy costume tonight. She's wearing a buttoned-up white cardigan, a pair of black jeans, and her trademark pearls. In other words…her regular clothes.

She's also not wearing her mask.

What the fuck is she doing?

Slowly, she trails her hand up the length of her arm, then up the side of her face until she reaches the white ribbon secured around the bun in her hair. She gives it a swift tug and long red locks spill down her back in a mess of silky waves, causing some guys to cheer.

She moves methodically—like a predator advancing on its victim—as she approaches the pole in the middle of the stage.

Only, she doesn't grip it right away—she teasingly runs a hand up and down—*stroking* it.

"Damn, baby," the guy next to me shouts.

I clutch my glass tighter, unable to take my eyes off her.

Keeping her movements unhurried, she coils her body around the pole like a snake before lowering herself onto the floor.

She looks like she's in a trance as she slips a hand down the front of her cardigan and touches her breast.

"Hottest thing I've ever seen, beautiful," some asshole calls out.

She then lies on the floor, jutting her hips—*writhing*. Moving her body like a goddamn serpent. The hem of her cardigan rises up, showcasing her flat stomach as her delicate fingers walk down her torso before dipping inside the waistband of her jeans.

Jesus fucking Christ.

I expected some meaningless booty shaking and a few clumsy spins around the pole.

Not this.

However, the shit she's doing is working, because the men are throwing money on the stage hand over fist.

My dick thickens when she unzips her pants and slips them down her hips, revealing a white G-string.

The move has my fingers tightening around the glass, and I want to kill a motherfucker when she begins unbuttoning her cardigan and it falls open, baring her white cotton bra.

She stands up then, stretching the length of her body against the pole before placing it between her perky tits.

"Fuck me," the guy in front of me says. "She's so hot."

I've never been the jealous type, but the thought of other men watching her do this has my blood fucking boiling.

Ginger belongs to them…

Aspen is *mine*.

She does one leisurely turn around the pole, slipping her sweater off her shoulders in the process.

Closing her eyes and gripping the rod, she tips her head back. I sit, hypnotized as her free hand finds the hook of her bra and she unfastens it before spinning around and letting it fall to the floor.

She raises her arms over her head—swaying her pert ass—before she turns to face us again, her perfect tits on full display.

Glass cracks under my fingers and liquid streams out over my hand and onto the table, but I don't give a fuck.

She does one gradual—*deliberate*—walk around the pole as the song begins to fade before coming to an end.

Aspen comes out of her trance, and as if realizing she just showed these assholes parts of herself they didn't deserve to see, she quickly picks up her clothes and clutches them to her chest before sweeping all the money into a bag.

I'm already out of my chair by the time she runs off stage.

Chapter 37

Aspen

*H*oly shit.

Adrenaline courses through my veins as I head back to the dressing room.

I can't believe I just did that. However, if there was ever a night to be bold, this was it because it's packed.

"Damn, girl," Heather says when I open the door of the dressing room. "There's not a dry seat in the house after *that* little performance."

After placing my bag of money on the counter, I put my bra on. "Well, hopefully it paid off—"

"You can't go back there," Bubba the security guard shouts before the door of the dressing room swings open.

My mouth drops when Knox rushes inside, looking like a deranged psychopath as his gaze lands on me.

"What the hell are you—"

I don't get to finish my statement because Knox picks me up and tosses me over his shoulder like some kind of unhinged caveman.

"Are you crazy?" I slap his back when he turns to walk out of the room.

"Do you know him?" Heather calls out as we pass the counter and I reach for my cardigan.

"Should I call the police?" Bubba asks, sidestepping Knox as he leaves the room.

No, you should fucking *stop* him. Then again, now that I've seen Knox fight…it wouldn't end well for poor Bubba.

"He's my stepbrother," I settle on because the club has a strict rule against boyfriends being here.

Not that Knox is my boyfriend.

He's nothing to me. He made that perfectly clear the other night.

"Put me down," I demand, but the asshole ignores me as he trudges down the hallway.

At least he's headed for the back exit instead of trekking through the club.

I try squirming out of his arms, but that only makes his hold on me tighten. "Jesus. Are you deaf? Put me d—"

"No," Knox growls. "You're done."

He can't be serious.

"My shift doesn't end for another two hours. I need to go back inside."

He shoves open the door leading to the back lot. "You no longer work here. You're fucking *done*."

For a moment I swear I must be hearing things because none of this makes any sense. "You're kidding, right?"

I jolt when I feel his palm slap my bare ass.

Holy hell. Did he just spank me like I'm a child?

"Does *that* feel like I'm kidding? Or do you need another one?"

I can't help but laugh because he's acting and talking like a crazy person.

My laughter only makes him slap my other ass cheek.

I punch the back of his thigh. "Quit spanking me, asshole." I pinch him for good measure. "And put me down. *Now*."

To my surprise, he obliges, setting me down in front of his jeep.

I quickly put on the only article of clothing I was able to grab and button it.

"What the hell is your problem?"

His sharp features twist and he blows out a ragged breath, almost like he's surrendering to something beyond his control.

His voice is low and guttural when he finally speaks. "I want to fuck you again."

I stare at him in disbelief because that was the last thing I expected him to say. However, if he thinks dragging me out of my job in a jealous rage and proclaiming that he wants to fuck me again is going to change anything between us, he's even crazier than I thought.

I shake my head, teetering on the verge of either laughing or crying because everything about this exchange—about *us*—is insane.

"You had your chance to do more than fuck me," I remind him, spinning around so I can go back inside. "But you blew it."

I've barely taken two steps when he snatches my arm and hauls me back to him.

"Leave me alone, Knox."

His free hand slides down the length of my torso. "I can't."

He's so full of shit. "Can't or *won't?*"

He grabs my hip with one hand and takes hold of my waist with the other. I can feel his erection pressing into my backside. "Both."

My head feels heavy and my eyes burn with unshed tears as he unbuttons my sweater and squeezes my tit through my bra.

His rejection hurt…more than any other time he's set out to cause me pain.

I was ready and willing to take the plunge with him.

All he had to do was be honest with me.

But he couldn't.

"Stop."

But he doesn't. Instead, he grabs the back of my neck, turning my face up to meet his before he kisses me like I'm the air he needs to breathe in order to survive.

He explores every inch of my mouth, leaving no stone unturned.

I feel the armor I've built around me begin to crumble like cheap plywood with every hungry stroke of his tongue.

I faintly register the sound of his jeep door opening before he tears his mouth away and bends me over the backseat.

I hate that he has this much control over me.

That he can hurt me so much, yet I still crave him.

I dig my nails into the seat, desperate to hold on to some semblance of control as he yanks my panties down my legs.

"No."

The sound of him tugging down his zipper has my blood pressure climbing and my nipples pebbling.

I hiss when he spreads my ass cheeks and holds them open—

exposing all of me—before I feel the head of his cock nudge my entrance. "Tell me you don't want this."

"I don't *want* to want this," I whisper, the last of my willpower shattering like glass.

Because everything was so much easier when I hated him.

His gruff voice cuts through the air. "That makes two of us."

With that, he pushes forward until he's buried deep inside me. "Fuck."

His thrusts are fast and brutal—*punishing*—yet rewarding at the same time.

I scratch at the seat, tearing the upholstery as he gives it to me exactly the way I need it.

"I hate you," I croak out, because I can't tell him how I really feel.

I can't tell him that he drives me crazy and he's a psychopath, but I feel like he's the only one on this earth who actually gets me.

I can't tell him I never felt for Leo even a fraction of what I feel for him…and I'm petrified I never will with anyone else.

Reaching around, he strums my clit like it's his personal instrument, causing little shocks of electricity to pulse through my body.

"That's it, Stray." He circles his hips before pumping them faster. "Give me what I fucking want."

Pleasure spikes through me and my orgasm strengthens like a brewing storm as he wrenches it from me.

A deep, throaty groan tears out of him, the carnal sound reverberating in my chest as liquid heat fills my pussy.

I can't tell him that even if he killed Candi and Shadow…my heart would still try to find a way to excuse it.

Despite my brain and conscience knowing better.

Tears spring to my eyes as I fight to catch my breath.

I have to know the truth.

"Did you kill them?" I choke out, and for once I almost hope he doesn't answer, because I don't want to lose him again.

His voice is so low I almost don't hear it.

"No."

Chapter 38

Aspen

*L*eaning against the headboard, Knox brings a cigarette to his lips and lights it. For such a terrible, disgusting habit, he sure makes it look sexy.

Then again, I'm still on a post coital high from our second round shortly after we came home.

Unfortunately, it doesn't last long because an image of Candi's necklace infiltrates my mind.

"Why was Candi's necklace under your bed?" I hold up a hand. "I believe you when you say you didn't kill her. I'm just wondering why…you know."

You had a dead girl's necklace in your room.

His dark brows pinch, and a stream of smoke leaves his mouth. "You sure you really want the answer to that?"

I blink, not understanding. "Of course, I do. Why wouldn't—"

I stop talking when I realize. *Goddammit.*

"You had sex with her."

He shrugs like it's no big deal.

Disgusted, I reach down for my money bag. After the incident in the jeep, I went back inside the club to collect my things. Of course, Knox followed right behind me like a bloodhound tracking a scent.

Fortunately, Heather and Violet worked tonight, so they kept it safe for me.

Knox takes another drag of his cigarette, studying me intently. "You're upset."

I dump the contents of the bag onto his bed so I can count the money I made. "Upset that my boyfriend's a whore?"

Yeah, I am.

He gives me a wolfish grin. "Last I checked, you benefited from my whore ways." The smile slips off his face and his expression grows serious. "Aspen."

I hold up a finger so I can finish counting the hundred-dollar bills in the pile. However, he doesn't wait.

"I don't do girlfriends."

My heart thuds, hard and pained because his words sting. Maybe I jumped the gun before by calling him my boyfriend, but I figured we were finally past the point of playing games and it was a given.

I mean, yeah, he's also my stepbrother and that will no doubt make things awkward, but…

I close my eyes when I realize. Once again, I found myself in a *relationship* with someone who can never truly be mine.

"But you have no problem making me your dirty little secret, huh?"

Just like Leo.

God, I'm such an idiot.

But at least I know exactly where we stand now.

Or rather, where we stood…because I will not be someone's surreptitious option again.

I deserve to be a priority, dammit.

To be kissed and claimed in front of everyone.

I'm worthy of more than the scraps he's offering me.

"I think we should just be friends."

A flicker of relief flashes across his face. "Right. Friends who fuck."

It takes everything in me not to smack him. "No…just friends. No fucking."

He looks like he smelled something rancid. "That's not gonna work for me, Stray."

I shrug. "Too bad. I'm not putting myself through another Leo situation."

I can tell I've made my point because he falls silent as he tokes away on his cigarette.

Turning back to the pile of cash on the bed, I continue counting my money. It's more than I've ever made in a single night before. A *lot* more.

"Looks like I'm going to have to do a repeat performance," I mutter. "I made over a grand tonight."

Knox's jaw tics. "There will be no *repeat* performance." He stubs his cigarette out in the nearby ashtray only to immediately pull another one out of the pack. "I told you, you're *done*."

"Sorry, *pal*, but you don't control me."

Reaching over, he grips my chin. "Read my lips. You're *not* going back to that shithole. I don't want you working there."

I hold his lethal stare. "I'm not quitting my job for someone who isn't my boyfriend." He opens his mouth, but I'm not done talking yet. "And no, I'm not trying to twist your arm or give you an ultimatum. I'm just saying that there's no reason for me to take your feelings about me stripping into consideration and leave the club when we're just friends."

His nostrils flare on an indrawn breath as he ponders this. "Okay, I won't fuck anyone else then. Happy?"

Far from it. He's acting like being with me is a fucking chore.

"Spare me." Exasperated, I shove the cash back into the bag. "I don't want someone who doesn't want me, Knox."

Now he's the one who looks annoyed. "I just said I *wanted* to fuck—"

"And I want more than that," I yell. "I want someone who actually wants to be in a relationship with me. Not because he's jealous and wants me to quit my job, or because I won't let him fuck me anymore. But because he actually wants *me*."

And Knox has already made it perfectly clear he's not that guy.

I'm about to leave, but Knox reaches for my wrist and gives it a tug. Without saying a word, he flicks off the light.

When I curl up next to him, he drapes his arm over me, pinning my back against his chest.

I swear if his hands start roaming inappropriately, I *will* deck him.

But the only thing he does is draw little circles up and down my torso, lulling me to sleep.

I'm dozing off when I hear him grunt, "Fine."

I stir as sleep claims my body and I fall into a slumber. "Huh?"

His lips find the shell of my ear, causing little shivers to run up and down my spine. "I want you."

———

After shutting the beeping timer off, I bend down and open the oven door. A quick check with a toothpick tells me they're done, so I take the tray out.

They smell *heavenly*.

Humming to myself, I place them on the cooling rack and focus my attention on piping the cheesecake frosting over the chocolate ones that have already cooled.

I also baked a carrot cake and apple pie for Knox to try, but I really want him to taste the cupcakes I'm making.

It seriously bothers me that he wasn't allowed to have sweets growing up.

Not only is it strange…it's *unfair*.

Every kid deserves to know what it's like to sink their teeth into something moist and yummy and catch a sugar rush right after.

I'm topping my now frosted cupcakes with some chocolate chips when I hear footsteps enter the kitchen.

When I glance up, Knox is looking at me, his expression inscrutable.

"How long have you been up?"

I shrug, suddenly aware that the only thing I'm wearing is his t-shirt. "Since six a.m."

Given I don't have a car to go to the store myself, I ordered groceries online.

He moves behind me, wrapping his arms around my waist before kissing the crook of my neck. "You've been busy."

"I wanted you to have a little of everything. I would have made more, but…"

"But what?"

"They'll be home in two days and I'm not sure you'd be able to finish it all."

At that, his lips twitch against my skin. "What makes you think I'll eat any of it to begin with?"

His words make me deflate like a balloon. "You don't have to—" I shake my head, annoyance climbing up my spine. "You know what? Fuck you. You might not have asked me to, but I wanted to do something nice for you because I ca—"

Reaching in front of me, he takes a cupcake from the cooling rack.

"It's fun getting you all riled up."

Smirking, he bites into the cupcake. Then his eyes close, as if he's savoring the flavor.

As usual, I don't know what to make of his expression.

"Well?" I say after another minute passes.

"Best cupcake I've ever had."

I start to smile, but then I remember it's the *only* cupcake he's ever had. Not exactly a ringing endorsement.

Nevertheless, it's a compliment, and God knows Knox isn't the type to dish those out.

"I'm glad you finally got to experience it."

Sidestepping me, he reaches for the knife and cuts into the carrot cake next. "Why do you like to bake, Stray?"

"Well, my dad bought me an Easy-Bak—"

"I didn't ask why or when you started, I want to know why you *like* doing it."

I bristle because no one has ever asked me that before.

He brings a fork full of cake to his mouth as I give him my answer.

"Well, most people think baking is simple, because you can follow a recipe. But there's actually a lot of creativity involved. The chance to mix in various ingredients and make it your own, turn it into something new and enjoyable." I close my eyes. "The smell and look is what lures you in first…attracts you. But the taste is what you're really after. And the moment it hits your lips and the flavor coats your tongue…you get to indulge your hunger. Give into your temptation." My tongue darts out to lick my lower lip. "I guess I like being responsible for someone's pleasure."

I squeal in surprise when Knox's hands find my hips and he hoists me up onto the island.

Some of the baked goods fall to the floor, but I'm too distracted by the dark carnal look in his eyes as he tugs my underwear down my legs.

"What—"

His teeth sink into my inner thigh and I tremble in response.

"I haven't showered today," I blurt out as he buries his head between my legs, his stubble scratching my sensitive skin.

His nose skims the length of me and he inhales deeply, his long fingers tightening around my hips. "I don't give a fuck."

He proves his point by licking and kissing my pussy the same ravenous way he does my mouth.

The vulgar sounds of him eating me fill the kitchen, causing my skin to tingle and my head to spin as he continues drawing incredible sensations from my body.

I place my hand on his head, keeping him right where I need him as he stabs his tongue between my legs. He makes tiny circles, causing the metal from the barbell to graze my inner muscles.

I whimper as pleasure coils my insides, and he shoves two fingers inside me before attacking my clit with his mouth.

"Oh, fuck."

With his free hand, he pushes my shirt up and squeezes my breast.

"I'm gonna come," I tell him. "Don't stop."

His hand wraps around my throat and I find myself welcoming the sensation as he propels me to orgasm.

I come with an audible gasp but unable to speak as I rock my pelvis against his mouth, my limbs jerking against the marble island.

The second Knox releases his hold on me though, an image of Shadow crying on the front lawn invades my mind.

I'm not sure what happened…but it's obvious Knox hurt her somehow.

"Why was Shadow upset that night?"

He's clearly caught off guard by my question as he wipes away the wetness on his mouth and jaw. "What?"

"You heard me. *Why* was Shadow upset that night?"

A knot of unease forms in my gut the longer he stays silent.

He doesn't look guilty, but he doesn't exactly appear innocent either.

The way his lips press into a firm line and the lock of his jaw makes it clear whatever happened that night is something he doesn't want to talk about.

"We have to be honest with each other," I whisper as I sit up. "No matter how bad it is…if this is going to work between us. We can't keep secrets."

His throat bobs on a swallow. He doesn't look nervous…just pissed off and unwilling to tell me.

I meet his eyes, imploring him to give me the truth. "Please."

I won't hurt him, and I won't judge him…I just have to know.

He glances up at the ceiling and I see the trail of tension ride down his jaw and neck.

When he speaks, his voice is gruff. "Because of you."

That doesn't make any sense. "How so?"

My gaze is paralyzed under the force of his when he says, "She was sucking me off and I accidently said *your* name instead of hers." Shrugging, he searches around in his pockets for something, but comes up empty. "She confronted me about it, but I reminded her we weren't together, and that *she* was the one who came over looking to screw me. Not the other way around."

Relief shimmies down my spine, but a trickle of guilt quickly follows.

That must have sucked for her. Shadow had feelings for Knox, and to hear him utter another girl's name while she was pleasing him must have felt like a punch to the gut.

Then again, Knox continuously told her he didn't reciprocate those same feelings.

And now *I'm* torn between feeling bad and feeling a little turned on knowing he was thinking about me while he was with someone else.

"I…uh. I had no idea."

"Yeah, well…now you do." He walks away. "I'm going out for a smoke."

I jump down and reach for his arm before he can leave. "Wait."

His nostrils flare as he peers down at me. "What?"

I get why he's upset. Not only was it the wrong time to bring it up…I probably came off accusatory.

"Did you call me Stray or Aspen?"

God, I'm so fucked up, but I can't help myself. He brings the bad side out of me. Causes the things I *shouldn't* want to rush to the surface.

Rising on my tiptoes, I kiss the vein bulging in his throat before licking it. It throbs under my tongue and I scrape my teeth against it.

His body tenses. "Aspen."

I trail my palm down his chest. "Because you wanted it to be my mouth around your dick?"

His lids grow heavy as his eyes track my every movement. "What are you doing?"

Moving my hand lower, I undo his belt buckle, release his fly, and slip my hand inside, grazing his length through his boxers. "Giving you what you want."

He raises an eyebrow in challenge. "What makes you sure I want this?"

Tugging on the waistband of his boxers, I reach inside. He's warm and hard for me. "It *feels* like you do."

There's a threatening look in his eyes. "Don't start something you can't finish, Stray."

"Don't worry." I circle my thumb around the drop of liquid on his tip. "I'll be a good girl."

Shoving down his jeans and boxers, he releases his cock. "Prove it."

I bat my eyelashes innocently. "Tell me what you want, and I'll do it."

His gaze burns as he stares at my mouth. "I want you on your knees. *Now.*"

I sink down as he fists his dick, watching the way his veins and tendons move as he gives himself a slow jerk.

My skin flushes when he moves closer and smears pre-cum over my lips.

I part them, tasting the salty fluid.

His thumb hooks inside my mouth, pulling my cheek. "Open wider." His jaw hardens. "So I can fuck your face."

When I do, he gives a forceful thrust, hitting the back of my throat.

I gag, my saliva dribbling down my chin as he ruthlessly shoves himself in and out of my mouth as if he were fucking me.

I try to stroke the part of his length that can't fit, but Knox shakes his head.

"Hands at your sides or I'll tie them up."

I go slack, doing what he says.

His thighs flex as he grabs a fistful of my hair, keeping me immobile.

I relax my jaw, taking everything he gives me. His hips roll as he meets my face, grinding against my mouth.

His muscles tense and contract as his face strains with pleasure. His intense eyes peer down at me like I'm the only thing in this world he's capable of seeing clearly.

And then I hear it. "Aspen."

His breaths sharpen, his hold on me tightening as I feel him pulse on my tongue.

"Swallow."

It's the only warning I get before his release fills my mouth.

A ragged sigh escapes him as he grips the counter. "Fuck." Smirking, he looks at me. "Get up."

When I do, he closes the distance between us and kisses me.

My knees go weak, because every time he kisses me senseless, I lose another part of myself.

He playfully tugs my t-shirt. Or rather, *his* t-shirt. "Take this off."

I fold my arms around his neck, not quite ready to put an end to his kiss. "Why?"

"Because I want to watch you shower." Reaching down, he grabs a handful of my ass and squeezes. "I want you to pretend you're all alone while I watch you play with yourself." His fiery mouth slides down my neck. "But you're not allowed to come." He sucks the sensitive skin above my throat. "Not until my cock is inside you."

It's a demand I wouldn't dream of turning down.

Chapter 39

Knox

"We're gonna be late for school," Aspen breathes as I unbutton her shirt.

I currently have her spread out on the couch in the living room.

I kiss and nip my way down her abdomen, pausing when I reach the top of her plaid skirt. "We're already late."

Might as well make it worth it.

Her eyes flutter closed as I open her blouse, revealing the white bra underneath.

My dick swells, throbbing and trapped inside my pants.

I unhook the clasp in the front of her bra, groaning when her tits spill out. "We're not going to school today."

My appetite for her is fucking insatiable.

"We have to," she says, but I capture one pale pink nipple in my mouth and bite down.

She hisses, drawing a sharp breath between her teeth. "Jesus."

I'm just getting started.

I want to spend the day biting and sucking every inch of her while she's trapped underneath me, begging for more.

And just when she thinks she can't take it and she's about to die from the torment I'm inflicting...

I'll feed her messy pussy my cock. Inch by excruciating inch, until she's full.

Aspen moans before finding her voice. "I have to finalize every-thing with the prom commi—"

My hands make their way under her skirt, effectively silencing her.

Sucking her other nipple into my mouth, I tease her pussy through her damp underwear with my knuckle.

Her brows furrow and her mouth parts as I continue my torture. "You're driving me cra—"

The sound of the front door opening cuts her off.

"Shouldn't you be in school?" my father booms from the foyer.

Fuck. They weren't supposed to be back until tomorrow.

I edge away and Aspen scrambles off the couch, buttoning her shirt in the process.

"You're such an idiot," Aspen yells.

When I give her a look, she silently urges me to play along.

Heavy footsteps travel toward the living room. "What happened?"

Aspen glares daggers at me. "Your son took my laundry out of the washing machine over the weekend and left it in a wet pile on the floor."

When my father scrunches his face she adds, "Now they're wrin-kled, and they smell." She gestures to her shirt. "I can't go to school like this."

It's not the best lie, but judging by my father's annoyed expres-sion, it works.

"You can and you will go to school like that, young lady." He glares at me. "Does someone need to teach you some goddamn manners since you obviously forgot them?"

The hairs on the back of my neck stand on end. "No."

Dark eyes narrow into tiny slits. "No, *what?*"

The word tastes like shit on my tongue. "Sir."

He hikes a thumb behind him. "Good. Now the both of you better get your asses to school or so help me God, wrinkled laundry will be the least of your worries."

Aspen opens her mouth in challenge, but I give her a look.

One she ignores because she places her hands on her hips and snarls, "Excuse me?"

He turns his furious glare on her. "Did I stutter?"

232

As usual, she doesn't back down. However, he's the wrong person to pick a fight with.

"No, but that sure sounded like a threat."

His face turns red with anger. "I'll show you a threat, you little bitch. It's about time you gave me some goddamn respect."

He lunges for her, but I'm faster and wedge myself between them in the nick of time.

"Get in the car," I bark, ready to rip his fucking throat out with my teeth.

To my surprise, Aspen actually listens for once and runs out of the living room.

Now it's just me and him.

"You seem to be forgetting where your loyalties lie, son."

"And you seem to be forgetting that *she's* not—" I catch myself before I finish that sentence.

"She's not what?" he prompts, daring me to say it.

I won't give him the fucking satisfaction.

"Nothing."

He smirks, reminding me we're not all that different. "That's what I thought." He scratches his chin. "By the way, the next time you fool around with your whore sister under my roof, make sure she thinks of a better excuse to give me. A liar is bad enough, but a terrible one is worse."

It's on the tip of my tongue to ask if he's just upset she won't give it up to him, but I know that will only goad him and make him have a point to prove.

Instead, I look him in the eye. "We weren't fooling around. I told you, I *hate* her."

His tone is low and clipped, but there's also a hint of amusement. "So you keep saying."

"Are we done here?"

I can tell he doesn't want to let me off the hook so easily, but the sound of his phone ringing has him waving me away.

I dig my keys out of my pocket and stalk out, suppressing the visceral urge to walk back in there and beat the living shit out of him until he no longer has a pulse.

One day.

The entire school is buzzing even more than usual as I make my way to my locker after lunch.

I'm about to chalk it up to the typical bullshit drama that goes on around here, but then I see Aspen talking to her friend Brie down the hall.

I'm not sure what's going on, but whatever it is has her paler than usual and visibly shaken.

The fact that she could mouth off to my father without so much as batting an eye earlier, but now looks like a cat being held over a tub full of water doesn't bode well.

The muscles in my chest tighten as I head toward her.

"It's not him," I hear Aspen whisper as I approach. "Trust me."

"How do you—"

"Because I've been with him all weekend."

Her friend's eyes widen before she gives Aspen's hand a squeeze and scurries off.

"What's wrong?"

When she doesn't answer, the predatory need to protect her takes over and I step into her space, intentionally crowding her. "What happened, Stray?"

Her eyes drop to the floor as her chest heaves. "Traci and Staci are dead." She releases a shaky breath. "Their bodies were found at Devil's Bluff. Just like Candi and Shadow."

A heavy feeling sinks into my muscles and uneasiness crawls along my neck.

Fuck.

Chapter 40

Aspen

*B*ack-to-back wakes for girls I used to see in school every day are definitely not something I ever planned on attending a mere five weeks before graduation.

At least now people have stopped acting like these murders are just random terrible things that happen in life.

Doesn't mean the local police are any closer to finding a suspect, though. Even my stepfather is growing frustrated with their efforts. Or as he put it—their *lack* of effort.

I peer at the pink coffin with a set of pom-poms placed on top. Yesterday was Staci's funeral...and tonight is Traci's wake.

Given this is the third one I've had to attend in such a short amount of time, I've grown a little desensitized.

Plus, it's hard to muster any sympathy for a girl who set me up to get raped at a party so she could film it.

Doesn't mean I wanted her to die, though.

I look around the packed room, wishing Knox were here. But he can't be because he has a fight.

Seeing as he made me quit stripping, I don't think it's fair that he keeps partaking in these illegal brawls of his—no matter how much money he makes—but arguing with him is like arguing with a wall.

I pull Knox's keys out of my purse. He told me to take his jeep to the wake and pick him up at the warehouse after I was done.

Perhaps I should go up to Traci's coffin and pay my respects, but that's hard when you had no respect for someone to begin with because they were a horrible human being.

Casting one last look at her pink casket, I say a silent prayer that her murderer is found before he or she strikes again.

I'm walking out to the parking lot when someone grabs me by the shoulder.

I spin around, ready to attack because there is a freaking killer on the loose, but relax when I glance up and see Leo.

Well, *kind of* because it's weird to see him here.

"Didn't mean to scare you," he says, raising his hands.

"It's fine. I'm just…jumpy." My nose scrunches as I assess him. "What are you doing here?"

Sticking his hands into the pockets of his suit slacks, he releases a long-suffering sigh. "Looking for you." Concern lines his features. "I've been worried about you."

I adjust the strap of my purse on my shoulder. "You could have just called."

He laughs, but it's devoid of any humor. "You don't pick up when I do."

He's got me there.

Guilt floods my stomach, which is weird because I have nothing to feel guilty about.

We broke up. Or as Knox would put it, we never even began.

How could we? I'm eighteen, he's forty-eight…*and* he's married to someone else.

Our relationship was immersed in secrets and only able to flourish in the dark.

I want someone who isn't afraid to be seen with me in the light.

"I've been—"

"Let me guess," he cuts in with a roll of his eyes. "Busy?"

I'm not sure why he's giving me the third degree, but it's not warranted because I no longer owe him any explanations.

"Yeah. Prom is next week and then after that it's graduation."

And then college.

I make a mental note to talk with Knox later about that, because while I know my plans, I have no idea about his.

Maybe we can get an apartment together, because God knows he must be sick of living with his uptight asshole father.

Leo's face falls. "Dammit, Aspen."

I bristle. "What?"

He shrugs helplessly. "When did we become strangers? When did you stop caring?"

"I don't—"

"Did what we have mean *anything* to you? Anything at all?"

Now I get it. He's still hurting and needs closure.

I tell him the truth. "It did. It taught me a lot of things. And while we didn't work out, I'll never take for granted that you were there for me when I needed someone."

And for that, I'll always be grateful to him.

Taking a step in my direction, he cups my cheek. "I can't stop thinking about you."

I don't know what to say to that, but it's obvious he takes my silence as compliance because he whispers, "I'm still in love with you."

He tries pulling me close, but I place a hand on his chest, stopping him. "I'm sorry you're hurting, Leo. Truly, I am. But what we had is over. You need to find a way to accept that and move on."

He looks so distraught—so ruined—my chest sinks. I never wanted to cause him pain.

Even though we had no business sleeping together…I think he did it to fill a void inside him.

Just like me.

"I can't move on. I *need* you, Aspen."

And I need him to let me go.

I'll never forget what we shared, but all I see when I look at him now is a broken man that I can't save.

Because I'm no longer tethered to him.

I take a step back. There's nothing more he can say to salvage this. "Goodbye, Leo."

Taking a cleansing breath, I start walking toward Knox's jeep.

"Knox is here?"

I stop in my tracks. "No. He lent me his jeep so I could come here tonight."

I don't miss the animosity in his tone when he drawls, "I see."

Chapter 41

Aspen

"*We* need to talk."

Sitting up, Knox reaches for his pack of cigarettes on the nightstand. I watch the muscles in his broad naked back stretch and contract with the movement.

I've been wanting to ask him about his plans after graduation for what feels like forever now, but every time I try, he either changes the subject, or distracts me with mind-blowing sex.

Seeing as we only have two weeks left until we cross that stage and receive our diplomas…it's now or never.

His voice is a rumble of smoke and ashes when he speaks. "About what?"

I pull the sheet around me. "What are your plans after we graduate?"

Closing his eyes, he sags against the headboard. "Don't know. I haven't given it much thought."

"Have you applied to any colleges?"

He brings the cigarette to his mouth and inhales. "Nope."

Not surprising. Knox doesn't really seem like the college type. Not that he isn't smart. He definitely is.

A knot forms in my stomach. I don't know why I'm so nervous. I shouldn't be.

I guess I'm afraid we're not on the same page. That maybe I'm rushing things.

Maybe I want this more than he does.

Despite him being my boyfriend, we still act like we hate each other when we're in public.

I get why we have to…with us being step siblings and all. But that's all the more reason we should start our lives together.

Far away from here.

"We should get an apartment together."

He raises an eyebrow as a stream of smoke escapes his mouth, but otherwise stays silent.

Neither agreeing nor disagreeing.

Annoyed, I toss the covers off my body and reach for my clothes. School ended an hour ago, but prom is tonight.

It was supposed to be two weeks ago, but Staci and Traci's murders kind of ruined that, so it had to be rescheduled.

I can feel him studying me like a hawk as I put my clothes on. "You're upset."

"And you're…indifferent."

"Indifferent?"

A groan of frustration leaves me. "Apathetic, unmoved…*cold.* How many more words do I have to use for you to understand why I'm so upset?" I glare at him. "Damnit, Knox. Do you even care about me at all?"

Or am I just some stupid girl with stars in her eyes because she's falling for someone who isn't capable of ever loving her?

He stubs his cigarette out in an ashtray. "You sprung this apartment shit on me out of nowhere, Stray."

I suppose he has a point there.

"Fine. If that's the case, take some time and think about it."

He nods slowly. "I will." He crooks a finger at me. "Come here."

I fold my arms across my chest. "No."

He stands up and I can't help but zero in on his abs, his strong, powerful thighs…and the big thing between his legs that's swinging like a pendulum with every step he takes.

My spine meets the wall behind me as he approaches. "You're sexy when you're angry."

My eyes flutter closed when he seizes my chin and his mouth finds my neck. "You shouldn't have gotten dressed." His free hand toys with the buttons on my shirt. "I wasn't done with you yet."

Arousal shivers through me when he licks a hot line along the column of my throat…but then I remember that I have to start preparing for tonight.

Pushing his hand away, I side-step him. "I can't. I have to get ready for prom." I find my shoes on the floor and put them on. "You probably should, too."

Confusion shadows his face when I look up. "What's wrong?"

"I'm not going to prom."

This is news to me. I mean, we never talked about it, but he sat there and listened as I droned on and on about everything the prom committee –the one *I'm* the head of—had planned.

He knows how important tonight is to me.

Not just because of all the work I put into it, but because for once I get to have something…*normal*.

Disappointment sinks like a brick in my chest. "Oh."

I don't even know why I'm surprised because this so isn't his thing.

Even still…he knows how much it means to me.

"You know what? Fuck you."

Brushing past him, I walk out the back door.

"Stray," he calls out after me, but I ignore him, the hurt in my chest growing worse.

I now know how Leo felt during our last conversation…because I'm forever wanting things from Knox I'll never get.

Chapter 42

Knox

"*S*tray," I grunt as she flies out the back door of the basement. I charge after her, but realize I'm naked.

Grinding my molars, I slip on a hoodie and a pair of sweatpants.

I know she's upset, but she should have known I wasn't attending that dumb shit.

Just the thought of dressing up and dancing in front of a bunch of stupid fucks I can't stand is enough to make my hackles rise.

Besides, there are much better ways we can spend the night.

I intend to tell her so, but Aspen's long gone by the time I make it to the backyard.

It's just as well. Nothing I say will make a difference, anyway. I'm not changing my fucking mind.

It's important to her, though.

Gritting my teeth, I turn to head back inside, however, I catch what looks like a red-haired fox digging a hole in the backyard.

Shit.

Bringing my fingers to my lips, I let out a loud whistle. The fox freezes and sizes me up briefly before making the smart decision to run off.

After he's long gone, I walk over and peer inside the hole.

Four severed fingers in various states of decomposition stare back at me. Tilting my head, I look at the nails lying beside them. One red, one black, and two the same shade of bubblegum pink.

Swiping my foot over the dirt, I cover the hole back up and fish around my pockets for my keys.

I'm walking past the gate in the backyard when I hear,

"Going somewhere, son?"

I stop at the sound of his voice.

Keeping my expression neutral, I utter, "I was gonna run a few errands. Need anything?"

Shaking his head, my father gets out of his car. "No."

I stride toward my jeep.

"Trenton."

I pause, my throat burning to lash out and my fists aching to bash them against his skull.

But I can't.

Because now there's too much at stake.

I just have to play his game for a little while longer.

"Yes...*sir?*"

His dark eyes narrow as he takes a step closer. "I gave you a new family, son. I'd hate to see you lose them."

A violent surge of anger burns through my veins and it takes everything in me to remain impassive.

"I understand."

With that, I open the door and get inside.

Nausea burns up my throat as I start the engine and put the pieces together.

I didn't think much of it when Candi was murdered. She was a stripper at a cesspool, and sometimes those girls hang around the wrong people and end up dead. It sucks, but shit happens.

It wasn't until Shadow was axed that I knew the person responsible was sending a subliminal threat to Aspen, and I needed to keep her close so I could protect her.

Staci and Traci showing up dead next only confirmed that.

Ice flows through my veins and my lungs lock up.

The one and only thing all these girls had in common was Aspen.

And me.

A torrent of anger kicks up my pulse.

But as it turns out...the murders weren't warnings for Aspen at all.

They're for me.

And if I don't handle this now, there's only one way it ends…

With her being his next victim.

My hand clenches around the steering wheel.

Maybe that's why he did it.

Because he knows the monster he created is even darker and more fucked up than he is.

And that fucking terrifies him.

He thought marrying Aspen's mother and making her my step-sister would teach me a lesson and keep me in line.

However, he fucked up.

Because if you're going to keep a wild animal in a trap and taunt it with its favorite toy…

You better make damn sure they don't end up loving that toy more than they fear you.

Chapter 43

Aspen

*J*roam my gaze over the dance floor, watching my peers dance in their elegant dresses and dapper tuxedos as colorful lights illuminate the large ballroom.

At least they're having fun.

I went with an Old Hollywood theme for prom, so there was a red carpet upon entry, and various movie film reel decorations placed around the room. I also managed to get a photo booth, so everyone could take pictures with their friends for an extra keepsake.

However, my favorite thing is the large movie screen depicting timeless actors and actresses via a projector.

Smiling to myself, I make my way over to the punch bowl. God knows I didn't have the best time at Black Mountain, but it's still a little bittersweet that it's all coming to an end.

Then again, I'm excited to see what the future holds. Especially at Stanford.

A weird twist goes through my chest.

I'm not sure what will happen with Knox and me. I want us to make it, but he doesn't seem interested in what happens after we graduate.

Or making me happy.

I peer down at my pleated satin floor-length yellow dress. It's fairly simple compared to some of the other dresses being worn tonight, but that's why I love it.

Too bad my boyfriend never got to see me in it.

Heart sinking, I reach for a paper cup so I can pour myself some punch.

I grip the ladle but freeze when I spot someone walking toward me out of the corner of my eye.

My breath catches as I take in Knox's dark jeans and black hoodie. However, it's the intense way he's staring at me as he moves that makes my skin hum and my knees go weak.

He's looking at me like no one else exists in the world.

Like I'm the only thing he can see.

I place the cup down on the table as he approaches. "I thought you weren't coming?"

He doesn't answer as he takes my hand. Then, to my utter surprise, he leads me to the dance floor.

The DJ switches gears to a slow song and Knox's arms close around my waist as the first few bars of, "Nothing's Gonna Hurt You Baby," by Cigarettes After Sex begins to play through the large speakers.

I want to pinch myself to make sure this is really happening.

I peer into his eyes as we sway to the music. I have so many questions burning a hole inside me...but suddenly none of them matter.

Because he's here...for *me.*

And that tells me everything I need to know.

Closing my eyes, I press my cheek to his shoulder, smelling his scent and sinking against his warmth.

His hands slip to my hips and his grip tightens, like he wants to touch me in all the ways only he can, but he's trying to control himself because we're in public.

My eyes flutter open and I'm suddenly hyper aware that everyone's staring at us. No doubt confused because not only is he my stepbrother...Knox and I hate each other.

Well, we *used* to hate each other.

Now we've found the other end of the spectrum.

My cheeks heat as an uncomfortable feeling brews in my gut. Knox prefers to lurk in the shadows and loathes being the center of attention, which we very clearly are right now.

I'm about to tell him we can stop, but his eyes darken, and he rasps, "I don't care."

My heart stops as he tilts my chin up and then races into a full-blown gallop when his lips crash against mine.

Strong hands move up my back until one is cupping my neck while his lips press against mine harder, urging me to open my mouth. The first touch of his tongue sends a jolt of electricity coursing through me. The second one lights my entire body up.

I lean in, opening my mouth wider as he kisses me with so much hunger, I shiver all over.

The hand on my neck constricts, demanding I stay in this moment with him. And I do, because I honestly don't want to be anywhere else.

I just want to be with him, because even though it *should* be wrong, nothing has ever felt so right.

A deep groan vibrates in his chest, and holy hell, I don't care who is watching or who might object. I want him to hike up my gown and take me right here.

We must be on the same page because he breaks the kiss and his fingers wrap around my wrist before tugging me out of the room like a man on a mission.

He's walking so fast I can barely keep up in my heels.

I expect him to open the door to the backseat when we approach his jeep, but he yanks on the passenger door instead.

"Get in."

I don't know what happened or the cause of it, but his demeanor is different than it was a moment ago.

He walks over to the driver's side and hurries inside. My senses sharpen with awareness when the engine roars to life and I hear the click of the lock on the doors.

"What's wrong?"

His jaw hardens before he turns and reaches into the backseat.

My confusion and concern reach new heights when he drops a small black duffle bag on my lap.

"There's some cash and clothes in there." He digs his hand inside the pocket of his hoodie and pulls out what looks like a bus pass. "Your bus leaves in forty minutes. It will take you to New York where you will hide out until the person I hired finds you and gives you a new passport and I.D so you can go to Canada."

My mouth falls open and I shake my head. I feel like I have whiplash because I don't understand what the fuck is going on.

"You're not making any sense, Knox. Why are you taking me to a bus stop? Why am I running aw—"

"Because I need to keep you safe," he grits out, the veins in his neck straining against his skin. "So, for once in your goddamn life, don't fight with me, Stray. Just do what I fucking tell you."

I want to argue—because this is *insane*—but both the uneasiness and conviction in his tone have me nodding.

"Okay. But first, I need you to tell me what it is I'm running from."

Because there is no way I'm leaving him and getting on that bus until I know what's got him so on edge to the point he expects me to willingly flee the freaking country.

His hand clenches around the steering wheel as he reverses out of the parking lot. "There's no time to explain. Just get on that bus."

I glare at him because you'd think he'd know me better than that. He can't demand I uproot my entire life in the blink of an eye without some kind of explanation.

"I'm not doing a damn thing until you start talking."

Tension locks his jaw as he drives down the road. I can tell he doesn't want to talk, but he knows I won't oblige if he doesn't.

After what feels like an eternity, he speaks. "I know who murdered those girls." Shock roots me to the seat as I process his statement, however the next words out of his mouth send me reeling. "And if I don't get you the fuck out of here *tonight*…you'll be next." His voice drops. "I can't let that happen."

Nerves tangle my insides, paralyzing my heart and lungs. "Who killed them?"

His nostrils flare on an indrawn breath, and he looks so disgusted —so *tormented*—I want him to pull over so I can wrap my arms around him.

His eyes cut to mine. There's a flicker of shame in them before they turn hard and he averts his gaze.

"My father."

I rub my temples, not understanding any of this. Yes, his dad is an asshole. Worse than an asshole—he's a horrible human being.

But a *killer*? How can that be? He's in the FBI for crying out loud. He's supposed to be the person catching murderers, not the person committing them.

"How do you know this?"

The jeep accelerates, like he can't get to our destination fast enough. "Trust me, it's him."

"I do trust you," I whisper. "But I need to understand how you know this. Why would he murder these girls?" I swallow. "Why does he want to kill me?"

He laughs, but it's strained. "Besides the fact that he's fucking crazy?" His expression turns grim. "To teach me a lesson."

That doesn't help clear anything up.

"Teach you a lesson about *what?*"

"Going against him." He pounds the steering wheel with his fist. "Everything that man does is a sick, twisted game, Aspen. He gets off on the control and trapping people. He enjoys stealing every ounce of power from you and leaving you helpless...right before he kills you."

"How do you know this?"

His features twist with revulsion. "Because he's been doing it all my life."

I'm trying to connect the dots, but he's speaking in riddles. "I don't—"

"Goddamnit, Stray." He makes a sharp left and turns into the parking lot of the bus station. "He killed my mom. After he spent years beating the shit out of her...*us.*" The engine cuts off. "Now, go...before he does the same to you."

Every instinct in my body is screaming at me to listen to him and run away so I can protect myself.

But I can't...not until I know everything.

I place my hand on top of his. "Tell me what happened, Knox."

His glare is ominous. "I just did."

"I need details."

Because something tells me he's never told a soul about any of this.

He's kept everything locked up tight until it turned him into a cold and unfeeling shell of someone he never got the chance to become.

The hard angles of his face strain with rage, and for a moment I think he's going to open the door and push me out...

But he doesn't.

Chapter 44

Knox

Past…

My heart beat like a drum as I rushed inside the house as fast as my legs could carry me. Excitement coursed through my limbs when I closed the door behind me and threw my bookbag on the floor of the mudroom.

I quickly scurried toward the kitchen. "Mom."

Not only was today my twelfth birthday, my mom promised to sneak me a special surprise before my father came home from work.

He had many rules we were required to follow, but the one I hated the most was that we weren't allowed to bake or consume any sweets.

According to my father, the sugar would not only rot my teeth, but my brain. He also didn't want my mother or me getting fat.

However, my mom agreed to go to the local bakery while I was at school so I could try a chocolate cupcake for the very first time.

My stomach rumbled whenever I saw my classmates eating baked goods, and it took every ounce of willpower to not snatch it out of their hands. But the fear of him finding out I broke one of his cardinal rules always prevented me from indulging.

But not today.

Today was my birthday.

Which meant I had a bit of luck on my side and nothing could go wrong.

"Mom," I called out again, making my way toward the living room.

She was always here whenever I came home from school—usually putzing around the kitchen getting dinner started.

However, she was nowhere to be found right now.

Unless she was downstairs doing laundry.

Realizing that must be the case, I opened the door leading to the basement.

I cupped my hands over my mouth, failing to contain my enthusiasm as I charged down the stairs. "Mom, I'm ho—"

The words jammed in my throat when the crimson trail came into view and a coppery, rancid stench invaded my nostrils.

She was hurt.

Bile surged up my throat as I rounded the corner.

I found her lying on the floor, a pool of blood surrounding her limp form.

I quickly rushed to her side. "Mom, are—"

Her body felt cold…stiff.

I didn't even have the chance to try to rescue her.

She was already gone.

My eyes welled with tears and my breath froze in my lungs as I took in the bruises coloring her pale skin, the deep gash in her neck…

The cupcake she was still clutching in the palm of her hand.

He always said he'd kill us, but I still hoped we'd find a way to leave before it happened.

Which was stupid of me.

Because good didn't overcome evil like all the books and movies claimed.

At least…not for us.

His brand of evil was too strong. Too resilient. Too powerful.

The tiny hairs on the back of my neck stood at attention when I heard heavy footsteps creak down the staircase.

"Welcome home, son," the rough, teasing voice belonging to my mother's killer said.

I didn't utter a word as my father approached.

"You have two choices."

I didn't want a choice.

I just wanted him to kill me and get it over with already.

Put me out of my misery so I could find her in the afterlife.

I hated myself for flinching when he placed his hand on my shoulder because I knew the reflex would only bring him pleasure.

He loved to be feared.

I refused to give him that. "Fuck you."

His hand wrapped around my neck and he hurled me to the floor before he climbed on top. "Excuse me?"

White spots formed in front of my eyes as he tightened his grip and I grew lightheaded. The joke was on him though because he'd have not one, but two corpses on his hands.

My body soon betrayed me, and the natural response to live took over. I clawed at his hands, desperate for him to release his hold as self-preservation kicked in.

My mother was dead—and it shattered what was still left of my heart and soul—but I didn't want to be another victim.

I wanted to live. To survive.

I wanted to be free.

But the only way that would ever happen was to let him think he was winning.

Do what he wanted…until it was time to get out for good.

Strike when he least expected it.

I coughed when he finally released me, my lungs burning like hot coals as I sucked in air.

"The police are going to think you killed her," he stated.

I shook my head, not understanding. "Why?"

"Because that's what I'm going to tell them."

A fresh wave of fear rippled through me. The fate he had planned for me was worse than death.

Because pinning the murder on me ensured I'd never be free.

He smirked as the realization hit me.

My stomach curdled when he leaned in, so close I could smell his coffee saturated breath. "Are you scared, son?"

I closed my eyes. Loathing that the ball was in his court and I had no way out.

I knew what he wanted to hear…so I told him. "Yes…sir."

He gripped my chin. "You should be."

Swallowing every ounce of pride, I choked out, "Please."

He raised a brow. "Please, *what?*"

A hot tear trickled down my cheek as a swell of disgust filled the empty spaces inside my chest, and I uttered the same words I silently begged God for each night before I closed my eyes.

"Please, help me."

Because God obviously wasn't listening…but maybe the devil would.

They say if he deemed you worthy enough, he'd strike a deal.

He rubbed his jaw with his free hand, not bothering to conceal his delight. "I supposed I could tell them an intruder entered the house, but he was wearing a ski mask during the assault so you couldn't see him." His grip on my chin tightened. "I could protect you, but every action has a consequence, son."

I nodded. "I know."

The corner of his lip curled up. "Since finding your mother dead upset you so much, you'll be spending some time in an asylum," he declared, as if he knew all along this was the hand he was going to deal me. "But don't worry. I'll visit you every weekend and make sure you're being a good boy." His cold, dark eyes bored into me. "Because the second you step out of line…the doctors are going to come to the conclusion that *you* murdered your mother and you'll be staring at those four walls for the rest of your life. Do you understand?"

I nodded again. "Yes, sir."

"Very well." He reached inside his suit jacket and pulled out a knife. "If you want me to come to your aid and for us to be a team. You'll have to prove your loyalty to me."

Needless to say, I was confused given I'd already agreed to his terms.

"How?"

He placed the knife in my hand, and it took everything I had not to stab him with it.

But he was stronger and knew how to fight off an attack.

And even if I managed to kill him, I was smart enough to know that once his friends in the FBI walked in and saw two dead parents, …they'd draw their own conclusions.

Plus, I had nowhere to go.

Nowhere to hide.

Just like he wanted.

His next words sent a chill blazing up my spine. "Cut out her heart."

No matter how much I wanted to, I couldn't refuse. This was my only out, and I had to take it.

I gripped the knife and turned toward my mother's corpse, forcing myself to detach and go numb. I convinced myself I was a doctor performing an autopsy as the knife sliced through her flesh, tendons, and muscles.

That it wasn't my mother…but a stranger I'd never met before.

That I wasn't doing this because I was an evil monster like my father…

I was doing it to survive.

He made me cut out her heart as a show of good faith, to prove that I joined the dark side in order to not suffer the same fate.

For the first time ever, pride illuminated his face when I held the organ up.

And then his expression darkened. "Now shove it in her mouth."

Vomit churned in my gut as I held her chin down and did what he asked.

I was positive I couldn't take anymore, but he wasn't finished quite yet.

"Cut off her finger."

A wave of dizziness washed over me and the knife slipped several times before I finally severed her pointer finger and dropped it into his gloved hand.

"Very good." A smile twisted my father's lips as he took the knife from me and placed it, along with the finger, into a zip-lock bag. "I'll make a man out of you yet, boy." He pointed to her body. "Now place your head on her stomach and sob. That's how I want the police to find you."

I did as he instructed, silently praying my mother would forgive me for my sins.

That she'd understand.

I recoiled when he reached into the pocket of my jeans and pulled out the yellow ribbon.

"It's mom's," I lied, hoping like hell he would believe me.

Because if he knew the truth, it would be one more thing he could use against me.

One more punishment he'd force me to endure.

Another thing he could take away from me.

My father didn't say a word as he stood and tucked the ribbon into the breast pocket of his suit.

I hated him. So much I could feel it immersing in my marrow.

The only thing that gave me any kind of solace was knowing that I'd eventually get revenge.

And one day...*I'd kill him.*

Chapter 45

Aspen

"*A*nyway," Knox states, his voice gruff. "After Shadow died, I knew something wasn't right. I thought maybe it was a warning from…someone." He runs a hand over his scalp and sighs. "But when I found the fingers buried in the backyard…I *knew* it was my father and he was preparing to set me up."

Oh, God.

I want to reach over, pull him to my chest, and console him—because what he's been through is so much worse than I could have ever conceived—but Knox shakes his head.

Respecting his request to not be touched right now, I sink against the seat.

Everything about him makes so much *sense* now. His standoffish behavior, the way he never lets anyone inside, the rumors going around school…even the way he has sex.

He needs the pain and to feel in control when he fucks.

Knox turns his head and gazes out the window, almost like he can't bear the thought of looking at me anymore because he's shown me his demons.

But I'm not judging him…because none of this was his fault.

He was just a boy.

"You're not a monster." Grabbing his chin, I force him to look at me because I need him to understand. "You didn't deserve what happened to you." He tries to turn away, but I don't let him. "What I feel for you hasn't changed."

It will *never* change.

"Then you're stupid," he mutters.

"I'm many things, but stupid isn't one of them."

I glance at the clock on the dashboard of his jeep. The bus leaves in twenty minutes, but the questions I have keep piling up with every second that passes.

I wonder why he never told anyone about the abuse? Although, now that I think about it, it's obvious. His father is a powerful FBI agent and instilled fear from the moment Knox took his first breath.

But still, you'd think someone would have noticed. A nurse, a teacher, a relative…

My mind flits back to what he said earlier.

"Before, you said you thought it was a warning from someone. Who?"

He brings a cigarette to his mouth. "You should go."

The way he's dismissing me churns my insides. It's clear he knows something important.

"Knox." My blood pressure rises because I *need* him to tell me. "Who did you think killed those girls?"

His expression turns hard and a stream of smoke wafts through the air. "Leo."

It takes everything in me not to laugh. Leo isn't a saint, but he's definitely not a murderer. The man wouldn't hurt a fly.

"Why in the world would you think it was Leo?"

His casts me a sad glance and that only makes this dreadful feeling forming in the pit of my stomach worse.

"Because he isn't who you think he is, Aspen." His jaw sets. "And he's killed before."

What? I clutch the duffle bag again, bracing myself.

"What do you mean he's killed before? Who?"

The groove in his forehead deepens and sorrow colors his face. The fact that he's looking at *me* with so much pity after what he just shared sends bile surging up my throat.

"Leo shot your father."

The words are like a bullet piercing my skin, puncturing my insides until I'm bleeding out.

But I don't want to believe it.

"No." I shake my head vehemently, unwilling to accept it. Leo was my dad's best friend and my dad loved him.

"You're *lying*." Blood rushes in my ears as I glare at him. I don't know why Knox thinks this, but he's wrong. "The man who shot my father confessed. Leo told me he didn't even try to deny it when the police tracked him down at his house." My hand flies to my chest. "Hell, the bastard said he deserved it when they dragged him out in cuffs."

The anger is back on Knox's face as he punches the steering wheel. "Leo *lied*, Aspen."

"What makes you—"

"Because I overhead Leo and my dad talking about how he shot him and my dad covered it up. My dad even found a suspect to pin it on. Some old guy who lived in a trailer park with a history of violence and schizophrenia." A muscle in his jaw bunches. "It didn't make sense to me because my uncle and your dad were friends. At first, I thought it was just about the money and Leo being greedy, but then it became clear there was another component."

"What *other* component?"

But he doesn't even need to tell me because something clicks painfully in my mind.

Me.

My breath stalls, and my eyes fill with moisture. I feel so sick. So gross and disgusting. Even though my dad's death isn't my fault, I can't help but feel like it is.

Knox wraps his fingers around my wrists, pulling me toward him as tears stream down my face and my lungs seize.

"Tell me you're lying," I beg, because the truth hurts so bad, I can't take it.

His fingers brush my wet cheek, wiping my tears. "I wish I was."

"How long have you known about this?"

"I overheard their conversation a few days after the funeral."

I mull this over in my mind, but it only makes me feel worse. Knox has been sitting on this for *years* and never once told me.

"Why didn't you tell me?"

Cupping my face, he scoffs. "You mean aside from the fact that you hated me and wouldn't have believed me even if I did?" His hand slides to the nape of my neck. "I couldn't trust you back then, Stray. For all I know you would have told Leo—the man you were not only sleeping with, but thought the world of—and he would have told my dad—"

"That's why Leo wanted me to stay away from you." Leo's words at the hotel that night play back in my mind. "He told me you weren't right in the head. That you were dangerous." I look down because I feel so stupid for believing him. "That you killed your mom."

But really, he was just scared that Knox would tell me *he* was the real psychopath.

Him and his brother.

Jesus. This whole thing is such a mess and I don't know how we can fix it or make them pay.

That's when another thought occurs to me.

Knox got *me* a bus ticket. Not himself.

Because there is no *we* anymore.

Heart hammering, I study him. "What are you going to do?"

His expression shuts down as he lights another cigarette. "Don't worry about it."

I balk because he can't be serious right now. He can't just dump this on my lap and tell me not to worry about it.

Not to worry about him.

"Knox—"

"I have a plan, okay? But if my plan doesn't work, at least the one I have for you will. That's all that fucking matters."

I have no idea what that ominous statement is supposed to mean, but it makes my chest cave in.

"Can you at least tell me what this plan of yours is? Maybe there's a hole in it. Maybe there's a better one we can figure out together. Maybe—"

He presses a finger to my lips, silencing me. "Your bus leaves in five minutes."

Before I can protest, he gets out of the jeep, walks around to my side, and opens the door.

Tears well in my eyes all over again. "I don't want to leave you."

His hand curls around my neck, drawing me into a kiss so intense

I feel it everywhere. I fist his shirt, not wanting to let go because I'm afraid of what will happen if I do.

My eyes flutter closed as he kisses a path to my ear and rasps, "I couldn't save her, but I *can* save you." Placing his hand on mine, he wretches the fabric from my grasp. "It's time for you to go, Stray."

Thinking quick, I undo the pearls around my neck.

It's the only thing in my possession that I actually value.

I can tell he wants to protest as I place them in his hand, but I shake my head. "You can give them back to me when we meet up in Canada, okay?"

Because we have to find each other again.

I don't know what to make of the dubious look he gives me. "Okay."

After giving me one last kiss, he pulls me out of the jeep and shoves the duffle bag into my hands.

"Make sure you throw your phone in the trash before you get on." He jerks his chin at the bus that's loading with people. "Now, *go.*"

Chapter 46

Knox

*R*elief flows through me as I watch Aspen turn around and head toward the bus.

After I'm sure she's on, I peel out of the parking lot. Time is ticking and if I don't get this shit over with now, it will be too late.

Thinking quick, I head down the highway, deciding to make a pit stop at the house to make sure everything is still copacetic.

Tying my stepmother up was the easy part.

Tying up my father—who always has his gun on him—was a lot harder.

However, there's one place he doesn't bring his gun.

The shower.

The look on his face when I opened the door and attacked him was like nothing I'd ever seen before.

Smiling to myself, I press my foot on the gas.

It's not over yet, though.

I've sat back—biding my time for *years*—while waiting for the perfect moment to strike.

But I had to be smart.

Sure, I could have just killed him and let them drag me out in cuffs, but I've spent enough time in a proverbial prison cell.

I needed to piece together the perfect plan that would give me the best chance to escape.

Fortunately, one formulated once my father married Aspen's mom.

He did it as a punishment.

Because no matter how much I insisted I hated Aspen, he knew the truth.

The girl with the yellow ribbon meant something to me.

Too bad for him his little *punishment* will end up being his downfall.

After parking down the street, I jog up to the house and run up the stairs to his bedroom.

Aspen's mother is still bound to the bed. She screams when she sees me, but it's muffled due to the duct tape I placed over her mouth.

Putting on a pair of black gloves, I walk over to her. "Don't worry. It will all be over soon."

Had she been a better mother to Aspen, I wouldn't have involved her, but alas, she's a fucking cunt.

I suppose I should be grateful for that though, because it enabled me to come up with the perfect murder.

I glance at my father, who's tied to a chair, looking more irate than I've ever seen him.

Or should I say…*murders*.

I amble over, double checking that he's still secured.

"I'm just waiting for one more guest to arrive before we get the party started."

My father's eyes widen, and a rush of satisfaction swells inside me.

The ball is finally in my court.

A sinking feeling pushes through my chest. *Not exactly*.

Because the knife—the one with my fingerprints on it—that I used to carve out my mother's heart is nowhere to be found.

And I wouldn't put it past the bastard to have left it with someone he trusts who will use it against me in the event of his untimely death.

But still…Aspen's on that bus.

So even if I don't make it out of this unscathed…I can take solace from knowing that she will.

Whistling, I head back down the stairs.

My aunt's nurse should be gone by now, and my uncle will be turning in for the night.

I find the spare key hidden in a plant outside.

Dumbass.

Everyone knows you shouldn't leave a spare key under your mat or in a nearby potted plant.

It makes it way too easy for people like me to break in.

After closing the door behind me, I creep by the kitchen and sneak past the living room where my aunt Lenora is watching television.

Surprise flashes in my aunt's gaze when she sees me.

The woman can't move, let alone speak, but I press my finger to my lips, anyway.

I'm not here to harm her…just her murdering, cheating, teenage-fucking piece of shit husband.

Aunt Lenora swivels her eyes in the direction of the hallway, indicating Leo's in his office.

I mouth a silent thank you as I make my way down the hall.

The way I see it, all three of them should pay, so I constructed a plan that will ensure they all do.

The police will find my stepmother naked in bed with my uncle Leo on top of her.

There will be a bullet in each of their heads.

From my father's gun.

My father's body will be found by the door of his bedroom, making it appear as though he interrupted his brother and wife while they were in the throes of passion.

I have no doubt he'll put up a fight about shooting himself with his own gun, but as he found out today when I yanked him out of the shower, tied him up, and dressed him in his work clothes again…I'm stronger than he is.

My lips twitch as I pull my father's gun out of my waistband and hold it out in front of me.

I can't wait to see the look of sheer terror on his face when he realizes I've got him by the balls and there's not a thing he can do about it.

However, everything I've arranged goes to shit the moment I open the door to Leo's office.

Because there's Aspen…holding a goddamn knife to his throat.

Chapter 47

Aspen

I can't do this.

I know Knox wants to keep me safe, but there's no way I can sit on this bus like a good little girl while he's off doing God knows what.

Rage erupts like a volcano in my gut.

Leo killed my father.

And then he looked me in the eye and told me he loved me and that he would always take care of me.

He killed my father.

Yet he had the nerve to console me and make me feel safe and protected.

To take my virginity while we were at his funeral.

All while knowing he was the one responsible for ripping the most important man in my life away from me.

The bus driver goes to close the door, but I quickly leap to my feet and rush to the front. "I need to get off."

"Sorry, miss. We can't wait any longer if we're going to arrive on time."

"Don't worry. I won't be getting back on."

With a shrug, he opens the door and I hop out.

The bus leaves and I try to gather my thoughts so I can formulate a plan for revenge.

Anger burns my throat and I dig my nails into my palms so hard I leave indents.

He *has* to pay.

On instinct, I reach around for my phone to pull up the Uber app, but remember I discarded it in a trashcan just like Knox told me to.

Making sure no one is looking, I walk over to the bin and pull it out.

I'm about to request an Uber, but think better of it.

The police will be able to track my whereabouts.

I suppose I could go inside the bus station and ask to use the phone so I can call a cab, but there are probably surveillance cameras everywhere.

Blowing out a shaky breath, I force myself to relax.

They'll only check the surveillance cameras if I give them a reason to.

I glance around, trying to figure out what to do next because I'm going to have to account for my whereabouts after I left prom.

There's a motel right next door. By the looks of it, it's definitely one of those pay by the hour and ask no questions type of establishments.

Perfect.

I can change out of my prom dress and call a cab company.

Hiking the duffle bag over my shoulder, I make my way over to the entrance of the hotel.

A thin man, who's missing most of his teeth, eyes me up and down like a prime piece of meat as I amble to the front desk.

"Hi. Are there any rooms available?"

"Sure are, pretty lady. Would you like one for the night, or just a few hours?"

That's a great question. "Uh. Can I rent one for a few hours, and then if I want to extend my stay, come back and do that?"

He winks. "Fine by me. And hey, if you're looking for some company, just say the word."

Ugh, I hate the way he's leering at me. Or rather, my tits.

"My boyfriend's right outside," I tell him because I don't want him getting any ideas. "Do you take cash?"

"Yup." His flirty demeanor fades. "Forty dollars for four hours. A hundred if you and your *boyfriend* want to spend the night."

I pull some money out of the duffle bag and slap it on the counter. "Here."

He hands me a key. "You'll have to pull around back."

"Thanks."

I trek around to the back of the building, but my next thought has my stomach knotting up.

If I use the phone inside my room, they can probably track that. And if I'm going to claim I spent time here after prom…why would I call a cab?

A woman wearing a short dress paired with fishnet stockings and smoking a cigarette a few doors down from mine snags my attention.

I don't want to assume she's a prostitute or anything, but I'm really hoping she has a phone.

"You lost, sugar?" the woman says, and I feel bad for staring at her.

"I'm sorry." I stride over to where she is. "You wouldn't happen to have a phone I could use, would you?"

She raises a penciled in eyebrow. "You know there's one in the room, right?"

"I know." I dig my teeth into my lip. "I…uh. Between you and me, I'm kind of running away from something. Or rather…someone."

I don't know what the woman sees in my expression, but I don't have to go into any more detail because she hands me her cell.

I quickly call a cab company and the man tells me they'll be here in five minutes.

"Thanks," I say, giving her back her phone.

She nods. "No problem."

I take a wad of money out of my duffle bag, but she halts me. "Are you sure you won't need that?"

Shaking my head, I place it in her palm.

I'm about to walk to my room so I can change…but pause.

"If someone inquires if a redhead wearing a yellow dress ever asked to borrow your phone—"

"Not to my recollection," she assures me with a smile.

"Thanks," I tell the driver as I step out of the cab.

I gave the driver an address that was a few houses down from Leo's, just in case a potential neighbor spotted a bright yellow taxi pulling up to his home.

After the driver is long gone, I trek up the pathway to the door wearing the black sweatpants and shirt Knox packed for me.

Leo once told me he keeps a spare key in a potted plant outside, and sure enough, it's still there.

Using the sleeve of my shirt, I wipe my fingerprints off the key and place it back.

A glance at my watch tells me the nurse left twenty minutes ago.

The house is quiet when I enter. The only light comes from the large flat screen television in the living room.

The living room where his wife is.

Her eyes turn into saucers when she sees me and my heart knocks against my ribcage.

She probably thinks I'm here to see her husband, and she would be right…but not for the reason she assumes.

I'm not here to fuck him. I'm here to *end* him.

Because he murdered my father.

And while I've never been one to believe in the whole *eye for an eye* thing…right now getting my vengeance is all I can focus on.

Being as quiet as I can, I walk over to her. I feel terrible that she can't move or speak, but the fact that she's unable to is a good thing right now.

Still, the woman deserves some kind of explanation.

Leaning over, I whisper, "Leo killed my dad."

Her eyes widen in surprise, and then just as quickly they fill with pity before they drop to my hands and linger there.

I'm confused as to why she keeps staring at my hands, until I realize she's probably looking for a weapon of some sort.

But I don't have one.

Thinking quick, I walk into the kitchen and grab a large knife from the butcher's block.

It's not perfect, but it will have to do.

Besides, they say a dull knife hurts worse than a sharp one…and Leo deserves every ounce of pain coming his way.

I walk past the living room again, this time holding the knife. If I had to guess where he was, I'd say he's in his office burning the midnight oil, but I'm not sure.

Pointing down the hall where his office is located, I look at Lenora.

'Blink twice for yes,' I mouth.

She does.

I'm not sure if she's playing me, but I take my chances and slink down the hallway.

My heart thunders in my chest the closer I get to the door.

Leo once mentioned that he had a gun at home, but said he kept it locked up in a safe.

Hopefully, I reach him before he has time to punch the security code in and grab it.

Taking a deep breath, I open the door to his office.

He swiftly spins around in the desk chair he's sitting in. "Aspen, what—" His gaze falls to the knife I'm pointing at him, and he pales. "What's wrong?"

What's wrong? Is he fucking serious?

"Stand up. *Now.*"

Holding his hands in front of him, he gets out of his chair. "Honey—"

"Don't you dare fucking *honey* me, you son-of-a-bitch." I bring the knife to his throat. "You killed my dad."

He shakes his head. "I don't know where you heard that rubbish, but it's not—"

Snarling, I bare my teeth. "Stop lying, asshole. He was your best friend, and you *murdered* him." I hate the way my voice cracks as I continue, "And then you fucked his daughter and made her believe you actually cared about her."

"I *do* care about—"

I dig the knife deeper and he winces.

"No, you don't. Because a man who cares about me would never—"

The sound of the door opening catches us both off guard.

Leo's mouth drops open in shock and it takes everything in me not to turn around, but I know if I do, he'll have the upper hand.

Nerves coil my stomach because I have no idea who's behind me.

The click of a gun cocking makes me want to shit a brick.

"Stray." Knox's voice wraps around me like a warm blanket during a snowstorm. "Put the goddamn knife down."

No way in hell.

"No." I peer up at Leo's terrified face. "He has to pay for what he did."

And I don't care what it costs me.

Because he took away the only person who ever loved me.

"Aspen," Leo breathes, like he's pleading with me to hear him out. "Your father was stealing money from innocent people. He had to be st—"

"He *will* pay," Knox grinds out behind me. "I have a plan, but in order for everyone to get their karma, you're gonna have to trust me and put the knife down."

I do trust him, but I still want to hear what he has up his sleeve before I agree. "What's your plan?"

Knox comes around so I can see him in my peripheral vision. The hood from the black hoodie he was wearing earlier is now pulled up, casting a shadow over his face as he aims the gun at Leo.

"I need to tie Leo up and bring him back to the house."

That makes no sense. "Why?"

"So the police can find him in bed with your mother."

Instinctively, I look at him. "I'm sorry...*what?*"

"Don't you even think about it, cocksucker," Knox snarls, and the lethal tone of his voice has my skin breaking out in goosebumps. "Touch her and I *will* blow your fucking brains out all over this office."

Leo swiftly raises his hands in surrender.

"Why would you want the police to find him in bed with my mom—" I stop talking when I realize.

He's setting it up to make it look like a double homicide *and* a suicide.

By making it look like Leo's screwing my mom behind her husband's back.

Jesus. I have to hand it to him...that is...brilliant.

There's only one problem. Actually, make that two problems.

"That means my mom has to die."

Knox's jaw bunches. "It's the only way it works. I can't take the chance that she'll talk."

While I don't think my mom deserves to die for being a heartless bitch who was more concerned with money and appearances than she was with her own child, Knox has a point.

It's the only way this goes off without a hitch.

"What about Leo?"

His brows pinch. "Leo will be dead, too, Stray. That's the fucking point."

It's all I can do not to roll my eyes. "I know." A renewed spark of anger heats my blood. "But I want to be the one to shoot him."

A sardonic smirk curves Knox's lips as he looks at Leo. "Anything for my girl." Briefly, he flicks his gaze to me. "Do you know how to use a gun?"

I nod. My dad kept one in the house and wanted me to learn how to use it for safety reasons.

"Good." He takes a step in my direction. "Now switch places with me so I can restrain him."

After we do, I point the gun at Leo's head. Adrenaline courses through my limbs as Knox ties him up and it takes every ounce of willpower not to shoot him right this second.

Knox stands behind a bound and gagged Leo and kicks him. "Let's go, asshole."

"Wait," I say as we haul him out of his office. "What about his car?"

It's going to need to be in our driveway.

Knox holds up a pair of keys. "We're driving it there. But I'm parking it down the block from our house so it looks like he was trying to cover his ass."

"Okay, but where's your jeep?"

"In the parking lot of a fast food place up the road."

That's good, but I have a better idea for it.

"Give me your keys."

He quirks an eyebrow. "Why?"

"I rented a motel room." Knox opens his mouth to yell at me, but I continue, "I told the guy at the front desk that my boyfriend was in the car, so we might as well park your car there and then take Leo back to the house."

He mulls this over. "How will we get back to the motel to pick up my car?"

He's right. One cab ride tonight is dodgy enough, but two?

I could call Brie, but there's no doubt in my mind that she'll have *lots* of questions about why she's dropping Knox and I off at a motel in the middle of the night.

And while I can trust her, she's too sweet and honest. She might crack once the news of the murder-suicide breaks, and God forbid they bring her in for questioning.

Violet, on the other hand…she'd be the person to ask for a ride.

She's quiet, keeps to herself, and won't say shit to the police no matter how hard they press her.

"I can ask Violet."

Knox makes a face. "Stray—"

"Violet's been my alibi every time I had a shift at the Bashful Beaver. She'll cover for me."

Leo's eyes enlarge at that, but I flip him the bird.

"No. We'll go back to the motel on foot." Reaching a gloved hand into the pocket of his black jeans, he pulls out his keys and tosses them to me, along with a pair of black gloves. "Put those on."

He pushes Leo, who's squirming to get free. "Start walking, dipshit."

Knox's steps slow when we reach the living room and he looks at his aunt.

For a moment, I'm afraid he's going to take her hostage too because of everything she's witnessed, but he ambles over and kisses her forehead. "Don't mind me, Aunt Lenora." A sly grin pulls at the corner of his mouth. "I'm just taking out the trash."

Chapter 48

Knox

*S*he was supposed to be on a goddamned bus heading to New York, not an accessory to the murders I'm about to commit.

Correction—murders *we're* about to commit.

Aspen's green eyes go big as she takes in the scene I've set up in our parents' bedroom.

For a moment, I think she's going to bail, but then she looks at me and utters, "What do we do now?"

I shove Leo until he falls on the bed.

"We need to undress them before we position them." I jerk my chin, gesturing to her mother who is still secured to the headboard via a pair of soft handcuffs. "You take her. I'll take him."

Aspen's mom starts sobbing—her muffled screams growing louder against the duct tape placed over her mouth—as her daughter unlocks one of her cuffs and removes her nightgown.

Despite her dramatics, Aspen continues, but I can tell she hasn't quite compartmentalized it the way I have, because she can't bear to look at her mom while she does it.

Perhaps I should feel bad she's a casualty in all this. But the woman only brought this shit on herself.

Not only did she not give a fuck about her own child, her lack of care and greed enabled my father to use her daughter as a pawn to punish me.

Gritting my teeth, I get to work removing Leo's clothes. Like Aspen's mother, his arms are secured behind him with a pair of soft handcuffs so as not to leave marks, but I had to fasten his legs, too, making the task that much more difficult because I have to do it one step at a time.

After it's done, I place the articles of clothing haphazardly around the floor.

Leo squirms as I spread my stepmother's thighs and position him on top of her. Whatever he's saying is inaudible thanks to the gag I placed in his mouth.

Grabbing my father's gun, I step back. I'm one-inch taller than he is, so I have to adjust the position of the gun ever-so-slightly. "We'll have to shoot them close together." I glare at my father, who's still bound to the chair. "We'll have a little more leeway with him, but not much."

Leo's still trying to speak, but I don't give a fuck.

Aspen, however, does, "What do you think he's trying to say?"

Grinding my molars, I aim the gun at his head. "Who the fuck cares."

"He's not screaming," Aspen notes, walking over to him.

I'm about to remind her that he will if she removes the handkerchief from his mouth, but she does it anyway.

"Please, don't kill me," Leo begs and it's all I can do not to laugh.

"Put the gag back in his mouth—"

"No," he pleads.

I'm about to shoot the motherfucker, but then he says, "I know where the knife is."

I freeze as I take in his statement.

Aspen looks at me, but I'm too busy looking at my father.

It's quick, but I notice his hand clench as his eyes briefly narrow on his brother.

"Where?"

Leo clears his throat, his gaze flicking to my father for a split second before he says, "In a safety-deposit box—"

I stop him right there.

"Look at me." When he does, I grind out, "You only have one shot at this." I jerk my chin at Aspen. "There are two of us, which means we can check if you're lying or not. Therefore, I suggest you choose your next words carefully, because you don't want to fuck this up."

He looks like a mouse stuck in a trap, because he knows the next words out of his mouth are the difference between life and death.

"It's buried in your backyard. To the left of the shed."

I look at Aspen. "There's a flashlight under the sink in the kitchen and a shovel in the shed. Try to be quick, Stray. We're losing time."

Nodding, she runs out of the room.

I glare at Leo. "You better not be lying."

Aspen returns after what feels like a goddamn eternity.

"He's right," she says, out of breath as she barrels into the room. "The knife is there." She makes a face. "Along with the skeleton of a finger."

A weird sense of relief combined with sorrow tangle in my chest.

The power he's wielded over my head like a guillotine all these years is gone.

But the fact he made me do those gruesome things to my own mother is something I won't ever forget.

Or forgive myself for.

A raging inferno erupts inside me, rushing to the surface and making my insides burn.

"Put the gag back in his mouth."

Leo squirms. "You promised—"

"I didn't promise shit, motherfucker," I sneer as Aspen stuffs the handkerchief between his lips.

Aiming the gun at my stepmother, I glance at Aspen. "You ready?"

The color drains from her face as she turns ashen. "I don't want her to suffer, okay? Just make it quick and painless and—"

I pull the trigger.

Aspen jumps as her mother's body goes limp and blood pours out of her skull. "Jesus, Knox."

I shrug. "You said quick and painless." Walking over to where she is, I hand her the gun. "Your turn."

She swallows hard as an array of emotions color her face.

I'm not surprised. Saying you want to kill someone is one thing.

Having the balls to make good on your word and going through with it is a whole different ball game.

Given she's almost a foot shorter than my father, I motion for her to stand on top of the crate I brought in.

When she does, I move behind her and adjust her aim.

"I can do it if you want."

"No." She tenses, and I can practically feel the contempt for the man who killed her father coursing through her body, despite the helpless way Leo's looking at her. "I want to."

Glaring at my uncle, I place my hand on her abdomen and kiss the crook of her neck. "Whenever you're ready, Stray."

I dip my fingers beneath the waistband of her sweatpants, because I want my hands on her body to be the last fucking thing he sees.

Aspen trembles and for a moment I think I'm going to have to take over…but then she pulls the trigger, and he slumps against her mother's corpse.

"Holy shit." She sucks in a sharp breath. "I did it."

Yeah, she fucking did.

Prying the gun from her hand, I kiss her neck again. "Hard part is over, Stray."

Only it's not…

Because there's still one more person to kill.

I'm practically choking on the cloud of wrath smothering me as I approach him.

Realizing he's next, he thrashes against the chair, putting up a formidable fight as I uncuff his right hand.

But I'm stronger, not just because of my strength-training, but all the hatred I've built up inside me over the years.

Fury claws its way through my chest, robbing me of air and sending me spiraling as I realize.

All the torture he's inflicted.

All the pain he's caused.

.   .   .

He's going to die without experiencing any of it.

Chapter 49

Aspen

I watch Knox pace back and forth, his expression stormy and uncertain—like he's waging a war against himself.

"Knox," I call out, trying to claim his attention.

Finally, he stops moving and looks at me.

Only he's not really looking at *me* because he appears unfocused and his eyes are glazed over, as though he's trapped some place inside himself.

A place I can't reach.

"Call the police," he instructs, his voice vacant. *Distant.* "Tell them I hurt you and held you hostage while I killed your mom and Leo."

My heart beats faster as the walls of the room begin closing in.

We're already two murders down. This isn't the time to be changing tactics.

This isn't the time for him to fall apart.

Because his plan is the only chance we have of making it out of this together, and I will not abandon him.

"Knox—"

"I need to torture him," he rasps, the anguish in his voice imploring me to understand. "I need to slowly drain the life out of him bit by bit and make him suffer…just like he did to her."

My heart sinks as I realize I'm losing him.

However, it's the sick, smug look of satisfaction in his father's eyes as he watches his son fall apart at the seams that shreds my insides.

He might be the one tied up while his son wields a gun...but it's evident he's the one in control right now.

"Knox," I remind him, trying to break through his fog. "We need to stick to the plan."

"No." His features twist as the inner turmoil he's undergoing illuminates his face. "He doesn't get to go peacefully." His tone darkens. "He doesn't get to escape his punishment."

"You're right." A sense of doom wraps around my lungs and pulls tight, but I have to try to get through to him. "Because right now he's winning."

That only makes Knox angrier.

Fear trickles through my blood like poison. I don't know how to pull someone back from the pits of hell, but I have to try.

"Look at his face," I tell Knox. "He *wants* you to fuck this up and you're playing right into his hand."

My voice cracks as a tear makes its way down my cheek, he's so far gone he won't even spare a glance my way.

I've lost him.

I try a different tactic. "A neighbor could have heard the shots. The police could be on their way here right now. We're running out of time."

Nothing.

Another tear falls as my heart folds in on itself. "I'm not going to tell them it was you...I'm going to tell them it was *me.*"

He angles his head ever so slightly, enough to let me know I might actually be getting through to him after all.

"Because I choose *you.*"

And maybe that makes me crazy, but I don't care.

His features contort as he breaks out of his haze. "Stray—"

"You wanted to protect me before, right? That's why you tried to send me away on that bus. Well, this is me doing the same for you—"

Out of the corner of my eye, I see his father take the gag out of his mouth with his free hand before he goes to unfasten the ties around his legs. "Knox—"

It all happens so fast, I barely have time to blink.

Knox lurches toward him. His father struggles as Knox pries his hand open and places the gun into it before forcing the tip into his mouth. However, he's no match for his son's strength…

Or his hatred.

"For every action there is a consequence," Knox sneers, his voice filled with venom as he presses down on his father's finger.

My ears ring for the third time that night as blood and bits of brain matter spray everywhere.

Knox's bloody face splits into a chilling grin as he takes a step back, taking in his father's corpse.

It might not have been what he wanted, and it sure as hell wasn't what the bastard deserved

But in the end…

He chose me, too.

Chapter 50

Knox

*T*he walk back to the motel took just over an hour, which means we have less than twenty-minutes until our four hours are up.

Aspen suggested we extend it, but I told her it wasn't a good idea and we needed to be the ones to find our parents and call the police, because the other way around wouldn't look good for us.

Grabbing her wrist, I make a beeline for the bathroom. We already wiped our faces and changed at the house in case someone spotted us on our way here, but we're both in desperate need of a shower.

"What are you going to do with all the evidence?" Aspen asks as I pull her t-shirt over her head.

I buried everything in the woods on our hike over, but it can't stay there forever.

I yank the dingy curtain back and turn the shower on. "I'll go back and burn our clothes once the coast is clear."

There's a fifty-fifty chance of that coming to fruition.

It will all boil down to how well Aspen can hold up while being questioned by the police—because they *will* question us.

I can play the part of the devastated son who just lost his *hero* FBI father over some unfaithful, gold-digging slut he married, but I'm not so sure Aspen can play the inconsolable, confused teen whose mom got a bullet in her head because she cheated on her new husband with her dad's old best friend.

It's also incredibly important we keep our stories straight, because one minor slip up will fuck us.

Which is why I'm prepared to take the fall if things go south.

She's not going down for this.

I peel her pants and underwear down her legs next. Splotches of blood that seeped through her old clothes mar her otherwise flawless flesh.

The sight probably shouldn't turn me on so much, but I'm a sick fuck.

Unfortunately, I won't get to indulge in my blood-stained reverie because she needs to wash up.

"Get in the shower."

She looks down at the blood streaking her skin, almost like she still can't believe the events that took place tonight. "Okay."

After stripping off my clothes, I join her.

She's quiet as I take the bar of soap and run it over her body. I'd use a washcloth, but it's white—make that more yellow—and I don't want to take any chances.

I wrap my arms around her waist as the water from the shower nozzle sprays over us and the blood from our bodies flows down the drain.

Flashes of my father's corpse zip through my mind.

I wanted to torture him.

To make him feel every single ounce of fucking pain he inflicted on my mother.

On me.

And so help me fucking God I would have... My cock swells, pulsing against her curvy ass. After bending her forward, I spread her little cunt and sink my dick inside her.

But I only allow myself one thrust. Just enough to collect her wetness on my shaft and drive us both crazy.

Then I shut the shower off and yank open the curtain.

"What—"

I drag my teeth along her neck, sucking and biting the tender skin above her pulse point. "Get on your knees."

She robbed me of the release I desperately needed back at the house, so she owes me this.

Aspen obeys, kneeling down on the filthy floor in front of me.

Whether it's because she wants this too, or she realizes this might be our last night together, I'm not sure.

And right now, I don't fucking care.

I fist her wet hair, wrapping it around my wrist so tightly she winces. "Open."

When her lips part, I shove my cock between them.

"You like the taste of that?"

She chokes and gags as I hit the back of her throat, her makeup-smudged eyes welling with tears as my balls slap her neck. The sight alone nearly makes me bust a nut all over her pretty face.

I thrust harder, so hard I know I'm pushing her past her breaking point. But she relaxes her throat and takes my cock like the good girl she is.

So fucking perfect.

I pull out and she tries to take me in her mouth again, but I yank her hair.

"Kiss it."

Pouting her lips, she gently presses them to my tip. I groan when she edges back slightly, causing a string of my pre-cum to appear between us.

Tugging her back to her feet, I bend her over the sink and spread her cheeks, exposing all of her.

She moans as I lick and suck her pussy, her breaths coming out in short, quick pants.

Her pussy clenches in that vise-grip way it does before she comes, so I change directions, teasing her little puckered hole with my tongue instead.

Tilting her head over her shoulder, she looks down the length of her body at me, a red flush breaking out over her skin.

I hold her gaze as I continue tonguing her, and that only makes her blush deepen.

She hisses when I replace my tongue with my finger, stopping when I reach my knuckle.

"Knox." She utters my name like a warning and a plea.

Standing up, I work my cock inside her pussy while I finger her tight little asshole. "How does it feel?"

"Full." Her teeth saw along her lip as she closes her eyes. "I can feel you *everywhere*."

Good.

Pumping my finger, I thrust deeper.

The walls of her pretty cunt squeeze around me, milking my dick as I give it to her harder.

But it's not enough.

I need the control that comes from holding her life in the palm of my hand.

I need to feel her fear.

Removing my finger from her ass, I wrap my hand around her throat.

Her pussy pulses, her cum dripping down my balls as she orgasms.

I constrict my grip, fucking her so hard she's going to feel the ache between her legs for days.

I glance in the mirror. Her green eyes are filled with panic as I deplete the air from her lungs, like she's afraid I might not let go in time.

White-hot pleasure sizzles up my dick and I come so fucking hard my head spins.

I let go of her throat, sagging against her.

"I'd never kill you," I rasp as she trembles beneath me.

Fuck knows I've thought about it plenty of times, but I could never go through with it.

Aspen's in my system. Pumping through my veins like sweet poison and surrounding the empty spaces of my cold, black heart.

She's in my head—like a whisper in the dark I can't ignore.

She's in my soul—like a siren I can't run away from.

She's the feeling in my chest I've never experienced before, but would kill to hold on to forever.

She's the home I never had.

Chapter 51

Aspen

"*C*an we get you anything to drink?" Detective Phillips—or is it Detective Avery?—asks.

I shake my head. "No, thank you."

They've already grilled me relentlessly about my whereabouts after they showed up at the house three days ago, but apparently, they aren't quite through with me just yet.

"I know this isn't easy for you, Aspen, but we have a few more questions for you."

"Okay."

"What was your relationship like with your mother?"

I force myself to remain calm. "Well, Detective Phillips—"

"Avery," he corrects.

Fuck.

"Sorry."

He takes a sip of his coffee. "Please continue."

"We had our fights like every teenage daughter and mother do." I look down at the table as I process Detective Avery's question. Knox told me to stay as close to the truth as possible, but it's a lot harder than I thought. "We weren't close. But the older I get, the more I realize we're a lot more alike than I thought."

Detective Phillips leans in. "How so?"

"Well, I pride myself on getting good grades and doing well in school. And my mother…she was—" I close my eyes. "I'm sorry. Talking about her in the past tense like this… it just…hurts."

Actually, it doesn't because she's always been a past-tense presence in my life.

Detective Avery gives me a sympathetic smile. "Understandable. But please, go on."

"My mother was a people pleaser. She always cared what others thought about her, always wanted to impress everyone." I shrug. "I guess I inherited a little of that from her."

They both exchange a glance.

Detective Phillips clears his throat. "Did you know your mother was having an affair?"

I shake my head. "No. Although, my uncle Leo—" I pause for dramatic effect as my stomach knots with anger. "I'm sorry. Leo was my dad's best friend, and I've known him since I was a child. I've always referred to him as my uncle."

They nod.

Phillips taps his pen against his notepad, growing impatient. "As you were saying?"

"After my dad died, Leo and my mother grew closer. I thought nothing of it. Especially since she married his brother."

"How was your relationship with your stepfather?" Detective Avery cuts in.

"Complicated," I settle on because Knox told me to stay as close to the truth as possible.

Avery raises a brow. "How so?"

"Well," I begin, looking them in the eyes. "She married Trent shortly after my father died. I guess you could say there was a little resentment on my part." Swallowing, I look down at the table again. "As far as Trent goes, he was a little…cold. I figured it was because he was a cop." I quickly glance up, as though I accidentally misspoke. "No offense."

Avery's lips twitch a little as he and his partner exchange an amused look. "None taken."

I take a breath, hating the next words out of my mouth. "But he was protective, and he was a provider. He offered numerous times to get me a car, but I declined."

Phillips stops writing. "Why?"

I give them complete honesty. "I didn't want him buying me… like my mother."

Avery's lips form a thin line as he takes this in. "Can you expand on that?"

A frustrated sigh leaves me. "It feels wrong speaking badly about her when she's gone." A tear falls down my cheek. "She didn't always do the right thing…but she was still my mom, you know?"

Phillips' eyes fill with sympathy. "I know this is very difficult for you, but we need you to tell us everything you know."

I brush my damp cheeks with the sleeve of my shirt. "We were broke right after my dad died. Leo gave us money here and there to help, but it wasn't enough." Because she didn't use it to pay the bills like she should have. "But then she started seeing Trent." My shoulders slump. "She once confessed that she married him so we could have a better life."

They exchange another glance. "I see."

Detective Avery scribbles something on his notepad. "You said you were at the senior prom the night of the murders. Is that correct?"

It takes everything in me not to scream. For fuck's sake, I was still in my prom dress when they showed up.

"Yes."

Avery brings the end of his pen to his mouth. "Did you stay until the end?"

Oh, boy. Here we go.

I feign embarrassment, like I'm hiding a secret. Knox told me this was the best approach to take because it would make me seem more honest.

Besides, they already know the truth.

"No…I wasn't."

Phillips leans back in his seat, his gaze scrutinizing. "Why is that?"

"Because I left with my stepbrother, Knox."

Avery brings his coffee cup to his lips. "There are reports of you two dancing and sharing a kiss on the dance floor before you left. Is this true?"

"Yes."

"What happened right after you left the prom?"

I lick my dry lips. "We went into the backseat of his jeep."

Phillips's expression grows curious. "Why?"

"So, we could hook up."

"Is that what happened?" Avery questions.

"Yes." I avert my gaze. "Kind of."

"Can you explain what you mean by that?"

"We started fooling around…"

"Fooling around how?"

My cheeks heat. "Seriously? What, do you need specifics?"

"Yes," Phillips deadpans.

"His hand was under my dress and he was…fingering me."

Safe to say I have their undivided attention.

"And then what happened?"

"Knox wanted me to give him head before we had sex, but I complained that there wasn't enough room and someone might spot us."

"How long have you and your stepbrother been *hooking up*?" Phillips questions, and I don't miss the judgment in his tone.

"A few weeks."

Avery rests his elbows on the desk between us. "When did it start?"

"The first time was last month. We were fighting—like we always did—but then it kind of just…happened." I curl my arms around myself. "And then it just *kept* happening."

"Back to prom night," Avery says. "You stated you were afraid someone would spot you while you were in the backseat of his jeep. What happened after that?"

"He suggested we go home and wait until our parents went to bed so we could screw in his bedroom like we always did but I…" I let my sentence trail off.

"You what?"

"I don't know…I wanted more. I wanted him to take me some-place a little more…special." Ashamed, I cover my face with my hands. "So, he took me to a motel."

"The Magic Motel," Phillips says, and it's clear he's trying to hide his amusement.

"That's the one."

Detective Avery, however, keeps a straight face. "What happened while you were there?"

"We had sex a few times—oral and intercourse—and then we took a shower together before we left."

They nod.

Phillips clears his throat before he speaks. "Were you afraid your parents might find out you were having sex with your stepbrother?"

At that, I snort. "Not just my parents."

"Can you clarify what you mean?"

"Knox is…not my type and not someone I can see myself being with long term. We're complete opposites. But as far as our parents finding out about us…they probably wouldn't have been thrilled with the idea, but it's not like we were planning on walking down the aisle or anything." I shrug, forcing the words out of my mouth effortlessly. "It's just a fling."

"So you didn't fear any repercussions from your parents?"

I shake my head. "Not really. They would have been annoyed, but like I said—it isn't serious between us, so they wouldn't have been mad for long."

Detective Avery caps his pen and places it on the desk. "All right, I think we've covered everything for now. We'll contact you if we need any more information."

Chapter 52

Knox

"What was your relationship like with your father?" Detective Phillips questions.

Anger warms my blood, but I know I have to spew the shit they want to hear.

Because once it gets out that a cop slaughtered his family... people start looking at *them* in a whole new light.

And they fucking hate that.

My best course of action is to be an ally.

"We weren't that close when I was younger because he was always working, but after my mom died, our relationship improved."

Detective Avery picks up his pen. "Did you ever get into any fights?"

Understatement of the fucking century.

I shrug, forcing myself to appear nonchalant. "Sometimes. My dad could be a hardass about my grades and doing chores. And there was one time he reamed my ass out for stealing his car in the middle of the night to meet up with some chick, but nothing crazy."

Phillips takes a sip of his coffee. "What did you think about your stepmother?"

This time, I let my anger break through. "Well, *now* I think she's a cheating, worthless whore."

Avery's eyebrows shoot up. "What did you think of her *before?*"

"Not much." I lean back in my seat. "I always knew there would come a time when my dad would remarry. As long as she made my dad happy and didn't try to take the place of my mom, that's all that really mattered to me."

Detective Avery gives me a sympathetic smile. "I take it you two weren't close."

"We got along just fine, but no. Eileen wasn't someone I confided in or sought to build a relationship with. I respected her as my dad's wife, but that's about it."

"So you had no knowledge of her and your uncle having an affair?"

"Nope." I pause, pretending to think. "Although, now that I think about it, there were signs."

Avery leans forward in his chair. "What signs?"

"Well, my uncle's wife—my aunt Lenora—has ALS. She's declined so much over the years she can no longer move or speak… let alone have sex." I take a breath and continue. "Evidently, Eileen was the wife of his old best friend, and after he was found dead in his car, my uncle asked my dad for help to solve the case. That's how Eileen and my dad met. However, there were a few times where I caught them looking at each other for a little too long. I didn't think much of it, though. Clearly I was wrong."

They both exchange a glance.

"What about your stepsister, Aspen?"

And there it is.

"What about her?"

Phillip's clears his throat. "She claims you two have a relationship. Is this true?"

I snort. "If by *relationship*, you mean we fuck occasionally, then yeah."

Avery rubs his chin. "Multiple witnesses said you showed up at the prom. According to them—you danced, shared a kiss…and then left together."

I nod. "All that's true."

He steeples his fingers. "She claims it's just a fling. Nothing serious."

"She's right."

"Forgive me," Avery says. "I'm having trouble understanding why you would dance and kiss your stepsister at a prom if your clandestine relationship wasn't *serious*."

I see where they're going with this.

"We used to hate each other." I laugh under my breath. "Hell, we still do. But we also have chemistry…chemistry that leads to great sex." I steeple my fingers, mimicking him. "For me, that's all it is. Because to be frank—the girl has a mouth like a Hoover and her pussy is every bit as up*tight* as she is, but for her…" Shrugging, I let out a sigh. "You know how girls are. They get clingy."

They exchange a humorous glance.

Phillips's expression evens out and his tone becomes serious. "Was Aspen getting *clingy*?"

"She wasn't boiling rabbits or anything, but she was definitely having a tough time separating sex from being a couple." I run a hand down my jaw. "To her credit, she tried to play it cool, like she wasn't getting attached. However, before she left to go to prom, she told me not to wait up because she was meeting up with some guy after."

"How did that make you feel?"

I laugh. "I mean, her attempt at making me jealous obviously worked. I showed up, didn't I?"

Philips nods. "So, what happened after you left the prom together?"

"We went into the backseat of my jeep."

"Can you go into more detail, please?"

"Sure." I smirk. "I finger banged her for a bit, and then I asked her to suck me off." I feign annoyance. "She complained that there wasn't enough room in the backseat and that someone might catch us. I suggested we go home so we could screw in my bedroom like we always did, but she bitched that she wanted me to take her somewhere special."

Phillips looks down at his notepad and I can't help but notice his lips twitch slightly. "You took her to The Magic Motel. Is that correct?"

I smirk, sharing his amusement. "It's not the classiest place, but I don't have a lot of money and it's cheap."

"Did you pay for the entire night?"

I shake my head. "No. I paid forty bucks for four hours. It would have been a hundred to stay the whole night."

Avery leans back in his seat, his gaze scrutinizing. "Just so we're clear. You were the one who checked in?"

"No, I was the one who *paid* for the room. I handed Aspen the money to secure the room while I stayed in my jeep."

He raises a brow. "Why?"

I cut my gaze to his. "Because I didn't feel like walking with an erection."

That answer seems to appease him.

Avery brings his coffee cup to his lips. "So, after you checked in. What happened?"

"I went down on her and she returned the favor. Then we fucked. Twice in the bed and once in the shower before we left."

Phillips makes a noise in his throat before he speaks. "Were you afraid your parents might find out you were having sex?"

I think about this for a minute before I answer. "Not really. Eileen probably would have gotten her panties in a bunch over it, because she was all about appearances. But my dad wouldn't have cared that much because it's not like we were raised as siblings. The only thing that would piss him off would be if I knocked her up, but she's on birth control, so there's no chance of that happening." I peer at the clock on the wall. "Not to be a dick, but I have an appointment at three. If you need me to stay longer, I'll have to give them a call and let them know I'll be late."

"That won't be necessary." After exchanging one last glance with his partner, Detective Avery puts down his pen. "I think we've covered everything for now. We'll contact you if we need any more information."

I get up from my seat and walk over to the door, but stop before opening it.

The next words out of my mouth are the equivalent of swallowing glass, but I don't have a choice.

"My dad was sad for a long time after my mom died. We both were. When he remarried, he finally started smiling again. I'm not saying that what he did was right...but I know he loved her." I close my eyes. "But people won't care about any of that when they read the paper. The only thing they'll care about is that he shot his wife and brother for having an affair. They won't give a fuck that he was a hero who spent his life protecting others."

They won't care that he was a lying, abusive piece of murdering shit.

They won't care…because no one will ever know the truth.

Because every action has a consequence…

And silence is still mine.

Chapter 53

Aspen

I bring the wine glass to my lips and take a sip.

I always swore I'd never drink—especially *merlot,* my mother's favorite—but here we freaking are.

To say my nerves are shot would be an understatement. The detectives asked Knox to come in for questioning after they were done with me this afternoon, but that was *hours* ago.

My heart sinks when I look at the clock on the stove. It's just after nine p.m.

It's not like I can barge into the police station and demand to know what's going on with my stepbrother, because I had to pretend our relationship isn't serious.

Nerves bunch in my stomach and my skin breaks out in a cold sweat.

What if they don't believe us?

What if one of us accidentally slipped up without even realizing it?

What if they think we killed our parents so we could be together without their judgment and disapproval?

My stomach churns and it feels harder to breathe.

What if Knox took the fall, and they locked him up?

Maybe I should hire a lawyer.

The thought has me laughing, because the only lawyer I know is —was—Leo.

But he's dead.

Because I shot him.

I take another sip of wine. *The bastard deserved it.*

I grip the edges of the island so hard my knuckles turn white.

Where is he?

My anxiety rapidly turns to fear and I'm about to lose my shit and implode when I hear the front door open.

I freeze—my mind flashing with images of men from the swat team raiding the house before they drag me out in cuffs.

"Stray."

My head snaps up at the sound of his deep voice.

Relief courses through me so rapidly, I grow lightheaded. "You're here."

Knox's eyes flick to the half-empty wine glass and he frowns. "You're drinking."

"I'm nervous." My voice drops to a whisper, "You've been gone so long, I thought they locked you up."

A weary sigh leaves him. "It actually went better than I thought it would." His strides eat up the distance between us. "Everything is fine. We're not suspects, and even if we were, they have nothing on us." He tips my chin. "And they never will...unless one of us confesses."

He's right.

Logically, I know this...but still.

I can feel him studying me like I'm a specimen under a microscope. "When was the last time you ate?"

I shrug because I'm honestly not sure, the last few days have all blurred together.

He walks over to the fridge. "I'll make you a sand—"

"No." Gripping my wine glass, I stand on shaky legs. "I'm not hungry."

Making a low growly noise in his throat, he stalks back over to me and takes the glass out of my hand. "Cut this shit out. You're not your mother."

That's where he's wrong.

Because just like her, I'm going to spend the rest of my life pretending to be something I'm not.

But that's not what scares me.

What scares me is not knowing what the future holds.

I've always had my life planned out. Even after my dad died and it lit my world up in flames, I still had my goals and worked toward them.

I still always knew who I was—despite what I picked and chose to show others.

But now…everything's different.

And all I can focus on—all I can think about—is *him*.

Because the thought of losing him is something I know I won't survive.

His irate face hovers inches above mine. His lips are slightly parted, his stubborn, chiseled jaw is tense, and his eyes—eyes that used to terrify me—are looking at me like I'm the only thing on earth that's significant to him.

"Knox—"

He captures my lips, stealing my breath and sending everything spiraling.

"Is this what you want?"

"No." I pull back and look at him, his eyes—one green and one blue—are hooded, and lust has shadowed all his anger.

I reach for his belt buckle and undo it. "I *need* it."

I need him.

A yelp of surprise leaves me when he lifts me into his arms, swings open the basement door, and proceeds to carry me down the stairs.

He drops me on the bed and kneels in front of me, his rough hands immediately going to the zipper on my jeans. I raise my hips as he tugs them off. My shirt, bra, and panties follow shortly after.

I reach for the hem of his shirt and bring it over his head.

I need to feel his skin on mine.

I need to feel him inside me…owning me, claiming me, fucking me.

Making everything make sense again.

I open my mouth to tell him so, but his lips brush mine and he kisses me again, siphoning all the oxygen out of the room.

My pulse skyrockets when he trails his fingers down my throat, stopping at my breast and teasing my nipple. He plumps it in his hand before bringing his hot, wet mouth down. Giving it greedy, urgent sucks.

"Spread your legs." His hands curl around my hips as his head moves between my parted thighs. He sucks and bites the sensitive skin above my pelvis, teasing me. "More. Show me every part of that wet pussy so I can eat it all."

I spread wider, and he presses his hands on my inner thighs, keeping me wide open for him as he begins devouring me.

"Fuck my face," he rasps before his serpent tongue goes back to licking me.

I arch my back, bucking my hips into his jaw as he attacks my clit, giving it just the right amount of suction to drive me crazy.

My orgasm hits me like a freight train, and I can only hold down his head as my eyes roll back and I fight for air.

He grabs my hips, flipping me so I'm on my belly before smacking my ass.

I know what he's about to do, and I know it will feel good, just like it always does, but I need something different right now.

Something deeper.

I flip back over. "I want to be on top."

I can tell he wants to argue, but I wrap my hand around his length, jerking him. "Please."

Reluctantly, he lays down and I straddle him. "Put your cock inside me."

With one hand on my hip, he reaches between us and lines himself up with my entrance.

His expression darkens as raw hunger illuminates his face. "Sit on it."

I squeeze my eyes shut as I rise up on my knees and then sink down, focusing on the way he stretches me as he fills me up.

Slowly, I start moving, tilting my head back as he raises his hips, matching my rhythm, our bodies in perfect sync.

His rough voice cuts through the fog. "Stray."

I know what he needs.

Reaching down, I take his hand and place it on my throat.

I expect him to start squeezing, but he doesn't. He wraps his arm around my back instead, pulling us into a sitting position.

His thrusts deepen as he kisses my cheeks, my chin, my lips.

Our skin sticks with sweat as we rock into each other and he presses his forehead against mine.

Oh, God.

This is so different...so *intimate.*

He holds my gaze as we exchange the same breath. "Aspen."

There's so much stark emotion contained when he says my name —hate, love, want, desire, obsession—all of it tangled into one.

Just like us.

He changes positions again, this time pushing me so I'm on my back.

I stare down between us, watching him enter me again, before his muscular body hovers above me.

His hands find mine, interlocking our fingers together before pinning them to the mattress.

His thrusts grow deeper...*hungrier.*

Like he needs this every bit as much as I do.

I close my eyes as a kaleidoscope of emotions pass through me and the friction between us builds, but he cups the back of my neck, demanding I look at him while I come.

I hold his gaze as my second orgasm rips through me, this one even more intense than the first.

A needy moan leaves me as I squeeze around him, giving him everything I have and holding nothing back.

I thought love ended the day my dad died. That I'd never be capable of feeling that emotion for someone ever again.

But I was wrong.

Because it's here between us—entangled in all our lies and ugly secrets.

It grew, despite our hatred—because it was stronger than we were.

And it will stay with us forever...like a scar that won't ever heal.

He licks the column of my throat before his teeth scrape my flesh. A deep groan rumbles out of him as he pumps one last time and spills inside of me.

All I can do is hold on to him—tighter than I've ever held on to anything before—as he collapses on top of me.

His eyes search mine as he sweeps my hair off my face, like he knows the words he wants to say, he just doesn't know *how* to say them.

But it's okay, because I know he will one day.

"I know," I whisper as tears blur my vision. "I feel it, too."

Chapter 54

Aspen

I wake with a jolt, wondering if I overslept until I glance at the alarm clock on the nightstand.

I breathe a sigh of relief when I see it's just after seven a.m.

I'm not sure if Knox is planning on going to school today. Although, there's really no point. There's only a week left until graduation, but for all intents and purposes we've already graduated, because we've both passed all our tests and classes.

Yawning, I turn over in bed. "Wake up, sleepy——"

He's gone.

For a moment I'm worried, but then I notice a note addressed to *Stray* on his pillow.

He probably ran out to get breakfast.

Smiling to myself, I unfold the letter.

My heart skips several agonizing beats as I take in his words.

Stray,

I've written this letter so many times now I've lost count, but no matter how I say it, or what words I choose to put on this paper…the end result will still be the same.
You'll be angry and upset.
Hell, you may even hate me again.

I get it. If it was me who woke up one morning to find you gone, I'd be going out of my fucking mind.

But this isn't what you think.

I know you think I'm leaving you while you're at your worst, but it's me.

I'm at my worst.

All my life my father said I'd never amount to anything, and for the longest time I believed him.

Because I never had a reason not to.

Unlike you, I didn't have a dream college. I also didn't have goals, aspirations, or an occupation that made me light up from the inside out whenever I talked about it.

Fuck, Stray. Most days, I didn't even know if I would make it out alive to see the next sunrise.

I'm not abandoning you, because that implies I'll never be back again.

I will.

I just need to get my shit together first and make something of myself.

For me and for you.

In the meantime, I want you to focus on you.

You've wanted to get into Stanford for as long as I've known you and I want you to have every single thing you've worked your ass off for.

I also want you to smile, go to parties, make new friends, blow a test or two, sip some fancy drinks with dumb pretentious names while you study at the local coffee shops, bake a fuck-ton of cupcakes, and turn down every guy who hits on you… because they will most definitely hit on you.

Point is, I want you to live, Aspen. More than live. I want you to grab life by the goddamn balls and fucking fly.

And no, I don't expect you to wait for me. But I'll sure as fuck be waiting for you.

Because you were the only person who ever helped me.

And you'll own every part of my fucked-up soul until they put me in the ground.

They say strays always come back…

But this time, I'll be the one coming back to you.

I don't know when…but I will.

I promise.

Always yours,
Knox

P.S: There's some money in my dresser drawer. It's only a couple thousand, but I'll send you more after the house sells. I know you don't want to, but take it. P.P.S: Seriously, Stray. Take the fucking money.

Chapter 55

Knox

*T*he muscles in my chest draw tight as the driver pulls up to the brown brick building.

This is it.

After pulling my wallet out of my pocket, I hand the driver some cash.

"Thanks." Smiling, he shakes my hand. "Although I should probably be thanking you, huh?"

Not yet.

Hiking my bag over my shoulder, I step out of the car.

You'll never amount to anything, you dumb piece of shit.

My father's voice echoes throughout my head as take in the block letters above the building that read,

Military Entrance Processing Station.

Maybe my father was right…

But there's only one way to find out.

Chapter 56

Knox

Past...

"*I* don't want to," I grumbled as my uncle Leo took hold of my arm and led me toward the playground.

"Tough shit," he bit out. "Your dad asked me to watch you while he and your mom ran a few errands. And since my buddy Miles has a kid the same age as you, I figured you two could play."

I planted my feet, repeating the same thing I said before. "I don't want to."

Everything still hurt from last night's beating, and the last thing I wanted to do was make nice with some stupid girl.

My uncle gripped my arm harder. He either chose to ignore the way I flinched…or he didn't care.

My guess was both…since he and my dad weren't just brothers, but friends, there was no doubt he knew what really went on behind closed doors.

"Let's go."

Reaching into my pocket, I fingered the scissors I stole from the kitchen earlier that day.

No one wanted to help me, but I knew a way to make the pain stop.

315

For good.

Leo pushed me forward. "Come on."

Reluctantly, I stomped toward the swing set.

The first thing I noticed was the way her long red hair blew in the wind and how she giggled. Like she didn't have a single care in the world.

Her ponytail was so long it seemed to go on forever, and my gaze fell to the yellow ribbon secured around it.

It matched the yellow dress she wore.

"Uncle Leo's here," the man pushing her on the swings declared.

"Uncle Leo," the girl squeaked before rushing over and wrapping her arms around him.

I wasn't sure why she was referring to him as *uncle* when she sure as heck wasn't my cousin, but she looked awfully excited to see him.

After their hug ended, he kneeled so he was eye-level with her. "Hey, honey. This is my nephew Trenton."

"Say hi, Kiddo," the man pushing her on the swings earlier urged with a smile.

Despite looking like she wanted to protest, the girl gave me a timid wave. I couldn't help but notice the freckles dotting her nose and cheeks. There were so many of them they covered her skin like a sundae with way too many sprinkles. Or too many ants on a log.

It was weird.

She was weird.

"Hi." *Freckles* shuffled her feet nervously. "I'm Aspen."

I said the first thing that popped into my head. "That's a stupid name."

"Trenton," Leo barked as he glared at me.

"It *is*," I defended.

Aspen's hands found her hips and she scowled. "My daddy named me."

"Well, your daddy is dumb."

The man standing behind her cleared his throat. For a moment I thought he was going to yell at me because almost every adult did, but Leo snagged his attention with his next statement.

"Why don't we let these two play so we can talk business?"

With that, they both walked over to the bench on the other side of the playground.

"My daddy isn't dumb," Aspen hissed. "Take it back."

I shrugged, secretly enjoying how irritated she was. "I'm sorry."

She started to smile, and I noticed her tiny teeth were crooked. "Thank—"

"I'm sorry your dad is dumb."

Her mouth fell open, and she looked like she wanted to rip my head off.

But for some strange reason, her anger actually made her pretty.

Frustrated, she stomped her foot in the sand. "Stop being mean."

"Make me."

I could tell she wanted to yell again, but to my surprise her expression softened, and she took a step closer.

Without warning, her hand found my cheek, her bright green eyes lingering on my face. "Are you okay?"

Before I could stop her, her thumb brushed over the bruise.

Bile rushed up my throat, but she held my stare…

Almost like she could detect the demons inside me.

Everyone ignored my bruises. Teachers, other kids, school nurses. No one wanted to get involved.

But not her.

This weird girl actually *saw* me.

Her free hand found my other cheek, almost like she was afraid I'd run away. "What happened?"

I couldn't tell her.

I couldn't tell anyone.

But I wanted to…so much it physically hurt.

"I—"

The words were on the tip of my tongue, fighting to be released.

But I knew if I did, he would hurt us.

Heck, maybe he'd even hurt Aspen for uncovering our family's secret.

I'd waited my whole life to be seen by someone and it finally happened.

I couldn't let him ruin that.

I was poison.

And maybe Aspen was the antidote, but neither of us would know for sure until it was too late.

I wouldn't take that chance.

So, I did what he did to me.

After breaking away from her touch, I pushed her. So hard she stumbled back.

But I wasn't done. I needed to make sure she stayed away.

That she no longer saw me.

That she feared me.

When she turned to walk away, I shoved her again. Harder this time.

So hard her face hit the metal pole of the swing set and she started to cry.

But it wasn't enough, so I crawled on top of her and pulled the scissors out of my pocket. I was planning on using them to kill myself later, but maybe I could hold on for a little longer now.

Maybe other people would see me.

Maybe eventually…someone would finally help me.

I'd only meant to cut the ribbon out of her hair so I could keep it, but I ended up chopping into her ponytail instead.

Aspen's cries were so loud they punctured my chest.

Her dad and my uncle quickly rushed over to us and pulled me off her.

My uncle's palm collided with my cheek. "What the fuck is wrong with you, you little shit?"

But I could only look at Aspen, who now had a mouth full of blood as tears continued to stream down her face.

I'm sorry.

I'm sorry I'm so messed up.

I'm sorry you saw me.

I'm sorry I had to make you hate me…

Epilogue

Aspen

Four years later...

*M*y heart beats so hard I can hear it pulsing in my eardrums as they gesture for my row to stand so we can accept our diplomas.

I fan myself with the program because it's hot as hell in this auditorium, which sucks because there are still a thousand or so students up after me.

It's going to be a long freaking day.

Beside me, Julie squeezes my hand. "Can you believe it's actually happening?"

I can't help but smile. "I know."

She prattles on about having dinner with her parents and boyfriend before going to a party that one of the Omega Delta *something* will be throwing later this evening, but I can't focus on that.

Because in a few moments, I'll be accepting my degree in business.

Then I'll be taking a few cooking classes over the summer before opening my very own bakery.

I always thought it was a pipedream, but I'm going to make it a reality.

"Are you gonna go to the party with us?" Julie asks as we make our way up to the stage.

I give her a nod, because why the hell not?

Over the last four years, I've not only studied and made friends. I've gone to parties, ate way too many carbs, spent way too much money on ridiculous, pretentious sounding drinks at the local coffee shop on campus, baked way too many cupcakes, and turned down every guy who hit on me.

Actually, that last part is a lie.

I kissed a few before I turned them down.

But I lived with no regrets, grabbed life by the balls, and got the full college experience.

My heart squeezes. *Just like he told me to.*

"Aspen Falcone," the announcer calls out.

Excitement courses through me as I walk across the stage and accept my diploma.

It's only when the room erupts in cheers and claps and I turn to look at the audience that disappointment slams me in the chest.

I don't have any family.

There's no one here to congratulate me.

No one here to take me out to dinner after.

No one here to smile and look on with pride because I made my dreams come true.

I walk off the stage and I'm about to head back to my row, but a man wearing a camouflage uniform stalks up the aisle like he owns it.

Not just any man. I realize as he gets closer.

Because I'd know those lips, sharp cheekbones, stubborn jaw… and those *intense* eyes anywhere.

Suddenly, he stops walking. His gaze rakes me in from head to toe as his expression fills with a mixture of pride and want.

My heart thumps against my chest, roaring back to life after four long years.

Knox said he'd be back, but so much time has passed, I started to lose hope.

But I should have known better.

Emotions tangle in my chest and I drop my diploma, my feet moving on their own accord as I run down the aisle to meet him.

Tears spring to my eyes as he catches me in his arms.

"You're here."

He holds me so tight it almost hurts as every ounce of oxygen leaves my body and I breathe him in.

His rough, familiar voice wraps around me like a thick fog, holding me captive. "Stray."

"You kept your promise," I whisper when he places me down.

He sweeps his thumb over my cheek, brushing away my tears. "Of course, I did." He closes the distance between us, his gaze falling to my lips. "I love you."

His mouth crashes against mine, kissing me like a man who's starved for four years.

"Wait," I say between frantic kisses that have my head spinning. "Is this for real?"

"Is what for real?"

"This…*us*." I peer up at him. "I can't do this if you're going to leave me again."

I understood why he had to do it, but I won't survive if he does it to me a second time.

He reaches for my hand and places it on his chest, right over the organ beating frantically. "I'm yours, Stray. For however long you want me."

I'll want him forever.

"In that case…I love you, too."

My breath leaves me in a rush because the sexy, cocky smile he's giving me is so beautiful it should be a crime.

"I know."

He leans in, cupping a hand around the back of my neck as he kisses me again.

This time, I don't stop him.

I let him kiss me until we both run out of air.

I let him kiss me until some old woman taps me on the shoulder and asks us to take a seat because there is still a ceremony going on.

I'll let him kiss me for as long as he wants to.

Because every action has a consequence…

And he's mine.

The End

Black Mountain Academy

Want to read more from Black Mountain Academy?
Drama, angst, love, lust, and everything in-between. Light
or dark, twisted or sweet, the BMA series has something
for every reader!
Check out the Black Mountain Academy webpage to see all
the books available:
https://black-mountain-academy.com

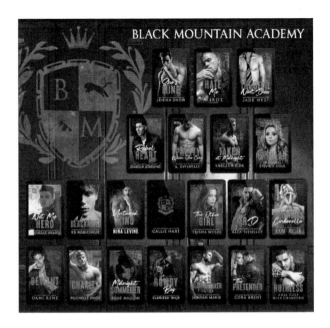

About the Author

Want to be notified about my upcoming releases? https://goo.gl/n5Azwv

Ashley Jade craves tackling different genres and tropes within romance. Her first loves are New Adult Romance and Romantic Suspense, but she also writes everything in between including: contemporary romance, erotica, and dark romance.

Her characters are flawed and complex, and chances are you will hate them before you fall head over heels in love with them.

She's a die-hard lover of oxford commas, em dashes, music, coffee, and anything thought provoking...except for math.

Books make her heart beat faster and writing makes her soul come alive. She's always read books growing up and scribbled stories in her journal, and after having a strange dream one night; she decided to just go for it and publish her first series.

It was the best decision she ever made.

If she's not paying off student loan debt, working, or writing a novel—you can usually find her listening to music, hanging out with her readers online, and pondering the meaning of life.

Check out her social media pages for future novels.

She recently became hip and joined Twitter, so you can find her there, too.

She loves connecting with her readers—they make her world go round'.

~Happy Reading~

Feel free to email her with any questions / comments: ashleyjadeauthor@gmail.com

For more news about what I'm working on next: Follow me on my Facebook page: https://www.facebook.com/pages/Ashley-Jade/788137781302982

Other Books Written By Ashley Jade

Royal Hearts Academy (Books 1-4)
Cruel Prince (Jace's Book)
Ruthless Knight (Cole's Book)
Wicked Princess (Bianca's Book)
Broken Kingdom

The Devil's Playground Duet (Books 1 & 2)

Complicated Parts - Series (Books 1 & 2 Out Now)

Complicated Hearts - Duet (Books 1 & 2)

Blame It on the Shame - Trilogy (Parts 1-3)

Blame It on the Pain - Standalone

Thanks for Reading!
Please follow me online for more.
<3 Ashley Jade

Made in United States
North Haven, CT
25 July 2023

39482955R00180